D1709948

ROARING
up the
Wrong
Tree

CELIA KYLE

chapter one

God hated Trista and the proof was taped to her door. The evidence fluttered in the breeze, words printed with black ink on bright yellow paper.

The wind picked up again, blowing harder this time. Empty cans clinked across the grimy concrete floor. A plastic bag followed in their wake, flying over the filthy ground. A ball of yellow, the hue matching the notice on her apartment door, tumbled by.

Someone else was being evicted. Well, at least she wasn't the only one who'd be miserable and homeless. Not that she wanted others to suffer, but misery loved company.

Clutching her keys, she traced the page taped to her door. It flapped, as if trying to flee, but she slapped her palm over the thin sheet.

Final Notice of Eviction.

Funny how she'd never received an initial warning. Then again, it'd only been a matter of time, right? She should have expected this after she heard of Bru's death, but she hadn't. She'd held onto hope that she could float idly along and pretend her landlord hadn't been killed and a new owner wouldn't be coming in to take over.

Trista slid her hand over the notice, letting her palm skim the rough door. Paint flaked off and pricked her skin, reminding her she was alive. And soon to be living on the streets.

Wouldn't be the first time. Except she hadn't been alone the first time, or the third or the fifth. No, she'd had her mother then. And now...

Her eyes stung, familiar tears welling, and she blinked them back. The piece of paper danced in the breeze again. Reminding her of what needed to be done. She didn't have time to cry. Besides, it didn't solve anything.

That didn't stop a tear from falling past her lower lashes and snaking down her cheek. It didn't stop the second either. Or the third.

"Fuck." She leaned against the door and balled her hand. "Fuck." She banged her forehead and fist against the scarred surface. "Fuckery Fuck McFuckerson."

With each syllable, more tears fell. One time, just once in her life, she'd love things to go her way.

"Fuck." She whispered the word and took a deep breath.

Memories of her mother filled Trista's mind. She imagined her mom pushing open the apartment door and brushing past her fifteen-year-old self. *Cry me a river, build a bridge, and get over it, Trista Ann. We've got work to do and no one but ourselves to do it.*

She allowed one last tear to trail down her cheek and one last curse to leave her lips. "Fuck."

There, now she needed to get her things packed before she left for her night job slinging drinks at the bar down the street. Come morning she'd apartment hunt between when she got off and her day job started.

2

Okay, she could do this. Even if she didn't have her mom by her side, she was an adult. She'd lived through worse, she could get through this.

Trista grasped her doorknob, careful to hold it in the right position to get the thing unlocked. It was a finicky bitch and it hadn't mattered how many times she'd complained to Bru.

It works, don't it?

God, he's an asshole. Oh, right, he was dead. Okay, he'd been an asshole.

Unfortunately, when she turned the knob just right—two inches right and then one back left—it didn't click like it should. Mainly because the door simply opened, swinging on silent hinges to reveal…

A bare apartment. Completely, utterly, empty of her possessions. The sagging couch remained along with the rickety table in the kitchen, but they'd come with the place. *Her* things were gone. Her pictures and mess of clothing that generally littered the floor. She had no doubt the money she'd hidden throughout the space was gone as well. She and her mom hadn't trusted banks, especially not those run by her father's "friends." When her mom pissed off her dad, their account typically suffered a "computer glitch."

Now, all of her belongings gone, it… it was too much. The rage that'd burned inside her from the moment her mother disappeared, the anger over fucking life fucking shitting on her every fucking day, boiled over.

Trista tilted her head back and screamed at the cobweb-laced ceiling, opening her mouth as wide as possible as she released the guttural roar. *"Fuck!"*

The yell went on and on, echoing off the concrete block walls of the hallway. The scream's never-ending boom mocked her, reminding her over and over that she was alone.

3

"My mim says you shouldn't curse. She says it's bad." The tiny, tinkling voice came from beside her, the tone of a high-pitched youth. She looked to her right, down at the child, and the little boy stared up at her with guileless eyes.

The part of her that hated being challenged, particularly by a *male*, roared its displeasure in her mind. God may hate her, but Trista *loathed* that piece of feral animal inside her even though she knew it'd never disappear.

Snapping her mouth closed she turned her raging attention to the little one at her side. She snarled at him, curling her lip. This behavior wasn't *her*, it was *it*, but she couldn't halt the aggressive attention she gave the boy. "When she pays my bills, I'll be fucking happy to quit my fucking cursing."

Now she was really going to hell. Squeezing her eyes shut, she leaned against the doorframe and slid down its length. In no time she went from standing to a dejected pile on the floor.

Working two part-time, dead-end jobs left her bone tired and now everything she owned was gone. Poof. The new owner must have decided he'd take her possessions in trade for her back rent. Nice.

When tears threatened once again, she swallowed hard and shoved them back. She'd had her little pity party, it was time to get her shit together.

A soft scrape of a shoe on concrete reminded her the child lingered. She opened her eyes to stare at him while he narrowed his and stared through orbs entirely too old for his little size.

As if her day couldn't get any worse, he took a deep breath and the brown of his irises bled to black. No, not amber like a lion or yellow like a wolf or even copper like a hyena, but black.

Yup, right there was proof that God declared Monday "Shit on Trista" day.

4

Because, of course, the small child before her *had* to be a werebear and Trista *happened* to be part werehyena and wonderful of wonderfulness, the bears hated the hyenas. Well, she hated them just as much and wasn't that *awesome*.

"You're not supposed to be here," the boy snarled, baring his rapidly sharpening teeth.

Right now, she really wished she could shift. If only her lovely father had given her that gift.

"And yet, I am," she retorted, but didn't expect him to understand the intricacies of the law and she wasn't about to get into that kind of argument with a six-year-old. At least, she thought he might be six. He seemed to be the right height, but he was also a shifter kid, so she wasn't all that sure.

It became a moot point when the distinctive *snap* and *crack* of bone echoed off the walls.

"You smell like *him*." The words were garbled as the child's mouth transformed into a cub's.

It finally registered in her mind that this was happening. She was truly sitting in the doorway of her ransacked apartment with an eviction notice attached to her door. She had two jobs and no money and now she was about to be attacked by a cub.

Trista's life had become a very sad, very twisted, werecountry song. The only thing missing was a dead dog. Though the dead dog could be her since she was part hyena and a lot of people thought they were dogs even though biologically they were more like cats and—

"Holy fuck!" She scrambled to her feet, the cub's claws barely missing her face and colliding with the door frame instead. Wood splintered and showered the ground with the small pieces, but she couldn't focus on the damage. Not when the little he-devil from hell growled and rushed after her, his little feet slipping on the mess he'd created.

5

"Parker!" A woman's voice rose above the growls, and the shout had the boy freezing in place.

Movement near the door had Trista wanting to look at her savior, but she didn't dare take her attention off the little ball-o-death.

"Parker, you back down right this instant, young man. Wait until I tell your parents." The yelling continued long enough for Trista to recognize the woman ranting at the boy.

"Lauren?" The boy narrowed his eyes, but didn't move closer. "Lauren, is that you?"

Please let it be Lauren. Especially if her friend knew Parker. Before Bru's death, Lauren had been her neighbor and passing acquaintance. Trista and her mom were always too busy to stop and chat, but she did exchange smiles with the woman often. Though, if she'd known the woman was involved with the bears, she wouldn't have done that.

"Trista? Shit."

In a split second the raging cub went back to a human child. He spun, presenting her with his little back as he propped his fists on his hips. "Aunt Lauren, Mim said—"

With the kid distracted, she looked toward her entryway and sighed. It truly was Lauren, and Trista changed her mind and didn't care that Lauren was involved with werebears. Not if she could prevent Trista from being dinner.

"Not another word, Parker. Not one," Lauren snapped and tore off her cardigan, wrapping it around the now naked child. That had the kid whimpering, but the woman didn't release her anger. "To the car. Right this second."

"But—"

"*Now.*"

The child kicked at the ground and shuffled away, his head hanging low. He grumbled the whole way. "Girl... Those... Dirty... Purge..."

Parker only repeated what others said about her kind. She was one of *those*, she was *dirty*, and she should be killed because of the *purge* ordered by the Grayslake Itan. The knowledge didn't lessen the pain, though.

"I don't want to hear it. *Get. Out.*"

Wow. Lauren could yell.

It didn't take long for the boy to disappear from sight and Trista didn't move until she could no longer hear the kid's stomping steps. Even when she figured he was gone, she was slow and careful in her movements. It was obvious Lauren knew of the bears; she hadn't blinked an eye at the cub's near attack, which meant this next bit would not be an enjoyable experience.

"Uh, Trista." The woman squirmed. "I don't know what to say. Do you need to be sedated? You don't have any guns, do you? I'm sure we have a therapist on hand to help, er... The thing about it is..."

Trista furrowed her brow. "What are you talking about?"

"So, sometimes, during evolution, nature takes a different course and..." Lauren nibbled on her lower lip. "Damn it, they need a handbook for this. What to Expect When Telling Humans About Shifters." The woman shrugged. "At least you're not running, screaming, and locking yourself in a room while holding the Itana hostage with an empty gun. That really pisses people off, by the way."

Oh. *Oh.*

"Lauren, you're not a shifter, huh?" Otherwise the woman would have identified Trista long ago. When Lauren shook her head, Trista breathed a relieved sigh. "Okay, well, I am. Sorta. The point is, I know about shifters, which is why I'm not freaking out. I'm fine.

You're fine. The psychopathic cub is fine but could really use some training in control. We'll leave it at that."

"But—"

"I'm good. No need to worry about me."

"But I haven't seen you at any of the clan runs. The Itana says—"

"If I had to adhere to clan laws, you'd be right."

"But—"

Argh, they were getting nowhere. "Look, Lauren, thanks for saving me from the crazy cub, but I have things to do. Mainly, work and find a new place to live." Trista flicked her gaze to the door and the woman's attention drifted to the eviction notice.

"Oh, but—"

She shook her head. "No buts. Regardless of what you think you know, it no longer matters. I'm moving."

Lauren nibbled her lower lip. "Okay, well, the clan is taking over the building and we have a new manager"—then Trista's day got so much more awesome—"and I have to tell Ty about you."

There was so not an ounce of caring left in her. Especially not if the clan took possession and not one of Bru's relatives. "Look, tell whoever you want—tell the NC for all I care—but I gotta go."

"NC?"

She hated being mean to someone who obviously hadn't finished her shifter education, but enough was enough. "Okay, I'm guessing you're real new, huh? You recently mated someone in the clan?" When Lauren nodded, Trista continued. "Okay, so go to your mate and ask him about the NC and the laws of visitation. Better yet, go to your Itan and Keeper. If you, or your clan, still has issues, they can find me at Jerry's Gas Station down the street until seven and then at

8

the Left Bank bar in Boyne Falls at eight." With that, she headed toward the bathroom. "Lock up on your way out? Just twist the little knob on the handle and it'll lock when it closes."

Not that she had much to steal anymore.

"Um, bye?"

Trista waved to Lauren over her shoulder and stepped into the bathroom. She remained inside the doorway, waiting to hear the front door close and the lock engage. The moment the familiar *click* reached her, she relaxed. Adrenaline still pulsed in her veins, the cause of the hormone now switching from her fear of Parker to the fear of being approached by the bears. Lauren hadn't known what she was, but it was only a matter of time before the little boy told someone else about her.

She shook her head. Not much she could do about it now. She had to shower, sleep, and then get to work. Okay, shower, *figure out what'd been stolen*, sleep, and then get to work.

She kicked off her shoes and shimmied out of her pants; her shirt and bra soon followed. Twisting the knob to get the water flowing, she waited for the liquid to warm and hopped beneath the spray.

And then she noticed it… she was devastated by the loss of her money and other mementos, but this… this was too much. Her wet/dry shaver was missing. It was the only thing that kept her hairy legs smooth and now it was gone.

Her life as a horrible werecountry song was complete.

* * *

Bleary-eyed and bone tired, Keen let himself into the Grayslake clan den. He stumbled over the threshold and grabbed the doorframe to keep himself upright. He'd spent all night in Helena's bed and it wasn't working with her any longer. Not like it used to anyway.

9

His bear prowled beneath the surface of his skin, stretching the flesh and begging to be released. Only… that couldn't happen. Not now, not when he'd walked into a home filled with people.

Later.

The animal growled, vibrating his bones with the internal sound.

I promise. Later.

It didn't relent and kept the rumble going. On and on it went, shaking him from inside out, and he dug his fingers into the wood beneath his palm. He needed to regain control before he stepped deeper inside. Otherwise, everyone would be in danger. Hell, they were already in danger, they just didn't know it.

If Keen had his way, they never would.

Turning his thoughts inward, he broke down and begged the beast.

Chill the fuck out. Please.

The grumbles eased slightly, and he no longer shook from the intensity of the bear's displeasure.

He freed a slow, relieved sigh and released his stranglehold on the wood. Glancing at the frame, he winced, bringing his shoulders up high and wrinkling his nose. Damn. He'd have to fix that. That and anything else his brothers decided he needed to handle.

His bear shook, jarring Keen's body with the action, and the rolling sounds began again. It responded to his frustration with his family and the disrespect they showed him. *Shit.*

Keen couldn't adopt his normal horn-dog, devil-may-care attitude this morning. He needed to hide in his room until he could present the attitude his family and friends had come to expect. The Keen who didn't care about anything. The one who smiled and pretended his world shined brightly. The male who hopped from bed to bed with not a care in the world.

10

Lies, all of them lies.

He forced himself into motion, placed one foot in front of the other until the welcoming scent of the den reached him. With a nudge, he closed the front door as quick as he could and leaned against it for support.

The solid panel at his back reminded him he still held his human form. Barely. His fingers tingled and ached with the need to shift, to bare his claws. Instead, he pressed the tips against the oak. Or rather, the thin layer of oak that covered a steel core. When he was fourteen, his father learned his fourth son was different and needed a little something extra to keep him contained.

He breathed deep, focusing on the scents of his clan members, hunting the flavors of someone who could calm his animal.

And... he found nothing.

Fuck.

Okay, if he could get to his room, lock himself in, he might be able to quiet his bear enough to get some work done.

Right. He had a plan.

Keen pushed away from the door, wincing when his nails clung to the wood. A quick glance at his fingers revealed what he'd feared. The pink of his human nails were replaced by beastly claws.

He stretched and flexed his hands, fighting the animal inside him, pushing and shoving the bear back. The ever-present rage that consumed him rushed him, the animal riding in its wake. He stumbled forward and managed to catch himself on the couch. Only this time he was careful. His palm hit the furniture, but he didn't curve his fingers around the back.

Forcing his feet into action, he pushed himself to stand once again and resumed his trek. He had the path memorized, ten steps to the hallway, turn right, four steps to the first doorway and another eleven to his bedroom door. Once he got the lock thrown, he wouldn't care about the rest.

He managed to make it to the hallway, hand braced on the corner while he took a few breaths.

The animal bolted onward once again, demanding to be freed. It wanted… something Keen couldn't give it. For years he'd been this way and for years he hadn't known how to appease the animal. Oh, it relented for a little while, soothed when he lay with a woman, but before long it'd return to its natural, agitated state.

How many women had he burned through?

Too many to count.

"Keen?" Ty's voice reached him followed by the heavy tread of his brother striding through the house.

Fuck.

"Yeah," he croaked and swallowed past the dryness of his throat. "What's up?"

He didn't need this. Not now. Maybe after he had some time for yoga and a little meditation.

"I need you in the kitchen."

He cleared his throat again. "Lemme shower and I'll be right—"

"Now."

Peachy.

Keen's beast wanted to chase after Ty, shove him to the ground, and show him who was the stronger bear. Instead, he slumped against the wall and willed his bear back.

12

He recognized the scents in the area and sorted through the strength of the aromas. Ty and his mate, Mia, were present. As was his other brother Van and his mate, Lauren. The sweet flavors of Parker were also around. Add in the smell of the den's cook, Gigi, and they had a full house.

Keen sought the peace that seemed so elusive, drew it forward as he imagined the nearby lake, smooth and serene. He pictured the scene in his mind. The early morning sun peeked over the mountains, illuminating the area and shining off the water's placid surface. Fog hovered over the water, shading the murky depths of the lake. No bugs flew through the air, no birds chirped in welcome. No, it was simply a place of nothingness, just Keen and the lake...

"Keen!"

Just like that, his tranquility vanished and the sounds and scents of the den invaded him once again.

"Coming!" He pushed away from the wall and headed toward the voices, but took an indirect route to his destination. Maybe the extra time would give him a chance to calm. He practiced his usual smile, the bit of swagger he always had in his step. Normal, he had to appear normal and then he could hide in his room, battle the bear in private.

He moved through the living room and brushed the mantel with his claw tips—the bear still hadn't let up—listening for the expected beep. Once it reached his ears, he continued. That installation of weaponry was operational and secure. Good. No one had tampered with it. That had him moving to the next in the dining room, and on to another in the family room.

When Ty mated Mia, a lot of trouble appeared on the clan's doorstep. Because of the fighting and violence, Keen placed several caches of weaponry within the house as well as their territory. Now, they had protection scattered throughout Grayslake. That also meant the occupants had protection against him if he ever lost control.

As he approached, the voices grew louder, echoing off the home's walls and ringing through him.

If only he'd been born deaf instead of crazy.

"We don't need Keen. Unless this woman is someone he's fu— *fallen* in love with before and he can smooth talk her." Van. Nice.

"He might know something we don't," Ty snapped.

"What? The color of her panties?" Van snorted.

"Isaac said Keen's smart enough to be our Keeper and he's done well, so far." Of course Ty tacked on "so far," though it was good to hear that Isaac at least had his back. Too bad the male was off helping Mia's father in Cutler.

"*Right.*"

With every word out of Van's mouth, Keen's bear eased closer to the edge of his control. The damned thing wasn't going to be happy until it bathed in his brother's blood. That'd be a nice cap to the day.

Keen's skin stretched, the tightness of his flesh beginning in his thighs and rippling up his abdomen. Despite burgeoning anger, he slapped a cocky grin to his lips and prepared himself to walk into the kitchen.

"Look," Van sighed and Keen imagined him running a hand through his hair in frustration. Well, welcome to his world. "I'm saying that things should be decided within the inner-circle and then we can go from there. Last time I checked, he isn't part of us. Am I wrong here?"

Wrong thing to say. In his mind, Keen's bear roared in a violent protest, rising to its back legs and bellowing his displeasure. It vibrated through him, rattling his bones with the force, and once again he found himself slumped against the wall. Someday, he'd show them why he and the Incredible Hulk had a lot in common. Keen didn't go green, but he did get very, very angry. And furry.

Fuck, why couldn't things with Helena have held a little longer? At least through today.

"Van…" There was more than a brotherly threat in Ty's tone. It was the voice he used when he acted as Itan, and that soothed Keen's bear a tiny bit.

"I'm just saying—"

Keen pushed away from the wall and strode into the kitchen, fighting his bear with every step. He put on a show of strength and bravado when all he wanted to do was curl into a ball in the corner of an empty room. He sank into his loose-hipped walk, and put a grin on his lips that said he'd just fucked his way through Grayslake.

"What you're saying is that you don't care about clan law." He strolled past his now silent brother and went straight for the fridge. He had to keep the bear occupied—distracted—and grabbing a sugary drink would do for now. The beast was a sucker for sweets.

As he moved, he kept talking, fighting to keep the tension from his body. "Volume Eight, Section Twelve, Paragraph Thirteen, Sub-section Five, Paragraph Two states any member of a clan holding an authoritative position within the clan is part of said clan's inner-circle. That includes and is not limited to the Itan." Keen pointed at Ty with one hand while tugging the fridge door with the other. "The Healer who is currently residing in Cutler, also known as Isaac." He snared a jug of milk and the chocolate syrup and let the door swing shut. "The Enforcer." He gestured at Van with the half-empty container. "As well as the Keeper." He dropped the milk to the counter, placing the chocolate to its left. He pointed at himself.

Keen snatched a glass from the drying rack and poured the liquid into the container before adding the chocolaty goodness. So far so good. The bear was occupied with pulling information and the impending sweet rather than on killing his brothers. "It goes on to list additional positions which represent the mates of those bears, regardless of their sex, as well as other titles which may become necessary as a clan grows."

He took a deep gulp of his drink, letting the cool liquid soothe his animal. One swallow turned into three and then it was all gone.

He lowered the glass and snagged a paper towel to wipe his face. "As educational as this has been," for them, not him, "are we going to let Van make up his own laws which means I'm done here? 'Cause," He waggled his eyebrows. "I got somewhere to be."

He let his question trail off as he waited for Ty to either step up or step off.

And... Ty didn't say a word.

Keen shook his head and placed the tumbler in the dishwasher as he ignored the others in the space. Soft whispers reached him, but he didn't bother trying to decipher the words. None of 'em mattered. The last six and a half months had obviously been a waste and he didn't know why he even tried.

With a sigh, he turned back to the small group of people. Lauren was angry, her eyes narrowed and focused on a frustrated Van. Mia, though... Mia was filled with rage, a fury he'd never seen before, and he was thankful it wasn't directed at him. Her face was red, eyes bleeding black. The Itana wasn't able to shift, but she did take on animalistic characteristics now and again.

Her rounded stomach rolled, telling him without words that her ire was upsetting her unborn cub. Not looking at Ty, he approached Mia and placed his hand on her abdomen, resting atop the baby pressing against her flesh, while he put the other on the back of her neck. A gentle squeeze and rub of his thumb had her relaxing into his touch with a soft sigh.

"Keen..." she moaned.

"Hush, relax." He winked. "Lemme cop a feel for a minute." He'd learned a lot about pressure points and relaxation—it was necessary as he'd grown from a volatile pre-teen to an even more dangerous adult. Now he was able to use it on his pregnant sister-in-law, which

16

pleased his bear and soothed some of the anger coursing through him.

No one said a thing as he worked, chastely rubbing and petting Mia until she was near boneless. Finally, he released her and stepped back. "All better?"

"I'm amazed every time you do that," Mia purred. "Can you teach—"

"If I was the Keeper, I'd happily share what I know. Since I'm not, I can recommend several physical therapists in the area."

"But—"

Ty overrode his mate and snarled at him. "What do you mean 'if I was the Keeper'?"

Keen raised a single brow and crossed his arms over his chest. There was no question that Ty was the Itan and he was dangerous as hell. What Ty still hadn't figured out was that Keen was as threatening, if not more so.

There's being strong and smart—like Ty—and then there's strong and crazy.

Keen happened to be strong and crazy smart. He just wasn't driven to lead like Ty.

"Van, as the Enforcer and second only to the Itan, indicated I'm not part of the inner-circle. Your silence was acceptance. If I'm not in the inner-circle, I'm not the Keeper. Follow the logic and if all else fails, I have the volumes in my now *old* office." With that, he turned from his brother, his family, and headed toward his room.

This was another encounter of many that reinforced one thought: the people who were supposed to mean the most, who were supposed to love him, didn't give a shit about him.

The bear rumbled its agreement even as it made fun of him for sounding like a girl.

Whatever.

He strode into his room and moved to kick the door closed only to have his movement halted by a soft voice.

"Keen, wait." Great. Mia followed him.

With a sigh, he turned to Mia. Even if she weren't his Itana, he'd always do as she asked. She was the sister he never had and never wished for.

"Yes?"

"They don't mean to be so…"

He dropped his head back and stared at the ceiling. "Yeah, they do and it no longer matters." He looked to her. "I'm goin' out for a while."

Mia frowned and padded toward him. "You don't look good. How are things with Helena?"

"It's over." Keen shook his head, regretting that he spoke the truth. His relationship with Helena was the shortest one yet and that had him more worried than he'd like to admit.

"Already?"

"Yeah," he nodded, no longer meeting her gaze. "I'm gonna get outta here. Maybe search for an apartment." He flashed her a half-grin. "A guy can't live with his brother forever, right?"

"But—"

Keen closed the distance between them and pressed a soft kiss to her forehead. He drew strength from the chaste, quick touch, allowing the skin-on-skin contact to soothe his bear. It was a quick recharge, a flash of calming, but it'd hopefully get him through the next few hours as he searched out a new place to stay.

Because staying in the clan den? Yeah, that just wasn't happening.

chapter two

"Jerry, that just ain't happening." Trista pressed two more buttons on the register and caught the cash drawer as it slid open.

"Aw, c'mon, Tris," her boss whined, actually *whined*. The man was pushing fifty and acted like a three-year-old.

"Nope. I've gotta be on deck at Left Bank at eight." She passed over the customer's change and hip-bumped the register closed. "That means no staying late today."

"But, Ronnie—"

Ugh. Ronnie always had something going on that ended with her not showing up and Trista staying late. "I get what you're saying about Ronnie, but I don't have a choice. I either stay here and work or get fired from my job at Left Bank. A job I really, really need."

He narrowed his eyes. "You need this job, too."

Yes, she did, but Left Bank paid better plus she got tips. Too bad she couldn't say that to him. "I know and I appreciate everything you did for me after…" After her mother disappeared. "But I need both jobs and I'm working the shift I got here. I can't stay late. Call Ronnie back and tell her she needs to come in or see if somebody else can fill the spot. I know Tommy was looking for extra hours. Call him."

Trista focused on the next customer, grabbing his twenty and presetting pump four so the guy could fill up. "All set, have a great day."

So intent on her job, she didn't notice Jerry's approach until it was too late. Suddenly his wide body was against hers, pressing forward until he had her cornered in front of the register.

"How appreciative?" The rancid scent of cigarettes and beer overwhelmed her, filling her nose, and that animal part of her snarled an objection.

Bile rose in her throat, but she swallowed it down, pushing it back. She opened her mouth and drew in a breath, hoping to avoid smelling him. Except doing that made her *taste* his aroma.

She was gonna puke on her boss.

"Huh, Trista? Just *how* appreciative are you? I gave you a lot of time off when you went looking for your momma…"

Yup, total pukefest coming right up. But what did she expect from him? A person couldn't get anything for free. It was always "give a little, take a lot" in her life.

"You needed to save a few bucks and you hadn't fired Pippa yet. You didn't have room on the schedule for me." She leaned away from him, fighting for clean air. She hated this, hated that she had to deal with sexual innuendo and the disgusting feel of Jerry's body on hers. If she didn't need this job…

"Pippa," he sneered.

Yeah, she was kinda in love in a non-lesbian way with that girl, who had placed a knee in the right place and sent Jerry to the ground when he'd gotten too close. She'd been able to throw away her job. Jerry's had been a part-time, summer position before she went off to college. Four months later, and the cold of winter bearing down on the towns, it still made her smile.

For Trista it was a won't-eat-without-it kind of position.

The bell announcing a new customer dinged and her boss eased back, but his presence remained.

She caught sight of the newcomer out of the corner of her eye and directed her attention to him with a wide smile. His presence saved her. At least, this time around. "Good evening."

The man grunted and kept on walking, disappearing between the aisles. It didn't matter that she couldn't see him any longer. The man's presence was enough to deter Jerry.

Her boss glared at her, narrowing his eyes as if he'd read her thoughts, and then he stepped away. Bodies no longer touching, his scent ceased to overwhelm her with the spoiled flavors.

"I'll be in the back doing inventory."

Also known as drinking.

"Sure thing." She flashed him a smile—relieved she wouldn't have to deal with him for a while—which earned her a scowl.

Jerry stomped through the small store, weaving along the aisles and snagging a bag of chips before he disappeared into the back. His absence let her relax and her shoulders slumped as she released the breath she'd been holding. The tangy scent of him still lingered, but at least it wasn't as bad as before.

Trista leaned over the counter and let her gaze sweep the interior of the small store. She noted the top of that guy's head rising above the aisle; damn, the guy had to be at least six feet to be visible like that. Part of her wanted to get a good look at him, but the other part of her wanted him to take his time. The quicker he finished, the quicker he left, and the quicker Jerry would be back.

Unfortunately, no matter how much time she wished he'd take, he showed up at the counter five minutes later. She glanced at the door Jerry disappeared through and mentally groaned. The man was peeking out at her, seeming to be waiting for her to finish with the guy.

Then he'd pounce. Again.

Pasting on an all-too-fake smile, she focused on her customer. "Find everything you need?"

He grunted. Wow, she got a talker. Which was okay since he was pretty to look at. He really was over six feet of lean, muscled hotness. His brown, shaggy hair nearly covered his eyes and he tossed his head to swing it aside. That gave her a good look at his face, at his chocolate brown irises, strong jaw, and slightly crooked nose. Someone had broken it at some point. Rather than take away from his appeal, it enhanced it. A dark scruff decorated his cheeks and she wondered if the hair would prick her palm when she stroked them.

That thought reminded her she didn't need a man, smoking hot or otherwise, when her life was so craptastical. Hell, even if it were fantastic, she didn't need the complication of a guy. He'd want her to lean on him, depend on him, and that wasn't happening.

Fool me once shame on you... She wasn't gonna be fooled twice. She couldn't afford to.

Snagging his items, she quickly scanned them, letting the register tally his purchases. When she announced the final cost, he still didn't focus on her. Nope, he handed over his credit card. One quick swipe and then she had his receipt.

"Here you go, Mister..." She looked at the card and gulped. Great, just what she needed. What the hell was one of *them* doing *here*? "Mr. Abrams."

Their fingers brushed as she returned his card, his callused skin scraping the pads of her digits. A sliver of desire tinged with unease traveled down her spine. Her body reacted to him, to his touch, and she fought to tamp down her arousal. Yet her inner-animal wasn't going to be denied. For some reason, she wanted him.

Even if he was a bear. Even if he was an Abrams. Even if he could blow her entire world to hell and back.

His gaze collided with hers, his eyes widening as his chest expanded, nostrils flaring as he drew in a deep breath.

Oh, fuck.

He furrowed his brow and repeated the action, drawing in more air. Anxiety attacked her, worry and fear rising to overwhelm her with the emotions. Adrenaline pumped through her bloodstream, pounding out an uneven rhythm. She immediately snatched her hand back, breaking their connection, as she stepped away from the counter.

Silence stretched between them, the rumble of cars and the whir of the fan in the back coolers the only things that filled the air. His deep breathing continued and she prayed he wouldn't be able to discern her scent, discover her true nature.

Lauren was one thing. The woman was human even if she was associated with the Grayslake clan. Besides, she hadn't said anything about her animal. Sure, the kid knew, but who'd believe a six-year-old? She was safe. Fine. Perfect, even.

Until Keen Abrams walked into the station.

Hoping to rush him along, she cleared her throat and finally broke the quiet. "Have a nice day. Come again."

Instead of walking away, he continued to stand there, tilting his head to the side as if he were trying to piece together a puzzle. Well, she was no man's puzzle.

Trista tore her attention from him, lifted her wrist, and glanced at her watch. Five minutes left. *Screw it. Good enough for government work.*

"Right. See ya next time." She gave a small wave and focused on the empty doorway in the back. "Yo, Jerry, I gotta go!"

It didn't take long for him to poke his head out, a scowl on his face. "You've got five minutes left on the clock."

"And I took a short lunch, so it evens out." Pressing on the register drawer, she confirmed it was shut before hurrying toward the end of the counter and abandoning her post.

A grumbling Jerry trudged toward her and she ignored his glare, more intent on getting the fuck out rather than talking to her boss. Of course, Keen Abrams kept pace with her, matching her step for step, and she was never more thankful for the counter separating her from the customers. At least it kept some space between them. For now.

The moment she reached the end, she darted down a nearby aisle, racing for the safety of the back room. Hell, who was she kidding? Safety? She mentally shook her head. If he wanted to follow her, he would.

He lurked in her periphery and she increased her pace, heart beating faster and faster with each step. It didn't matter that she was within her legal rights, it didn't matter that the law was on her side when it came to her work and her residence. She knew if he wanted her gone, she'd be gone.

Like her mother.

Trista practically dove for the back door. Hell, she really did dive. She rushed forward and jumped through the doorway, grasping the edge of the panel and shoving it closed. Almost.

The slap of flesh on metal echoed through the small stock area, Keen's hand stopping her bid for safety. "Hey, wait—"

"Sorry." She pointed at the sign on the panel. "Employees only. Jerry can help you with what you need. Have a good day." She pushed on the door and it didn't budge, his strength keeping her from a clean escape.

"You're—"

26

"Late for my other job." The animal in her growled. It knew a bear stood before them, a powerful bear, and it didn't like being in this position.

"You shouldn't—"

"Really gotta go." Adrenaline pumped through her veins, urging her to run, to hide, to be anywhere but Jerry's Gas Station.

The shrill ring of a cell phone broke into their battle, dragging his attention from her enough for her to shove the door closed. Damn it, she wished she could throw the lock, but that'd piss Jerry off when he couldn't get in. Hell, it might anger him enough to fire her.

Though, dead or fired, which was worse?

She wasn't sure.

Keen's muffled voice reached her. "Lauren? What's up?"

Trista winced. Crap. He knew Lauren, which meant he'd soon know about her. Maybe he wouldn't connect the dots. She snorted. Right. The bears were assholes, but they weren't stupid.

"The laws of visitation?"

Yeah, she was so caught.

Trista ran into a bear cub who figured out what she was and then told Lauren and then Lauren told Keen while Keen had already scented her and... Bum, bum, buuummm... *My life is over.*

Not waiting for the bear to figure things out, she snatched her purse and strode to the back entrance. Apartment. Shower. Change. Left Bank.

Just because she was about to be run out of town—or worse—by the bears, didn't mean she didn't have to work.

A girl's gotta eat.

* * *

Keen was tempted to shift and confirm what his nose told him. A hyena? In Redby? Nah, he couldn't imagine Reid, the werewolf Alpha, allowing a hyena in wolf territory. And yet… He'd stood not five feet from the woman as she'd rung up his purchases. He'd had to fight past the stink of the gas station owner, but beneath the stench he'd found the sweet scent of the woman.

Then the battle began. The bear's desire for her warred with the man's objection to her species. The man eventually overruled the bear. For now.

His human half was ready to run her out of town. At least, until Lauren called, fussing at him for bolting before they could talk, and distracted him.

When Lauren went back to her old apartment to check on the new owner, she'd run into her friend Trista. Trista who'd almost been eaten by Parker when he'd sniffed her. Parker who assured his Aunt Lauren the woman smelled like the bad man who'd kidnapped him over six months ago.

Was that who he'd met? It seemed too coincidental. Did they really have a hyena living in Grayslake and working in Redby?

Actually, she worked in Boyne Falls at the Left Bank bar, too. That information cost him a hundred bucks and had him suffering through a conversation with Jerry.

Keen scented the air, drawing in the flavors of the parking lot and hunting up the identity of those inside the bar. The aromas of bears and wolves reached him, the flavors sinking into his lungs. None of the patrons were particularly strong, mostly regular members of the Grayslake clan and Redby pack. After purging Boyne Falls of all hyenas, wolves and bears took up residence. The fact that their clan and pack managed to mingle without bloodshed said a lot about Ty and Reid.

28

He also found Trista's scent lurking beneath the surface of the others. A hyena in Boyne Falls. He breathed deeper, drawing in more; was she just a hyena though? Half maybe? But there was something else in there... Keen shook his head, unable to believe the balls on the woman.

He pushed away from his SUV and headed toward the front door. He and the woman had a bit of a reckoning coming. She needed to get gone. His brothers wouldn't stand for her presence and he didn't even want to think about how Reid would react.

Except his bear didn't want her lush, curvaceous ass going anywhere other than his bed. Unlike nearly every other woman he'd come across, his animal wanted her writhing beneath him and screaming his name in pleasure. It had a singular focus: her. It roared and snarled, demanding he hunt her, find her, and claim her. No one else would ever place a hand on her skin.

Fucking crazy-assed bear.

He tugged on the door and strode through the portal. He stepped to the side, allowing others to come and go as he adjusted to the bar's atmosphere. Loud music assaulted his ears while the heavy scents of many bodies filled his nose. This was why he rarely went to places like this. It was hell on his senses.

Men and women packed the space, some settled at seats while a few were on an impromptu dance floor toward the center. His feet almost stuck to the concrete as he wove his way through the room, occasionally sliding when he stepped in a puddle of who the hell knew what. The smash and tinkle of glass breaking cut through the music but no one seemed to care. Okay then.

Left Bank looked to be about one step above a total dive and the only thing helping it cling to that dubious distinction stood behind the bar.

The place was dim, the lights shining on the bartenders, and there stood the reason Left Bank couldn't be considered a total loss. Her hair shined in the low light, bringing out the different shades of brown. Hints of red glistened and caught the glow. It also highlighted the curves of her body, tracing each rise and fall of her form. Including her deep cleavage exposed by the V of her shirt. It clung to her chest, outlining her breasts, seeming to offer them up to whoever would accept the invitation.

It sure as hell wasn't gonna be the guys drooling over her. And he wasn't going to think about the fact that his bear was ready to destroy the next man who touched her.

At all.

Keen waded through the press of customers, ignoring the purrs and strokes from the women he bumped. Normally, his bear would take comfort and solace in the contact, but today it wanted to snarl at the females. Damn it, his world was whirling through the air and he wasn't sure where he'd land.

He pushed between two large males, shoving one and then the other aside. The one on his left, a bear whose name he couldn't remember, bared his human-shaped teeth. At least the man managed to keep his animal at bay. Otherwise, he'd have to haul him off to face Van.

Keen knew the laws; Van enforced them.

And that thought brought him back to what sent him tearing out of the clan den earlier in the day.

Keen knew the laws, but he no longer had the power to act. Not like he would have if he were still in the inner-circle. Which meant he could face Trista as a man free of obligation and that thought lifted him. If he found out she posed a threat to the clan or pack, he'd take her to Ty, but he doubted she was one to cause trouble. Ty would have heard about it by now if that was the case.

The wolf on his right curled his lip and he revealed a very non-human fang. Obviously the guy didn't know who he was fighting with.

Leaning forward ever so slightly, and careful to keep his voice low, he spoke to the male. "You should think long and hard about your attitude."

The wolf's nostrils flared, chest expanding as he drew in a breath. His eyes widened and he stepped back, putting more distance between him and Keen.

Smart wolf.

Trista continued to walk past him, smiling at one customer or another as she slid drinks over the smooth surface and pocketed tips. That's when he noticed the rest of her. While her top was snug and new, her jeans were frayed, ragged, and loose. From the waist up, she looked like any other laughing bartender. But waist down told a different story. She didn't have a lot of money and had probably been nursing those pants along for months if not longer. The seams were white and there were several patches where the cotton was so thin, he could see the creaminess of her skin.

She had two jobs and lived in a dump like Lauren's old apartment and she still had trouble with money.

The bear didn't think she should have problems ever again since they'd take care of her.

He told his bear to fuck off. They were too screwed up to attach themselves to a woman. Females like Helena were one thing, but Trista seemed like she'd be a hell of a lot more.

His animal was good with that.

Raising his hand, he waved to get her attention. When her gaze finally landed on him, he didn't miss the slight widening of her eyes or the way her chest rose and fell, straining her shirt. He recognized the beginnings of panic in her. It was the same reaction she had at the gas station.

She was like a scared rabbit, even if she was a hyena.

31

Trista remained frozen in place, the beer in her hand obviously forgotten. One second turned into two and still she didn't budge. Finally, the gruff voice of another man got her moving.

"Trista!"

She jerked, spilling some of the brew, but managed to slide it onto the bar mostly full. The smile she flashed the customer was fake, her happiness obviously dimmed by his presence.

Just because she didn't want to see him didn't mean he'd leave.

She slowly made her way toward him, checking in with different patrons, filling a glass or mixing another drink before she moved on. The closer she came, the slower she moved, as if dragging her ass would make a difference. She'd soon learn it didn't.

Finally she stood before him and he looked his fill. He traced her features with his gaze, noting her round face and the dimple that appeared when she smiled as well as the pale blue of her eyes. Combined with her beautiful body and her gorgeous hair... She took his breath away. Right then, right there, Keen couldn't breathe.

"What can I get you?" The words were flat and without emotion, but he knew better. The vein along her throat pulsed and pushed against her skin, belying her indifference.

"Beer. Whatever you've got on tap." He placed a twenty on the bar and slid it toward her. When she moved to take it, he grasped her hand and rubbed his thumb over her flesh. "And ten minutes of your time."

"I'm working." She snatched her hand back, taking the cash with her.

Keen kept his attention on her as she strode to the register and collected the change before turning and pulling his drink. In just over a minute, he had his beer and a handful of bills, but instead of taking it, he pushed the money back toward her.

Of course, she shook her head in denial. "No. Keep your money."

"I'm tipping you." He raised a single brow. "You're so rich you'll turn away that kind of tip?"

Red suffused her face and—after thinking through what he'd said—he prayed it was in anger and not embarrassment. The last thing he wanted to do was mock her. He... wanted to take care of her.

Even if it was wrong for him to have those desires. A bear and a hyena?

No.

Just no.

She moved to shove it back at him and once again he pushed it back. "Take it as a tip or I'm giving it to this guy." He tilted it toward the bear beside him. He would have selected the wolf, but wolves were assholes and he wasn't sure the guy would refuse the cash.

With another glare, she shoved it in her pocket and turned away as if he were already forgotten.

Nah, that wasn't gonna happen.

"Ten minutes, Trista." He raised his voice enough to be heard.

She spun on him, eyes shooting fire in his direction. She stomped back to him and leaned over the bar. At the same time she snatched his shirt, fisting the material and dragging him toward her.

She kept her voice low, hissing at him before spitting her words in a furious whisper. "You may have every woman in Grayslake sniffing after you and you may spend the night in their beds, but I'm not some bear *whore* you can buy, Keen Abrams."

Damn his reputation, and damn him for letting it get out of control.

His heart squeezed and his dick went hard. He hurt for her even as he wanted her. Damn it. Based on the fierce reaction, he knew others had done the same except while he wanted to talk to her, they wanted something else.

The thought enraged his bear and the animal stretched his skin, pushing and shoving at his control until he thought he'd bust out his fur in the middle of the bar. Fuck. He breathed deeply, fighting the need to gag as the sour scents of the room filled his lungs. At least battling the urge to vomit distracted the bear from its desire to destroy the place.

Keen settled on his stool and resigned himself to watching her work. He glared at one male after another, shifter or not, when they got too friendly with her. It didn't take long for word to spread amongst the shifters in the building. The men went from leering to respectful in less than a half hour and it only took the humans a full hour to catch on. Trista still got her tips, still pulled drinks, but she didn't get the fast grabs and tugs as the males tried to get real friendly.

He couldn't understand why the bear wanted her so much, but while it remained steadfast in its desire for her, he'd humor the beast. The animal wanting to pounce on Trista was better than the animal wanting to gut the nearest shifter to prove his dominance.

Hour after hour passed, the men beside him ever changing, but he remained in place and kept his gaze on her. It was only a matter of time before she got off for the night and he'd be there. Ready to speak to her. Ready to find out the truth. Ready for... more?

chapter three

Trista stepped into Left Bank's darkened parking lot. Several streetlights were out, broken by one drunk customer or another. Apparently it was fun to throw empty beer bottles at the lights. Right.

She waved goodbye to her boss, leaving him as he locked up, and headed toward the sidewalk. Two in the morning and she had a good forty-minute hike to her apartment.

She strode over the glass and rock-strewn asphalt, avoiding the deep cracks and several potholes that littered the area. At some point her boss needed to clean the place up, but his favorite word was "soon."

Rolling her eyes, she hit the sidewalk and began her long trudge homeward. Thankfully she was allowed to wear black boots instead of the "fuck me" heels the waitresses wore.

Shoving her hands into jeans pockets, she refocused on her journey, careful to keep her attention on her surroundings. She'd been hounded by men during her walks in the past. Though they tended to find her difficult prey. It was hard to be scared when she was stronger than they were. She didn't get fangs and claws, but she had the reflexes and strength. She'd left more than one guy whimpering in her wake.

Occasionally a car zipped past, the residual wind whipping through her while also sending the trash littering the ground spinning and flying through the air. A can rolled into her path and she kicked it, the aluminum tinkling over the hard surface.

The sounds brought forward old memories of her and her mother doing the same, hand in hand as they walked along the road. Thoughts of the past brought a pain she'd been shoving to the back of her mind for months. She wasn't going there ever again. Thinking about it couldn't change anything.

The deep rumble of an approaching vehicle reached her just as its headlights painted her back. Her shadow danced on the sidewalk, reminding her once again she should think about cutting back and slimming down a little.

Well, going hungry will help that right along.

She had to be one of the only fluffy—never fat—shifters. Then again, Lauren hadn't been all that skinny. Oh, wait, she was human. Damn it, she didn't have a sister in solidarity.

The vehicle that neared her actually slowed instead of speeding past and she groaned. Not another one of *those*. Did she have "I'm a whore" stamped on her ass or something?

She ignored its presence as it slowed enough to keep pace with her. She also ignored the tell-tale sound of a window being lowered. Maybe the person would just go away.

"Trista!"

God hated her.

Trista glanced at the SUV riding alongside her and glared at the driver. "I'm pretty sure I told you I'm not a whore."

Keen grumbled too low for her to hear and then he raised his voice. "I know you're not a whore. I just wanna talk."

36

"Sorry." She shrugged. "All talked out."

"No, there are plenty of things to say. Such as: what are you doing alternating between Grayslake, Redby, and Boyne Falls when you shouldn't be anywhere near here?"

She huffed and stopped, turning toward him with a glare. "Sleeping, working, and working. There, done."

She returned to her journey homeward, stomping instead of walking. Panic and worry assaulted her and she prayed he wouldn't see how much he upset her.

The law is on my side. The law is on my side.

Even if the law hadn't done a damn thing for her seven months ago. Nor had the asshole in the Southeast inner-circle, but she wasn't a bear and neither was her mother and blah, blah, blah...

"Trista, I know what you are." His voice was lowered, but still audible to her. She had no doubt that had a human been present, they wouldn't have picked up his words.

"Do you want a gold star?" There, sarcastic was better than sobbing and begging.

Had her mother begged for her life?

She shouldn't think about that.

"No, I want you to get in this SUV before I haul you in here myself."

Trista paused and stared, focusing on him instead of her path. There was no doubt he'd do what he threatened. The resolve was there, written in his features, in his rigid posture. He'd chase her if he needed to, run her to ground and then shove her into his vehicle.

"C'mon, Trista. I just want to talk."

Her stomach rumbled, gurgling with anxiety. "And take me to your brother, or the wolves? I think I'm safer out here."

He grimaced. "I swear nothing will happen to you." He sighed. "Look, whether you talk to me or not, riding with me has to be better than walking. Tell me where you wanna go and I'll take you. I already know where you live."

Trista was torn in two with indecision, but one solid fact stood out from the rest. Even if she didn't go with him, he knew where she lived. She was no safer standing on the street than she was inside her home.

"Fine." She snapped off the word, hating that he'd won.

She took a step toward him and then, in the most graceful move ever, went tumbling to the ground in a rolling heap.

Stupid curbs with their stupid drops and... damn that'd hurt.

Tiny rocks dug into the heels of her hands, scraping her skin, and her purse dumped its contents on the asphalt.

God could totally cease to exist now. All over, all kinds of ceasing.

"Trista!"

Yeah, well, yelling at her as she fell didn't do much for stopping the falling.

The heavy thump of his door preceded his rapid stomps as he came toward her. In no time he had his large, warm hands on her, helping her upright. He grasped her hands, cradling them in his as he brushed the debris from her skin. Small droplets of blood surfaced and just as quickly, the wounds healed until they were pink freckles. Go team Hyena.

He traced the longest line of red skin with his thumb, following it from the base of her pointer finger to her wrist. The sand and dirt fell away beneath his touch.

"I wasn't sure," he whispered.

"Wasn't sure what?"

He continued to stroke her and each pass sent a shiver of want down her spine. "Whether the bear was right."

How could a shifter not trust their animal? Nine times out of ten it was spot on. And that one time was usually because it wanted to fuck instead of eat or eat instead of fuck. That's when it became the human's call.

Looking at Keen Abrams, she figured he picked fuck... a lot.

No man should be that gorgeous.

Based on his reputation, a lot of a lot.

Trista cleared her throat, fighting back the snakes of arousal traveling through her blood. Now was not the time to wanna bang the big, bad bear. "What was he right about?"

"You really are a hyena, but there's something—"

"Yup."

He brought his gaze to clash with hers. "Why did no one report your presence? Those shifters in the bar? The ones you run into at the gas station? Even those at your apartment?"

"Yeah, well, I've known most of them since I was a kid or they know—*knew*—my mother. It's hard to hate someone—turn them in—when you know death is very likely. When they've been slinging your drinks or selling you honey buns for years, they aren't too keen on losing someone they've called a friend." Trista tugged her hands from his grasp and bent to toss her belongings back into her purse. There wasn't much—she didn't have a lot at the moment—but whatever she had left, she wanted to keep.

"But you shouldn't be here. The pack was—"

"Purged. The definition of which is to deem a specific species, family, or other type of cohesive group with a definitive, if not solid, hierarchy from inhabiting a specified area."

He blinked once, jerking his head back in surprise. "That is... surprisingly accurate."

Trista shrugged. Her survival depended on knowing and using the laws to her advantage. "It is what it is."

"So you know that your *kind*"—he said the word as if it tasted vile— "shouldn't be in Grayslake, Redby, or Boyne Falls."

Pushing to her feet once again she shrugged and then flashed Keen a smile. Patting him on the cheek, she grinned even wider. "Why don't you think of the laws of visitation coupled with the stated definitions and see who's right about that one?"

With that, she strode around him and toward the SUV. She'd let him stew on her challenge for a little while and in the meantime, she'd enjoy riding in glorious, leather-lined style.

*

Trista was a mystery. Gorgeous, tough, a fighter, and smart as hell, and still a puzzle.

It made his dick hard.

It made the bear want to roll in her scent. The scent of human, hyena, and something that didn't make sense. Something he couldn't quite nail down.

Regardless, it made both halves of him crave her.

But he wasn't about to act on his desires. At least not until he knew more about her, before he ferreted out all of her secrets.

40

The SUV trundled along the rutted road, turning left and then right as he headed toward her place. "Sunwell Apartments, right? Where Lauren Evans used to live?"

"Yup." Her attention remained on the passing scenery, which was fine with him. It gave him the chance to watch her as he drove. "Eyes on the road," she snapped.

Or not.

Silence continued to reign and he cleared his throat, determined to fill the empty space. "So, you know a lot about shifter laws."

"Yup."

"Is there a reason?"

Trista snorted. "When someone wants you gone or wants to treat you like shit, and you disagree, it's a good idea to tell him why continuing would be a mistake."

"And you can do that?" Keen turned down Sunwell Street and then left into the community parking lot.

The moment he popped the SUV into park, her hand was on the door handle, tugging it to enable her escape. It took every ounce of strength he possessed to stay put. The beast in him wanted to snatch her back and take her to his den.

Instead, he remained frozen when she hopped down and stepped away. Hand clutching the edge of the door, she focused on him once more. "I know I can. We," she coughed, "*I've* been doing it for twenty years and as long as you realize you're wrong, and tell your Itan, I'll continue to do so."

His gut clenched when she'd said "we" and it nearly turned inside out when she slammed the door closed and dashed toward the apartment building.

That's when he finally noticed the place, took in the details, and he frowned. The roof toward the left side sagged and seemed to be waiting for any reason to collapse. Several shutters dangled precariously from the windows and at least one pane of glass looked like it'd been smashed in.

Half the lights in the parking lot were out while the other half were so dim, they didn't make much of a difference. Cracks littered the asphalt, some so large and jagged that they rose above the flat surface. Trash and debris were scattered everywhere, dancing in the breeze. Several splashes of neon yellow caught his eye, some balled and others flitting in the wind.

Keen remembered the place used to belong to one of the bears who betrayed the clan and tried to kill both Mia and Lauren. He wondered who'd taken possession of it and why they hadn't bothered fixing it up.

A high-pitched, feminine curse split the air, reaching through his windshield and grabbing him by the throat.

Trista.

He was out of his SUV before the desire to go to her fully formed. One moment he sat behind the wheel of his vehicle, the engine softly purring, and the next he was on the move. He bolted toward the stairwell, hunting her. His bear lent his assistance, allowing him to sniff out her path as he ran. He raced up one level and then sprinted up another before sliding to a stop on the landing.

Another curse, this one louder than the last, reached him and he hurried to her. He paused in an open doorway and gripped the door frame. The scent surrounding the area told him this was her place and he scowled. The room was sparse and that was being generous in his description.

There was literally no furniture in sight. No couch or dining room table and the walls were bare. Just... nothing.

42

"Fuckery Fuck McFuckerson!" Trista came stomping into the living room and froze, glaring at him. She pointed a finger in his direction and sneered. "Don't tell me what to say. And if you even think of going furry on my pissed-off ass I will cut you."

"Um... Okay?"

He wasn't sure what the problem was, but he wanted to fix it. He and the bear wanted to put a smile on her face and keep it there. Forever.

That thought gave him a gut-check. After all these years, all the women, the bear really had settled on a single female.

Trista.

"I can't believe he did it. He fucking did it." She ran her hands through her hair and then down her neck, lifting her face to the ceiling. The move exposed the smooth line of her throat. Or rather, not smooth. Scars littered her pale skin and he opened his mouth to ask about them, but she kept speaking. "It's all gone."

"Gone? This isn't how it normally is?" He knew she didn't have money, her clothes attested to that.

That earned him a wide-eyed stare. "Seriously?"

"Uh..." He was so out of depth with her.

Trista took another look through the room, glaring at the blank walls, and then stomped toward him. "Fuck this. The bastard took my bed and I want that shit back."

When she got close, he stepped out of the way and let her pass. She tramped down the stairs, speed increasing as she neared the first floor. She broke into a brisk walk once she hit the sidewalk, feet moving faster and faster with each step. By the time they rounded the end of the building she was practically running.

He didn't know where she was headed, but he refused to leave her side, even when she glared at him. Instead of justifying his presence, he shrugged and kept up with her. Something obviously infuriated her and he wanted to be there when she confronted whoever she was poised to challenge.

She finally halted before a battered, dented door and instantly began pounding on it with her fist. "Hey! Asshole! Open this fucking door!" She kicked the metal panel. "I want my shit back! I want my bed, dickhead!"

Keen's bear rose to its feet, a threatening rumble filling his mind. "He took your things?"

His voice was soft, but the threat lingered in his tone. He would take on the male behind the door and get Trista's belongings back whether the man had a right to them or not. Period.

Trista glowered. "Why are you here? I can take care of myself. Go home to one of your girlfriends or something. Find Bambi or whatever." She pounded on the door some more. "Hey, asshole, open up."

He ignored the dig and the denial sprung to his lips. He didn't have a woman in every corner of the town. There was a reason. Without them he…

"Obviously," he drawled. "Is this the new owner's apartment?"

"Yes," she snapped and then kicked it again.

"Stand back." He eased her aside and her frown returned in full force. He'd accept her anger if it meant making her happy when all was said and done. Mimicking Trista's earlier actions, he knocked and raised his voice. "Open the door."

Where she'd failed, he succeeded. Not because he yelled louder or was male. No, he allowed his bear to come forward, fill his voice, and his deep baritone crawled through the door to the male on the other side. Pure power filled him and was then directed at the male he had yet to face.

In less than a second, the panel swung wide, revealing the new owner of Sunwell Apartments.

A hint of fear coated the man's features which pleased the bear, but the rest of the male disgusted Keen. He looked much like Jerry from the gas station: pot belly, stringy hair, and a scent that curdled his stomach. It took a lot for a bear to gain so much weight and get fat that way. The male had obviously been working at it for a long time.

"Sir?" The man's eyes were wide with fear and he tilted his head, acknowledging Keen's dominance. His inner-animal was pleased with the show of submission and then the owner looked at Trista, giving her a loathsome scowl.

That did *not* please the beast.

"What are you doing with this garbage?"

The scent of Trista's rage surrounded him, pummeled him with her anger, and he caught her wrist before she could strike the man. Not because he didn't want her to defend herself. No, he just didn't want her to get in the way when he punched the asshole.

But he had a few things to discover first.

"Your name?"

"Craven Simmons."

"And you own Sunwell now?" He raised his eyebrows.

"Yeah, after that—" Craven swallowed the words, which saved his life. As it was, he'd earned a beating simply because he upset the woman at his side. "Yes."

"So, what happened to Trista's things?"

"Is that what this is about?" Craven curled his lip. "She owed rent and I took payment."

"Uh-huh." He looked to her. "That true?"

"Depends who you ask," she hedged.

"I'm asking you."

She sighed. "Here's how things go with people like me." She pointed at herself. "I'm a half-hyena—"

Craven spat on the ground at her feet and Keen reacted without thought. He went after the male before he could blink, grabbing him around the throat with one hand and yanking him from the apartment. With hardly any effort, he slammed the werebear against the brick wall and held him steady even as he fought to get free.

"You were saying?" Craven gurgled and Keen tightened his hold. "Sorry about that. Continue."

"I'm half-hyena and have—*had*—difficulties with the local pack before, well, before. That meant we—*I*—had problems finding jobs and a place to live. Some people like Bru don't give a damn what you are as long as you pay rent. In my case, it was double the price of anyone else."

That shit was going to stop. "Go on."

"When Bru was killed, this guy"—she waved toward the still gasping Craven—"raised my rent again. People like me don't get rental agreements. We get a wink and a nudge. So he raised it and I can't pay it. I've been doing the best I can, but…" She shrugged and the insecurity and unease in her gaze made him want to hug her close. "But it's not enough. I got home this morning and found an eviction notice on my front door and my place was empty." She focused on Craven and before Keen could blink, she kneed the asshole in the balls. "You took all my cash, dickhead."

46

Had the man been able to breathe, he probably would have cried out in pain. But he couldn't. So he didn't.

"Your things? Your money?" Rage suffused him, filling his every breath. "What made it worse tonight?"

"I at least had a couch, a table, and a bed in there. They came with the apartment. Now I've got nothing." She rushed forward again, but this time Keen managed to catch her with his free arm.

"Easy now." He noted the trembles that wracked her body. She was pissed and—he breathed deep—scared as hell.

Yup, not happening. Not to his Trista.

"I left the SUV running. Why don't you go get in there for me?"

The shakes increased. "But—"

"I'll take care of this, you go."

"I—" She stared at him, hope, fatigue, and anxiety filling her gaze.

"I'm going to chat with Craven and then you and I can talk in the SUV. Let me help you, Trista. You don't know me, you have no reason to trust me, but take a deep breath and know I'm just trying to help." He prayed she could smell past his rage at Craven and discover he spoke the truth.

"Keen..."

Carefully, so damned carefully because he valued his junk, he pulled her close to him and wrapped his arm around her waist. "Let me do this and then we can speak."

She took so long to reply that he wondered if she could suddenly no longer form words.

"Okay." The word was barely a whisper, but his beast rejoiced in her small measure of trust.

He watched her walk away, watched the sway of her hips—damn she was something—and the way her hands trembled as her arms hung limply at her sides. That took the small ounce of pleasure he'd experience away in a heartbeat.

Hand still wrapped around Craven's throat, he focused on the male. "Now, with very small words, explain to me why you felt your behavior was acceptable."

He eased his hold enough to let the male to breathe. "That bitch—"

"Ah, ah, ah." He allowed his nails to prick the man's skin. "That was too big. Try again."

A good fifteen minutes later, Keen left the male in a quivering, whining mess. When he rounded the corner and spied a decidedly pale Trista huddled on his front seat, he wondered why he hadn't slaughtered the asshole landlord. The bear wanted to know why, too.

Good point.

Keen spun and headed back the way he came. Trista could wait five more minutes.

*

Trista had one thought whirling through her mind as Keen placed the SUV in reverse. It had nothing to do with a plastic bag filled with her belongings that he'd tossed into the backseat. Nor were they centered on the wad of cash he'd pushed into her hands.

No. The only thing she could focus on was the fact his knuckles were bloody.

Because of her.

Not because he'd hit her, but because he'd fought for her. He'd fought and then gotten back some of her things. Staring at the ball of money in her lap, she realized she wasn't poor any longer.

48

Okay, she wasn't rich, but she could at least spring for a hotel for a few nights and actually *eat*.

It made her wonder if there was more to Keen than a pretty face and quick, seductive smile.

"Thank you." Her words broke the silence. "I know I didn't deserve your help and I've been nothing but a bitch, but thank you."

Keen grunted.

He drove farther along Sunwell and then turned onto Main Street. They traveled along in silence, the rhythmic thump of the tires rolling over asphalt warring with the sound of their breathing. Moments passed and she spied the sign for the single hotel in their small town.

They approached and he didn't slow, the SUV maintaining its speed as he flew by.

She half-turned in her seat, pointing behind them as she faced him. "You passed the hotel."

"Yes."

That was it. A single word, a single syllable.

"And amazingly enough, I'm staying at the hotel for the next few days."

He flicked his blinker and the harsh clicking of the indicator stung her ears. "Not really, no."

The SUV eased right and she gripped her seat to remain steady. "What do you mean 'no'?"

"Well, my discussion with Craven—"

She snorted. Apparently bloodied knuckles constituted a "discussion" in his world. He grumbled something about not killing males who deserved it, before he spoke.

"After my *discussion*"—he glared at her—"with Craven, it's best if you stay with me at the clan den for the time being."

"You?"

"Me."

"But you... I'm... It's just..." She shook her head. "I really appreciate what you did for me. I mean..." She swallowed past the lump at her throat and stared at the money once again. It wasn't a lot to some people, but it was huge to her. "Thank you. But I'm not staying with you. I'm not going anywhere with you but to the hotel. You and I being near a bed ain't happening."

Ever. Because he was too tempting and probably knew a million ways to seduce someone. Not that he'd seduce her or want to seduce her, but she did have a vagina...

"Uh-huh."

Trista tried again. "Don't you remember? You're supposed to be running me out of town on a misguided concept of authority and righteousness, not leading me to my potential death and dismemberment. Hopefully in that order if it has to happen."

This time they turned left, bouncing over the rutted road, but she couldn't be bothered with their surroundings. The important thing was to get him to swing his happy SUV-driving ass around and take her to the hotel. Going anywhere with an Abrams was a bad, bad idea.

Really bad.

"Misguided?" He glanced at her, a single brow raised.

Trista winced. "Misguided may not have been the right word. Maybe ignorant. That's better. It's more ignorance and authority than anything."

Based on his frown, she didn't think she'd made things better. A closer look revealed she may have made it worse.

"I'm ignorant? Do you know who I am?"

"Is that a trick question? We've already established you're Keen Abrams. Your brothers are Ty, Van, and Isaac. The Itan, Enforcer, and Healer respectively. Also, in case you were wondering, they'd probably enjoy me being on the 'die today' menu."

Suddenly the SUV came to a jerky stop, the action causing her to thump against her seat with a grunt. He cut the engine and shoved his door open, leaving her to gawk at her surroundings. The house that loomed before them was massive and yet it appeared welcoming. It had that old-world, southern charm thing going on with its high pillars and white exterior.

It also had a very large glaring male standing next to a very pregnant female who was bracketed by a familiar, very evil bear cub.

Keen appeared at her door, tugging it open before reaching across her and freeing her from the seatbelt.

"You really did bring me to the clan den." He didn't deny it and her doom stood on the porch and crossed his massive arms over his chest. "Please remember: death *then* dismemberment. That part is important."

Yup, dying, dead, and gone.

"Hush."

She shook her head. "Keen—"

He placed his finger over her lips. "Hush. You need a place to stay and, for now, this is where I'm at. So, you're crashing here. I'll keep you safe."

She licked his finger to get him to stop touching her. No matter their age, boys did not like getting licked by surprise. "You're tying the words 'you' and 'where I'm staying' together and I don't like that."

"Trista," he sighed. "Right now, I need you to let it go."

She looked at him then, stared into his eyes that should be brown and were now black. Allowing her gaze to shift to the male on the porch, she quickly redirected it to Keen.

"I'm going to be safe? I'm really not ready to die." She wasn't prepared to join her mother.

"You're going to be safe," he nodded.

"Even from him and the spawn from the seventh level of hell?"

Keen glanced over his shoulder and then turned back to her, a smile on his lips. "Yes, even from the spawn."

"Why should I trust you?" That was the big one. When she moved past everything that'd happened in the last several hours there was one thing glaringly obvious.

Token protests. She'd given half-hearted objections when he'd done this or that. For some reason, that snarly part of her wanted to be near Keen and worked to push aside every objection she had.

Keen brushed strands of her hair from her face and tucked them behind her ear. His fingertips skimmed her cheek, callused skin abrading hers, but she didn't want him to stop touching her. The scent of Craven's blood hit her nose, but beneath it lurked Keen's and she was okay with that.

Okay with his nearness, his touch, his decisions…

Stupid animal thing that trusted him and accepted that he could—would—defend her.

"Because I understand the laws of visitation and you know the textbook definition of purge. Because I think dealing with people like Craven is pretty standard for you and maybe I'd like to show you it doesn't have to be." He cupped her cheek and his tenderness nearly brought tears to her eyes. *Nearly.* "And worst case, I'll take you wherever you want to go in the morning. For right now, give in and sleep."

Rhinos stomped through her stomach, bringing along a good dose of panic and fear.

"I won't be safe here, Keen." She wheezed out the words.

"Yes, you will. You'll be here as my guest."

She snorted. "Of the bears? The ones who drove out an entire pack of hyenas? Which, by the way, I happen to be one."

So was her mother. Kind of. Sorta, but not really.

"Trista?" His gaze remained focused on her while he caressed her cheek. "I'll take care of you."

She wanted to believe him so, so badly. For once in her life, she wanted to be able to lean on someone else. Just once...

Making a decision, she brushed aside his touch and straightened. She drew her emotions back into her body, hiding them. She'd try and believe in him, but she'd keep her heart locked away and out of reach. "I have to be out of Grayslake and at the gas station by eleven."

He frowned, but nodded. "I'll get you there. C'mon."

C'mon. Like it was so easy to crawl from the SUV and follow a man toward the male who may have ordered her mother's death.

Right.

53

chapter four

Keen kept his grip tight on Trista's hand, twining their fingers together as he held her captive. He sensed her resistance, her desire to flee, but he couldn't let that happen. Not when this simple touch of skin on skin soothed his bear like no other. How many women had he been through while searching for this sense of calm?

Too many to count.

Yet, with this simple connection, his bear was focused on *protection* and not *destruction*.

A novel experience for him.

He drew her closer to the clan den, his feet crunching over the pale gravel driveway. Eventually the rocks gave way to grass, the soft earth welcoming him, and then he stood before the steps leading to the home.

Steps that led to the porch which, in turn, led to Ty and Mia. Mia's expression was open and welcoming with a touch of wariness. He couldn't blame her for the emotions, her reaction to Trista.

Hyenas had ripped their lives apart, had been responsible for deaths and scarring wounds, but that wasn't Trista's doing.

"Ty, Mia." He bared his neck and his bear snarled in protest. He was stronger, faster, and bigger than his older brother.

But they sure as shit didn't want to be in charge. Which was why he showed Ty the deference due the clan's Itan and kept a lid on his beast. Unless the fucker wanted to lead the Grayslake clan, it'd shut its trap. Reminded of that, the animal quieted pretty damned fast.

Ty narrowed his eyes, attention shifting between Keen and Trista before finally settling on Keen. He tilted his head toward Trista. "What's she still doing in town? I purged Boyne Falls. I think it's pretty obvious that I don't want hyenas anywhere near here. Redby either. This part of Georgia is closed to them."

Keen nodded. "Yes, if she were making her home in Boyne Falls, she'd be violating your decree. Since she's not," he shrugged, "she's not. She's abiding the laws of visitation."

"You can spout laws all day, Keen"—Ty's glared hardened—"but she's not coming into this house. Hell, I don't want her in Grayslake."

Keen raised his eyebrows. "Not coming in? Amazingly enough, she is. Laws of visitation with a dash of occupation. It boils down to the fact that she can visit the territory and she can safely stay with anyone who grants her shelter. Since I live here, I'm granting it. Step aside, Ty." Focusing on his older brother, he placed his foot on the bottom step and then rose to the second. Ty didn't look like he was gonna budge. "Move. Aside."

Finally, Mia spoke. "Ty," she whispered. "You know he's probably right."

Keen almost snorted. Probably right? There was no question. He'd happily flip through the books in his office, his ex-office, and point out his justification for Trista's presence.

Ty breathed deeply and then froze as a ripple, a gradual wave, overtook his skin. Brown fur quickly followed in its wake, coating his brother's arms and neck. It snaked higher, slithering until his cheeks were equally covered. "I know that scent, Keen."

"I'm sure you do. You met a lot of hyenas that day."

That day. The day Ty waded into Boyne Falls and with the help of the wolves, rid the town of their infestation. Rid the area of shifters like Trista. He had no doubt there were many who deserved to die at the time, but what about women like Trista? What about them?

His brother shook his head. "No, it's more than that. It's—"

Mia placed a hand on Ty's arm, cutting his brother off. The Itana's attention was entirely on Trista and Keen refocused on the woman at his side. She tried to put on a brave front, but even he saw the stark whiteness of her face. It was then he sensed the trembles that traveled from her hands to his and her whole body seemed to buzz with suppressed fear. Cold. Hard. Fear.

She'd been more pissed than afraid of Keen, but she quivered beneath the strength of Ty's glare.

Unacceptable.

He opened his mouth to blast his brother, but Mia beat him to it.

"Ty, she's coming inside."

His brother flung his arm out, gesturing toward Trista. "She smells familiar, Mia. And there's something else. She's—"

"She's part hyena and from Boyne Falls. I'd be surprised if she didn't. Now, she's coming inside. Right this second." Mia looked at Keen. "Do you want her in the guestroom that connects to yours?"

That had Trista freezing, but he didn't take a moment to ask her why. He knew she didn't trust him and he hadn't given her reason to. But he had sanctuary within his grasp and he wasn't going to squander the opportunity.

"Yes. That room is perfect."

Mia flashed him a smile, wide and with a hint of happiness. "Good." She removed her hand from Ty and turned toward the front door. "Come on in, then."

Ignoring his brother's glare, he tugged Trista up the steps. He made sure his body remained between the woman at his side and Ty as they passed. A low, rumbling growl came from Ty, quickly followed by renewed tremors from Trista. Keen curled his lip and exposed a rapidly lengthening fang.

He would take on Ty for Trista. Take him on and win.

He didn't realize he'd stopped until Trista tugged on their joined hands, urging him to continue moving forward. He fought to keep his gaze intent on Ty's, but eventually he was forced to look away, to follow the woman into the clan den.

They moved down familiar hallways, delving deeper into the house until they came to a stop near Keen's suite.

When they reached the two doorways, Mia turned back to them. Her hand continued to stroke her large belly, palm gliding over her roundness in what he assumed was a soothing motion. The larger she got, the more often he found her rubbing her stomach.

"Here you are, then." Her smile was a little more forced, but still held a hint of welcome. "I'll just get Trista settled and then I'll see you two in the morning."

Keen wasn't sure it was a good idea for the two women to be alone. In fact, if Ty found Trista's scent on his mate, it might send him over the edge.

"I can—"

Mia cut in. "Go to bed and we'll see you in the morning."

Trista's expression pleaded with him, begged him not to allow Mia to pull her away, but Mia was the Itana. And while his inner-bear had problems with Ty, it had nothing but respect for their Itana.

Mia reached for the door on the left and turned the knob, allowing the panel to swing wide and grant the women entrance. He knew what they'd find. The room was decorated much like his own. Solid dark wood furniture with deep colors that weren't overly masculine, but weren't feminine either. Dear God, it was unisex. Plain. Interchangeable with any other guestroom in the world.

No hint of his personality lingered in the two bedrooms and it made him realize even more about himself. He was a guest in his own home. His mother had decorated the rooms when he was younger and it was as if his parents knew he was only passing through. He wouldn't settle in the clan den.

They knew he'd leave someday and they hadn't bothered trying to suit his tastes.

"Keen?" Trista's soft voice tugged him from the sudden realization that he'd never been meant to stay in the clan den—hell, maybe even Grayslake—for the rest of his life.

"Sorry," he cleared his throat. "Right. I guess I'll see you in the morning."

His hand shook as he reached for his bedroom door, arm trembling as the truth sunk into his bones.

Keen's home wasn't in Grayslake, maybe not even in Georgia. Catching one last glimpse of Trista as the door swung shut made him realize one other truth. He might not be meant for Georgia, but maybe, just maybe, he *was* meant for Trista.

*

Trista was gonna die. Plain and simple. Dead and gone and buried before she had a chance to finish her horrible, hand-to-mouth existence.

Was this how her mother felt?

She didn't have time to follow that line of thought because suddenly she found herself following a waddling Itana into a bedroom. The space was filled with solid furniture. Nothing fancy, but obviously high quality with shining dark wood polished to a smooth shine. The bedspread sported a deep red. Not one of passion, but of comfort and warmth.

"Well, this is it." Mia made her way through the room. "There are extra clothes in the dressers. Just sweats and stuff. Nothing fancy." The woman turned and pointed at a closed door nearby. "That's the bathroom. It's got a shower and all that. It's a Jack and Jill which means Keen uses it as well. I'm sure he won't just come barging in or anything." The Itana blushed. "You can trust him. More than anyone else here, you can trust him."

Trista stared at the closed door. The white, carved panel taunted her. It scared her and intrigued her in equal measure. Would he come in while she slept? And if he did, what would happen?

"Why?" She refocused on Mia. "Why can I trust him?"

Mia frowned and turned her attention to the ground as if gathering her thoughts. She finally sighed and waddled toward a chair near the large bay window. "Keen is…" She leaned back, hands resting atop her protruding stomach. "Sit down for a minute."

Trista did as asked, climbing onto the bed and settling on the soft mattress. As soon as she was situated, Mia spoke again.

"I know he seems like a ladies' man and all that. He pretends to be so lighthearted and uncaring, but that's not…" Mia paused, seeming to gather her thoughts. "Keen is the brother they don't think about." Trista furrowed her brow and opened her mouth to comment, but the Itana kept going. "He's much younger than Ty, Van, and Isaac. And he doesn't have an official purpose in the clan. Well, he did, but he stepped down this morning."

60

Mia shook her head. "Anyway. Ty was raised as the Itan, Van as the Enforcer, and Isaac as the Healer." She shrugged and continued. "Unfortunately, that left Keen to his own devices. It allowed him to grow and develop without limitations. I don't want you to think his parents didn't care enough to raise him, but with securing the clan's future…" She shook her head and fell silent. "He's strong—stronger than even Ty realizes, I think—and could lead his own clan if he wanted."

"That's… but…"

"Yeah." Mia gave her a rueful smile. "I know. He just… he's so much more than this clan, than being disrespected as the Keeper and constantly thought of as simply a bothersome younger brother." The Itana looked at Trista. "I'm hoping you can help with that."

"I'm nothing, Itana."

"Mia. And you are something."

Trista gulped. "No, I'm nothing. I'm the bastard daughter of—" She swallowed the words. Admitting her parentage at this point would only cause problems. Problems she didn't need. She already had enough. "I don't see where I could help anything."

"Are you aware of what happened between the bears and hyenas?"

She shook her head. No, she'd just known that her kind pissed off the Itan. A lot.

"It boils down to the hyenas helping my uncle in his attempt to take control of my hometown. The Alpha held my adopted son—my baby cousin Parker—captive while my cousin Griss attacked the clan house." The Itana seemed lost in memories. "Keen had the den outfitted with caches of guns. Without a word, he'd prepped the den with ways to defend us. And when I wandered after him into the living room, he took bullets for me. Several hit his chest, and his only thought was for my safety. He's more than he seems and better than most bears in the clan." Mia lowered her voice to a whisper. "Sometimes even better than Ty."

61

Trista swallowed past the lump in her throat and pushed down the desire to hunt Keen, to assure herself and that hint of beast inside her that he was safe and whole. She didn't want to ponder the desires, didn't want to examine them too closely, but she couldn't banish them entirely.

"Before then, he worked to capture Griss and his accomplice. Then he negotiated and collaborated with the Southeast Itan." Mia focused on her. "All without fanfare or acknowledgment from his brothers. Hell, even after everything was said and done, no one said a word. He's the one no one considers or thinks about, Trista. Only... only I don't think that's the case with you."

She swallowed her agreement, refusing to admit that from the first instant she'd seen Keen, she'd done nothing but think about him. True, it'd only been a few hours since their paths collided, but he'd filled every inch of her brain. And when her mind told her to run far and fast—she was screwing with her safety by staying with him—her heart said "fuck off."

"He even became Keeper by default. No one gave him the title or completed the ceremony to welcome him to the inner-circle. He just... was."

Keeper. That's how he knew the laws, how he knew she was able to stay in Grayslake and spend time in Boyne Falls and Redby. "How long has he been the Keeper?"

"Almost seven months."

Trista closed her eyes. "He knows the laws as well as I do."

And I've been living by them since I could talk.

"I imagine so, but for different reasons."

Trista opened her eyes and looked to the Itana. The knowing look on the woman's face had her jumping from the bed and moving away from Mia. She walked around the room, looking everywhere but at the woman seated near the window.

"I should"—she licked her lips—"I should get to sleep. It's late and I have to be out of here in," Trista looked at her watch, at the countdown that displayed on the face, "five hours."

The rustle of cloth followed by a low grunt announced Mia's rise and the soft shuffle of her feet across the carpet allowed Trista to track her progress. The woman paused beside her. "I suppose the time is significant."

"Yes." She wouldn't say more, wouldn't admit to the loopholes that let her flit from place to place.

"And Keen knows its importance."

"Yes." There was no doubt he knew. A Keeper would understand, would see the laws from all angles and advise the Itan. Maybe he was more than a guy who jumped from bed to bed.

But he wasn't a Keeper. That thought made her wonder if he'd explain things to Ty or just let it go. She prayed he'd let it go, that she'd get out of Grayslake before it became an issue.

"Good night, then." Mia rested a hand on Trista's shoulder, rubbing her back slightly, and she fought the urge to flinch. "Remember that you're safe. I'll see you in the morning."

"Good night," she whispered and held her breath as she waited for Mia to leave. When the door clicked shut, she released the air in her lungs. Without hesitation, she rushed to the bedroom door and flicked the lock, securing her against… no one.

If a bear wanted in, it'd get in. With luck, the time it'd take to bust down the door would give her a chance to escape through the window.

Trista judged the distance between the bed and the door. A lot of luck.

Maybe sleeping in the chair would be a good idea. She could prop her feet on the window sill and—

A low rumble reached her, a sound not familiar to her, and she spun to face whatever approached. Instead of finding some sort of threat, she spied Keen standing in the bathroom doorway.

She jumped and gasped. "You scared me."

Way to go, Captain Obvious. He was a full werebear and could rely on his animal's senses. He could smell that he frightened her.

Keen grimaced. "Sorry. I just wanted to make sure you have everything you need."

She nodded, pointedly ignoring the bed that lay between them.

"Good, good," he nodded. "I, uh…" It was his turn to ignore her. "I'll see you in the morning, then."

He pretended that he hadn't heard Mia's words. But there was no way he didn't know what they'd discussed—she didn't imagine the doors were all that thick—but she let him cling to the pretense.

Keen stepped back, sliding the door shut behind him, leaving her alone in the strange room.

She didn't sense movement in the bathroom and she was half tempted to take a shower, but stopped herself. Stripping and stepping beneath the water would leave her vulnerable to him, to the others in the den.

Instead, she settled for digging through the drawers and snaring a pair of large shorts and a T-shirt. She undressed and then tugged on the borrowed clothing, much more comfortable now.

Leaving her clothes in a folded pile, she moved to the bed and grabbed the top comforter and a few pillows. In no time she'd set up a comfy bed in the large chair and propped her feet on the window sill. Not the best bed, but better than some she'd endured through her life.

With a sigh, she settled in to sleep. It was one night. One night in the lion, er, bear's den and then she could hunt for a place to stay tomorrow.

And she would not think about the delicious Keen Abrams who slept in the room next door. She wouldn't entertain any thoughts of him in his bed—shirtless or nude?—and what it'd be like to touch him.

Trista demanded her mind leave daydreams of his hands on her alone.

Instead, she was faced with other things. Her thoughts were awash with Mia's words and her own memories.

Thinking about Keen's childhood, his life until now, had her wondering which was worse: indifference or hatred.

With that question tumbling through her, she relaxed into her makeshift bed, ready for sleep to pull her from her worries and allow her to push them aside for the night.

Even as she drifted to sleep, one question continued to swirl inside her.

Is it worse to have your family not care enough to know you or for your family to care so much they want you dead?

chapter **five**

Dreams had always troubled Trista. Good or bad, the annoyance with them always filled her because she knew they weren't real. She couldn't revel in a wonderful fantasy that captured her mind as she slept because it was only a matter of time before she opened her eyes and the real world intruded. Of course, she thanked God for the knowledge that nightmares would end the moment she woke.

Unless it was a memory. Unless it was parts of her past that came calling when her eyes drifted shut. Unless it was a tiny piece of her personal hell that eased forward.

Then she was in there, deep in the middle of the bloody action.

Tonight she was thirteen and she learned, not for the first time, that pretty words weren't always pretty, but claws were always sharp.

Trista tugged on her favorite shirt and let it wrap around her like a comforting blanket. Next were her baggy jeans and looking at her outfit, she was kinda glad she stuck to wearing black a lot. It meant her mom didn't have to buy her new clothes for the funeral.

"Tris, you coming?" Her mom didn't have to yell. Heck, half the time she whispered so Mrs. Montfort in 1A didn't bang on her ceiling for them to be quiet.

"Yeah." She raised her voice a little louder than her mother's and then…

Thump. Thump. Thump.

Good old Mrs. Montfort.

Ignoring the banging, she slipped into her ratty sneakers and left the bedroom she shared with her mom. The apartment wasn't much, none of theirs ever were, but it was home. For now.

Trudging through the small space, she spied the pictures of her growing up. They lined the small hallway and were scattered throughout the tiny living room. Her mom said poor didn't mean unhappy, it just meant occasionally hungry.

Though, with Mr. Scott giving them cash, they weren't hungry too often. They still didn't have money for much, not with all the laws they had to duck, but they at least had food to eat.

She wondered if that'd continue now that he was dead.

Trista didn't think so.

The second she met her mom at the door, she was enveloped in a hug, her mother's scent wrapping around her like a snug blanket. Her mom always smelled good. Sweet and happy.

Yeah, happy had a scent. She learned that when she was younger, when she first realized she was different than other kids. It was also when she figured out that hate stunk.

For now, she'd stick with smelling the happy. She'd be surrounded by the hate soon enough.

"Ready?" Her mother's voice vibrated through her and that weird part of her that her mom called hyena, rumbled in pleasure.

"Yeah." Trista rubbed her cheek on her mother's shoulder.

"Okay, then." Her mom became all business, stepping away and snagging her purse before opening the door and moving into the hallway.

The stench of the space hit her like a truck and she sneezed, trying to clear her nose of the aroma. Blech. Someone puked on the stairs again.

Instead of commenting on it, they stepped around the puddle and kept on going. No sense in complaining when there wasn't anything they could do about it. Mr. Scott's money went for food and Mom's went toward paying the rent. Since her mother got pregnant with Trista in her senior year of high school and barely managed to get her diploma, she wasn't exactly qualified for much beyond working at the diner in Grayslake and manning the counter at the fast food joint in Boyne Falls.

And then she couldn't even work at those all that often because of the stupid bitch in Boyne Falls. Mr. Scott's wife didn't like her mom, but the woman couldn't get around the laws of visitation which meant they were safe. For now.

Who knew what'd happen after today.

"Come on, Tris. We're gonna be late," her mom called to her as she slid behind the wheel of their clunker. The car looked like it was on its last legs, and it was more rust than metal, but it got them around.

But why did she have to hurry? They were gonna be late no matter what.

Flopping into the passenger seat, she tugged on her seatbelt and then looked at her watch. Out of everything they owned, their watches were the most expensive.

"Atomic" watches. Ones that always kept perfect time. It was super important which was why they splurged on them. Her mom never wanted to give the local shifter "people" a reason to hurt them for hanging around too long. Twelve hours and one minute was one minute too long for them.

Well, for Trista really. Being part hyena meant *she* couldn't hang around. That didn't apply to her mom since she was human.

What. Ever.

Stupid furball rules. Those rules, those "people," were another reason they were still hanging around.

It didn't take long for them to reach the border between Grayslake and Boyne Falls, but her mom didn't cross the line. Her mom had to juggle several shifts and really work out the timeline in order for them to go to Mr. Scott's funeral, but she'd said it was important.

Trista didn't see how.

Because he was your father.

Blech. It wasn't like she'd seen him for more than five minutes in her entire life. Even his checks came in the mail and were sprayed down with some disgusting cologne. He couldn't be connected to Trista and her mom. His "mate" wouldn't like that he still had contact with them.

Throwing the car in park, her mom slumped in her seat, her attention focused on the road before them.

Two hyenas paced the street while a human-shaped, gun-toting man leaned against a nearby SUV.

"A welcoming party. Again," Trista sneered.

"Well, Mrs. Scott doesn't like us. You know that."

"Yeah." Trista wiggled and settled into a comfortable position. "I don't know why she can't just let us go already." Not that they had the money to leave, but whatever. She sighed and glanced at her watch again. Only a minute had passed. Crap. "How long do we have to sit here?"

"Another eleven minutes."

She sighed again and watched the animals down the street watching them. They drooled on the asphalt. Gross. Then she remembered why they were drooling—they were looking forward to making them dinner. Even grosser. And scary as hell.

Finally the wait was over and her mom popped the car into gear. She pulled onto the street and they approached the city's border. The hyenas quit their pacing, but kept on with their drooling. Ick.

As they passed the three "people," the human guy pointed his gun at them and the two hyenas jumped and scratched the side of their car.

She wondered if she was gonna die now, if Mr. Scott's order had died along with him. Instead of cowering and showing fear like she had when she was little, she stared the man in the eye, kept her attention right on him. They moved forward and she remained focused on him, not breaking his gaze as they passed.

He flinched first and dropped his eyes.

Score one for her.

"You shouldn't antagonize them like that." Her mom's voice was half censuring and half prideful.

Trista focused on the pride and shrugged. "Not my fault he's weak."

Her mom hummed, but didn't say anything else. Not while they finished their drive, nor when she pulled into a parking spot at the cemetery.

Trista stepped from the car, only her mom… did not. She bent down and caught her mother's attention. "Ma, you coming?"

She shook her head. "No, this is something for you alone."

"Mom," she whined.

"They're your people, Trista. You need to go and pay your respects. I'm not allowed there."

"But what if…" What if Mr. Scott's order really did die with him?

Her mom shook her head. "No, Mrs. Scott may not like you—"

Trista snorted, but her mom continued.

"—but she will follow the law."

"What about *Heath*?" She spat the guy's name.

She'd call him a man, but he was hardly eighteen and still pimply-faced. God, did the guy *ever* shower? Shifters were supposed to be all heal-y and stuff and yet the kid ended up with more pimples than stars in the sky. She really felt bad for the pack. Mr. Scott was a jerk, but Heath was an asshole. Too bad the hyenas didn't make the heirs wait until they hit twenty-five to take over the reins. Not like the bears.

"Heath knows the law. Otherwise the men at the border would have stopped us." In mom-speak, "stopped" meant "killed." As if Trista didn't know.

Trista turned her attention to the gathering of "people" on the other side of the graveyard. The hyena shifter graveyard. She had no doubt the individuals milling about were other hyenas, and any minute now they'd catch her scent.

In three, two, one…

It was like they were one person. All heads turned toward her, everyone's eyes suddenly glowing copper.

Panic assaulted her, burrowing into her heart, and she very, very much wanted to cry. And run. The animal part of her rumbled its objection. It begged to stay and fight and demand their due. She didn't think they were due anything other than their lives once this was over.

72

"Trista." Her mom's firm voice pulled her away from the men and women who wouldn't mind seeing her dead and gone.

"Yeah?" She gulped.

"You'll be fine." She shook her head and her mom spoke again. "You will. Mrs. Scott may not like you," understatement of the *century*, "but she and Heath know better than to do anything. Harming you will bring down their Southeast Alpha and they don't want that."

No, no one wanted one of the territory leaders hanging around. Least of all that one.

"Now, go pay your respects and then come back. We've got a few hours to kill. We'll head over to the falls."

The falls. She'd always loved the sound of rushing water, even if her animal thing in her head hated it.

"'K." She took a deep breath and fought for calm. Heading into a group of blood-thirsty shifters while scared out of her mind was *not* a good idea. With a jerky nod, she stepped back and pushed the door closed. She didn't know why she was surprised that her mom wasn't coming along. From the moment Trista was born, Mr. Scott told her Mom she wasn't welcome at pack gatherings. Trista and Trista alone. Never a human.

Even if she'd been banged by a furball at some point.

Okay, ew, no thinking about Mom and sex. Ever.

Rubbing her hands on her jeans, she made her way toward the group, ignoring the sneers, growls, hisses, and high-pitched cackling laughs that chased her. Those laughs… They scared the shit out of her while also poking her animal. Trista couldn't shift, couldn't even get slightly furry, but she sure could make the screeching sounds.

73

She swallowed them now, pulled them deep into herself. No sense in antagonizing the "people" who could kill her without blinking.

They hated her, but still stepped aside as she approached, making a path straight to the gravesite. Mr. Scott's casket remained perched above the hole, waiting to be lowered into the ground. She wondered if someone would throw a rose in after he'd been put down there. Or toss a handful of dirt on top like they did in the movies.

Tired of rubbing her sweaty palms on her jeans, she tucked them into her pockets. No sense in showing how nervous they made her.

Eventually Mrs. Scott and Heath were revealed. Mrs. Scott sat straight-backed in a fold-out chair while Heath stood directly behind her. Both of them were focused on Trista, their eyes the orange-tinted brown of their animals. It'd freaked her out when she first met others in the pack. Honestly, it still freaked her out.

Stopping five feet from them—Mrs. Scott's reach tended to be about four feet—she tilted her head slightly as she'd been taught. "Mrs. Scott, Heath, I'm sorry for your loss."

She supposed it was her loss, too, but she didn't care.

Mrs. Scott glared at her while Heath smiled wide, exposing his hyena's teeth.

"Trista." His smiled grew even more. "Come, sit beside my mother. You're part of the family, after all."

Oh no, she really, really wasn't. But he was Alpha now, so that meant she had to listen. Taking a deep breath and praying she didn't end up in tiny pieces, she stepped toward the empty chair beside Mrs. Scott. A chair she hadn't noticed until now.

Slowly she made her way to the seat and lowered herself to the surface. She perched on the edge, afraid of relaxing too much and being unable to run. Even if she did, she knew she wouldn't make it far, but she'd try.

Her mother was sure of Mrs. Scott's adherence to the law and that she'd keep Heath in line. Trista was not.

A large, claw-tipped hand rested on her shoulder and yanked her back, forcing her to rest on the seat fully.

"Relax, Trista." Heath's voice was a menacing purr, his lips brushing the shell of her ear.

Relax. Right.

When his mouth left her skin, one of the other males stepped forward and stood at one end of the coffin. He was old, as old as Mr. Scott, she thought. He launched into a prayer, words asking God to send Mr. Scott's soul to Heaven.

Trista hoped the man went to hell, but she wasn't sure that was a popular opinion. Looking at all the others, she realized it wasn't.

Heath's hand tightened on her shoulder, his claws piercing her shirt and digging into her flesh. She forced herself to remain still, to not react. He'd prick her, cause her to bleed, and then laugh when she cried.

It started when she was barely able to walk and still continued today. He'd been ordered not to kill, but that didn't mean he couldn't maim her. At least, that's what he said each time he caught her. Of course, thanks to being part hyena, he still hadn't managed to scar her.

She watched the ripple of awareness travel through the crowd, the rise and fall of chests and the flaring of nostrils. They scented her, smelled her blood, and it excited them.

Nice.

The wounds on her shoulder burned, the pain sinking deep into her body and searing her from inside out. She fisted her hands, her human nails digging into her palms as the agony twisted its way along her veins.

It hurt. God, it hurt so much. It hadn't ever felt like this before and she didn't know why and she almost cried out when he tightened his hold even further. Usually the animal thing took care of wounds by now, but it was as if something stopped it from healing her.

The man speaking kept droning on and on only now his attention was on her as well. He'd moved on to blessing the pack, licking his lips between statements.

Heath wrapped his other hand around her throat, his thumb pressed against the hollow beneath one ear while his index finger stroked the other. His palm spanned her neck and it'd take one rapid move to tear her throat from her body.

From the corner of her eye, she watched Mrs. Scott's gaze swing to her and then flick to Heath. "You can't kill her. Your father wouldn't have wanted that, more's the pity. Just be thankful that his will requires her to stay near her 'family' in Boyne Falls."

Heath leaned down, speaking to her once again. "I won't kill you, will I, Tris? This is just a game we play, Mother. One that I'll win this time around and with father's last wish, we'll get to play this game for a long time coming."

Trista didn't hear the rest of the speech. No, she was too focused on the pack watching her, on Mrs. Scott staring at the blood that now soaked into her shirt, and on the wounds Heath inflicted.

The fingers in her shoulder weren't the only ones that burned her. No, he tightened his grip on her throat, squeezing harder and harder with each passing second until his claws pierced her skin.

More burning assaulted her. More heat and agonizing pain pumped through her veins in an increasing tempo. Even she smelled her blood now and she cursed her mom for making her come to this stupid funeral with this stupid pack.

She cursed herself, too. She'd never told her mother about Heath's treatment. Her wounds had always been healed by the time she got home from school. There was no point worrying her. Besides,

Trista's pain was nothing when compared to what her mom would endure if her mother went to Mr. Scott and complained about Trista's abuse.

Trista complained once, and only once. After her mom came home covered in bruises and smelling like Mrs. Scott, Trista never said anything again. Ever.

She shoulda said something before they left the apartment.

While Heath dug his fingers deeper, she held onto Mrs. Scott's words. *"You can't kill her. Your father wouldn't have wanted that, more's the pity."*

She just had to endure.

Tears pricked her eyes, gathering as more agony filled her body. It was so much worse than ever before and she wondered when it'd end, *if* it'd end before she passed out from the pain.

When spots danced before her eyes, she wasn't so sure.

Heath dragged his index finger across her throat, digging into her skin, and she wondered if he'd cut her there, too. When another round of rolling pain hit her, she decided he had.

She gasped as it joined with the rest of the hurts bouncing through her, assaulting her with invisible claws.

This was different—new—and she decided she'd never, ever, come to Boyne Falls again.

The man speaking finally finished his speech, still not talking to the crowd, but focused on her. They were all intent on her, on her wounds.

Hungry.

They looked so very, very hungry.

Trista swallowed, forcing Heath's nails even deeper, and she tried to remember some of that stupid biology class she was taking this year. Was he near one of those "holy crap, I'm dead in a minute from blood loss" artery things?

She hoped not.

Then again, that'd be killing her and Mrs. Scott said—

"He's been laid to rest. Are you ready to go to the house?" Heath murmured and she remained still, fighting not to flinch. "Or would you like to go home?"

Home. She wanted to go home.

"We'll leave the territory now, if that's okay, Alpha." She prayed that using his new fancy title would make him happy and he'd let her go.

The pain was overwhelming her now, pushing deeper and deeper until she wondered if it'd reach her soul and crush it.

"Hmm..." He straightened and tugged his hand free of her shoulder, scraping furrows into her flesh.

Tears streamed from her eyes then, coursing down her cheeks, and she didn't care if all the stupid hyenas saw.

"I suppose you're free to go." He gave the same treatment to her throat, drawing a line over her skin.

The second she was free, she bolted to her feet and headed toward the gathered crowd. It was the quickest path to her mom's car, to her mom, to safety.

Heath's cackling laugh chased her and she increased her speed, forcing her to move faster, to almost break into a flat-out run.

Other chuckles flowed in her wake, the sounds of their animals and not men. Then—she was gonna die—the snap and crack of bones reached her. They were shifting. One or all? It didn't matter. It didn't matter because Mr. Scott told Heath and Mrs. Scott they couldn't kill her, but she didn't know if that applied to the rest of the pack.

Trista shoved past the last line of shifting hyenas, breaking free of the crowd. Blood flowed down her neck and stained her shirt, but she forced herself to run, to push beyond the bone-melting pain that filled her.

They'd swarm her, attack her, if she faltered. Hell, she didn't even know if she'd make it to her mom's car.

Her mother's vehicle came into view just as the first hyena snapped at her jeans, jaws barely missing the cloth. Stricken eyes met Trista's, her mom's face paling, and she could only imagine what she saw.

This was what she'd hidden over the years and now it was being shoved in her face.

Her mom reached for the door handle and Trista shook her head. She needed to start the car. When indecision covered her mother's face, she shook her head again. Then she clutched her shoulder, squeezing it in an effort to stem the pain. It burned so hot and she thought she'd die from the agony of the wound.

Teeth finally did snag her pants, almost tripping her and sending her to the ground, but she righted herself and kept moving. Stopping would get her killed.

As soon as she neared, her mother unlatched the passenger door, allowing it to swing open.

The heated breath of a hyena on her left teased her, telling her of its closeness, and she shifted right just as it snapped at her shirt.

When it came near again, she focused, bent her arm, and elbowed the animal in the face. If she had the energy, she would have smiled at its pained yelp. Instead, she pushed harder, ran faster.

The car was only fifteen feet away. Then ten.

Another bite had her jerking away from the attacker on her right and she fought to keep her balance. She was so close…

It did it again and this time she spared a moment to kick at the animal, nailing it in the shoulder. She smiled when it went tumbling to the ground. They seemed to forget who they were chasing, who'd fathered her. Even if her mom was human, Trista was still strong as heck.

Another thing that pissed them off.

Trista stumbled the last few feet, grasping the edge of the door, and she used it to stay upright. She scrambled into the passenger seat, snatching her foot back just as one hundred fifty pounds of hyena slammed into the panel, shoving it closed.

Her mom didn't utter a word, didn't make a sound as she slammed the beat-up car in reverse and peeled out of the parking spot.

The rest of the pack flowed toward them like a claw—and fang—lined river, swarming their car.

"Go, Mom!" Trista yelled over their snarling attackers while she waited for her mother to slam the car into drive.

One furred body slammed into the side, sending them rocking. Another jumped on the trunk and fell against the back window, cracking the glass. Yet another hyena vaulted onto the vehicle, sliding across the hood with an earsplitting screech. Finally orange-brown eyes met hers; familiar eyes. Its paws were soaked in her blood and the redness surrounded his maw. Hers or someone else's?

When he dropped a shoulder and attacked the glass, it didn't matter. One slam became two, became four, and still her mother sat frozen as Heath fought his way through the front windshield.

"*Go!*"

Before it was too late. Before Heath succeeded. Before— A final crunch gave him space to reach his arm past the glass and Trista ducked. He caught her hair, yanking the strands, as well as a hint of her flesh. The claws scraped her jaw, sliding along the curved line.

Trista's fear filled her voice, pain on its heels, and she screamed once again. "*Go!*"

chapter six

A scream rent the air, snatching him from his restless sleep and into wakefulness in an instant. Keen's bear recognized the source before his human half realized his eyes were open. Fur burst from his pores, his hands transforming into claws, and his teeth pushed through his gums in a stinging rush.

He gained his feet in a fluid dash, rolling from the bed and striding toward the bathroom. He shoved the pocket door aside, sending it crashing into the wall, and the one leading to Trista's room received the same treatment.

His bear scanned the area, its senses focusing on their surroundings while the human part of his mind got his body into further motion. He flew over the carpet, racing to the struggling pile of woman and blankets near the window. Her heavy panting reached him as did the rapid beat of her heart. The bear was attuned to her, intent on securing her and assuring her well-being.

Nothing—no one—lurked in the shadows which meant he could focus on Trista. He lowered to a crouch and clawed his way through the blanket enveloping her. His nails sliced the material into floating ribbons, revealing Trista with every cut and tug. It didn't take long to find the baggy T-shirt that covered her upper-body, nor did he have trouble getting to her loose shorts.

Then he focused on her body, running his hands over her arms and legs, ensuring she wasn't hurt. All the while, she panted and moaned, struggling against him, her hands clawing at her throat.

Her scent finally penetrated his focus, smacking him in the face with her emotions. Panic. Fear. Pain. Hyena and... what?

He pushed the question away and focused on her terror. A nightmare... or memories. He couldn't imagine what caused her terror, but he needed her to calm before she hurt herself.

Redness surrounded her throat, her fingers clawing at her flesh, and he snatched her hands, gathering her wrists into one fist while he tugged her close with his free arm.

"Hush. Easy. Trista..." His bear raged at her fear and the scrapes now peppering her skin. "I've got you."

The words were garbled, warped due to his beast's muzzle, but she seemed to recognize him. She slowly quieted, the gasps and cries gradually lessening to low mewls and whimpers. He stared at the woman in his arms, the tears streaking her face and the redness of her eyes.

"I've got you..." This time he sounded more like his human self and he realized his bear had retreated. It still paced in his mind, grumbling and growling, but seemed to have accepted that his human half could better take care of her. "I've got you."

I'll always have you.

The thought ricocheted through his mind, pinging off his memories and thoughts of the future. The bear snatched the idea from its travels and held it close, growling when Keen attempted to mentally wrench it from the animal. It was then he realized one thing with pure clarity. He wanted to have her as his. Now. Forever. Longer if it were possible.

"Keen?" Her eyes focused on him, shifting from glazed to laser sharp. "What...?" She shook her head. "What happened? Why am I on the floor?"

He released her, convinced she wouldn't hurt herself any longer, and used his free hand to stroke her face. He brushed aside lingering tears, capturing the droplets with his fingertips and making them disappear.

"You had a nightmare," he murmured, watching her gaze for recognition.

It was swift in coming, her eyes widening as she sucked in a harsh breath. Her heart rate picked up once again, the rhythmic beating reaching his ears thanks to his inner-beast. Air whooshed in and out of her lungs and the scent of panic, terror, filled the air in a resurging wave.

"Shh... You're fine. You're okay, Trista."

She brought a hand to her neck and he tensed, worried that he'd have to subdue her once more. Except, this time her touch was light, fingers fluttering over her skin. She danced across the line of her throat and paused by her ears before retracing her path. She sought something, but what?

With one final pass, she brought her hand before her gaze, flipping from one side to the other, staring at her pale skin. Finally, a soft sigh escaped her lips and she relaxed in his arms.

He reveled in the embrace, knowing it probably wouldn't last long once she realized a bear held her close. His animal enjoyed it as well, begging him to breathe deep so they could memorize her sweet scent. Honeysuckle and sunshine. Sweetness paired with happiness. She could be his happiness if he could just convince her to put away her prickly, defensive exterior for a while.

It lasted exactly two seconds. She went from dazed and panicking to furious and fighting in two seconds. She shoved and pushed at his hands and he allowed her to pull away.

She scrambled backwards, finally colliding with the wall. "I'm—"

The click of the bedroom doorknob being turned cut her off and a jiggle of the metal immediately followed. Then there was a heaving crash of wood and plaster as the panel was crushed beneath the weight of his eldest brother. "What the hell?"

Keen pushed to his feet, his animal rushing forward for the second time in less than five minutes. What should have tired him, exhilarated him. The partial transformation sent a rush of energy through his body as the bear took over. He snarled at Ty, baring his teeth and allowing the animal to increase his size.

His clothing stretched taut over his muscles, straining the fabric, but he didn't care. Ty had invaded Trista's space while she was a trembling, crying wreck and he'd be damned if someone else frightened her.

Keen's inner-bear gave him a mental high-five followed by a roar he interpreted as "fuck, yeah."

Ty froze in the doorway, the frustration and anger in his brother's expression quickly transforming to trepidation. "Keen?"

He growled in response. Ty was still in the room, still standing within Trista's space, and he nearly lost his shit when she whimpered. "Get out."

The bear didn't want him here, didn't want anyone near her. Especially not a male who looked down on her for being part hyena. His animal didn't care about her heritage, about the animal that lurked beneath her skin. It wanted *her*. Period. Full stop.

"Keen?" Ty's eyebrows rose, eyes wide.

"Get. The fuck. Out."

"Ty? Keen?" It was a voice he recognized, one soft and sweet. His Itana. She could come in. Maybe she could calm Trista. That would, in turn, allow his bear to quiet so he could reassure the woman behind him.

"Mia…" Ty's voice held a warning tone, but that didn't stop Mia from pushing past her mate.

The woman seemed to take in the scene in a single glance. "Well, then." She propped her hands on her hips. "First things first." Mia turned on her mate and shoved at his chest. "Out you go. I can't believe you broke down a door in your own house. Why would you do something like that?"

Ty frowned. "I heard a scream."

Keen didn't see Mia roll her eyes, but her exasperated sigh told him enough. "And you think big, bad Keen can't handle one little woman?"

Keen wanted to correct his Itana. Trista wasn't "one little woman." She was lush and curved and his. The thought, combined with Mia's presence and corralling of Ty, soothed his bear. Mia poked and prodded Ty, pushing and nudging him from the room until his eldest brother was no longer visible. His scent still lurked, but he was at least out of sight.

The moment Ty disappeared, Mia turned on him. "And you," she pointed at Keen. "What's with the fur? And the cursing! I'd yell at you for your language, but Ty's the same way when I get all teary." She propped one hand on her rounded hip while the other went to her protruding belly. "Now, is everything okay here? Keen? You're still rather furry." Mia peeked around him, her gaze dropping. "Trista?"

Trista coughed and cleared her throat, but her voice still warbled when she spoke. "I'm…" She swallowed, the sound audible in the quiet room. "I'm fine."

"Do you need me to—" Mia stepped forward and froze when he growled. That earned him a dark glare. "Really?"

Keen closed his eyes and swallowed the sound while mentally whacking his bear on the nose. "Sorry. Just... sorry."

Trista was his, his, and his again. He didn't want anyone near her.

"I had a nightmare. I'm fine. I'm sorry I woke up the house." Trista's voice shook and the rustle of cloth followed her words.

He glanced over his shoulder and found that she'd stood. The moon shined its pale light on her, highlighting her rumpled clothes and messy hair. Her tear tracks were easy to see, as were the scrapes and bruises she'd caused herself.

"Keen?" After reaffirming Trista was okay, he turned his gaze back to Mia. "Are you okay?"

He cracked his neck and urged the bear back, begging it to retreat so everyone would just get the fuck out already. He wouldn't truly be calm until he had Trista alone and safe. His inner-beast saw reason and slowly retreated. Fur receded while his face and body returned to its normal, human shape.

"I'm good." He shrugged. "Just got surprised."

And enraged, but he didn't have to reveal that to Mia. She'd seen the evidence for herself.

"Okay, then. I'll leave you two for tonight." Mia nodded at him and then looked at Trista once again. "You remember what I said?"

Keen glanced at Trista, caught her nod, and he wondered what the women had talked about during the short time they'd been left alone.

"So, no more cursing and maybe it's best if you two bedded down in your room, Keen. I'm sure it'd make Trista feel safer since *someone*," Mia glared at Ty, "busted down her door."

He wanted that more than anything in the world. He'd love to have her close even if it meant he slept in a chair while she took the bed.

88

The bear wanted her safe and nothing would calm him more than having her in his den.

Den. He'd have to think about moving. He couldn't have Trista in the clan den. They needed a place of their own.

A new scent drifted to him from the woman at his back. Worry tinged with a flare of interest. He wouldn't call it arousal, the aroma wasn't even close, but at least she wasn't indifferent. Plus, it was true worry and trepidation, not fear.

When she stepped forward and leaned close, gently brushing him, his bear calmed with a soft rumble of pleasure.

Yes, they definitely needed a place of their own.

But first, he needed to convince her that she didn't want to be anywhere but at his side.

Staring down at her, at the vulnerability in her gaze, he didn't think it'd be too difficult.

*

Trista could do this. It wouldn't be difficult. The animalistic part of her urged her to take his comfort and she didn't have the strength to deny its wants. She could lean on him for a little while. Just one night and then she could go back to being alone. Depending on someone only led to heartache and pain. So she'd take what she could, tuck away the memories, and move on.

The past still attacked her even though she'd snapped awake. While she stared at him and listened to Mia, it continued playing through her mind. She still saw Heath's arm burst through the glass, the feel of his claw-tipped fingers wrapped around her throat and squeezing tight.

The blood… the poison… the *scars*…

"Trista?" Keen's tone no longer held the angry rumble of his bear and she noticed fur no longer coated his skin. The animal had retreated.

She'd been startled when he finally freed her from her blankets. First by his presence and then by the lightning-fast partial shift as he squared off against his brother.

Over her.

No one had ever defended her before. Well, her mother always stood against her father and other hyenas, but a male had never put her first. He'd put himself between her and the Itan.

And he hadn't backed down.

That sent a wave of awe through her. She'd never heard of a male able to stand strong when faced with their leader's displeasure unless the challenger was sure he'd win. And Keen stood tall and unshakable, immovable.

The level of power frightened and intrigued her in equal measure and she fought to banish the fascination. He was a level of protection, security, for a night and then tomorrow would begin her struggles again.

But one night of safety was a fierce draw.

"Trista? Do you want to sleep in my room? You can have the bed. I'll sleep in a chair." His voice flowed over her like a comforting river and she fought to calm her thundering heart.

She knew what she wanted, knew what her half-beast craved, and pushed the words that lurked in her heart past her lips. "You can sleep in the bed with me. I don't want... You can't..." She shook her head, unable to finish her sentence.

"Sleep, Trista." He slowly eased his hand into hers and gave her a gentle squeeze. "You need your rest and I'll be there in case you have another nightmare."

Right. Nightmare. If only…

When she hesitated, he spoke again. "You can trust me. Like I said, you have no reason to, but you can."

It wasn't a matter of belief, but of desire. She didn't want to put her faith in him.

Swallowing the words, she simply nodded and allowed him to draw her toward the bathroom, through the small space and then further to the massive king-sized bed. His blankets and sheets were a tangled pile on the floor and he shot her a rueful smile.

"I was in a hurry to get to you." He reached down and snagged the ball, tugging and yanking until he had them fairly straight. When he leaned over the bed and began remaking it, she forced herself not to stare at his body.

His body. She finally realized what had her so intrigued. Keen was shirtless, baggy shorts barely clinging to his hips as he moved around the furniture. His muscles flexed and stretched with each movement, outlining the dips and grooves of his body. Most shifters were fit, strengthened and body honed due to their inner-animal. But Keen seemed like he had so much more. More strength, more power, just… more.

When he next tugged on the sheet and released a low groan, she went into action. She'd been standing there like an idiot and ogling the man when she could have been helping. Snaring one corner, she pulled it into place and then moved to the other corner as he did the same. In seconds they had the bed remade and they stood on opposite sides of the mattress.

Unease that matched her own filled him and she realized that he was merely reacting to her emotions. She needed to get herself under control. She didn't want this, and yet she did, and that indecision was tearing her in two.

Taking a deep breath, she crawled onto the mattress and pulled the sheet atop her.

Seeming to take her movement as silent permission, Keen did the same, resting on his side beside her. His gaze remained intent on her and instead of making her feel awkward, it gave her a sense of peace. He worried about her as if he cared, truly cared, about her.

Without saying a word or uttering a sound, she slowly slid her hand toward him, fingers seeking out his skin. Just as gently, Keen did the same until their fingers met and twined beneath the sheet. They didn't say a word and she was thankful for that.

"Thank you," she whispered, unwilling to break the soothing quiet.

"For what?" He spoke just as low.

For standing up for me. For protecting me. For letting me lean on you.

Instead, she simplified her feelings. "For being you."

Pleasure flared in his eyes, his bear peeking out from behind his brown irises and darkening them to black. She didn't want to see that, didn't want to see her hope and attraction reflected back to her. Because then she'd come to depend on him, would allow herself to lean on him until she couldn't live without him.

And then he'd leave or disappear or die and then she'd be flat on her face and alone in the world. Again.

So she closed her eyes, closed them and pretended to sleep, pretended not to feel his lips as they brushed her temple or the heat from his body as he eased closer.

Most of all, she pretended not to like it.

"Goodnight," he murmured.

Goodbye.

chapter seven

Yelling woke him, a shout quickly followed by a bellowing roar. The sound had Keen rolling from the bed and landing in a low crouch as he sought out danger. Just like last night when he'd heard Trista's scream, his bear stretched his skin, pulling and pushing at his flesh in an effort to break free. He'd been calm, content even, since being close to Trista and he'd nearly forgotten what it was like to fight his unstable beast. Facing off against his brother had been a controlled rage as he'd defended her, but this was wild and violent.

Then a new sound, one that chilled him to his core, battled against those that'd woken him.

Almost… a laugh. Only it wasn't a child's giggle or Mia's tinkling joy. No, he'd heard it before—as he'd fought to protect the clan den from attack—and he knew there was only one source. Something, someone, had come upon Trista and her inner-beast was responding in kind.

Another growl, another bestial chuckle that signified her unease and fear.

The sound caused Keen to rush into action. His bear thundered, releasing a noise that he'd never heard before, and shredded his tenuous control. The transformation came upon him, tearing at his skin, turning him inside out with the shift from human to animal.

His bones snapped and cracked, severing for a split second before reforming to his beast's shape.

He pulled and fought the bear, reminding it they couldn't finish the change before entering the hallway. Otherwise they'd be battling the doorway which would slow their progress.

The bear faltered in its fight, giving him the chance to rush through his bedroom door. He was anxious to get to Trista, to calm and soothe her as well as maim whoever had caused her distress.

Another shout, another scraping cackle, and he burst into the hall in a flurry of shredded cloth and reshaping limbs. By the time he'd taken two steps from his room, he'd acquired his bear's form. With rapid, lumbering thumps of his massive feet on plush carpet, he ran toward Trista, using her voice as his guide.

Another roar and this time, he answered it with one of his own. No one would touch her. No one. He'd made the decision last night. No matter what it took, no matter how long he had to fight through her protective layers, he'd have Trista.

New sounds joined in the cacophony of the attacking bear and the nervous hyena creating a jangled, macabre symphony that echoed through the house. The coppery tang of blood hit his nose, filling his lungs with each inhale, and it made him run that much faster. It wasn't Trista's, not yet, but he didn't want to see how long it'd take for hers to join the party.

He bolted down one hallway and then another before racing through the kitchen and on into the main areas of the house. As the roars and rumbles gained in volume, he realized his mistake in bringing her here.

Ty hadn't been happy, but had grudgingly accepted her presence based on Keen's word that she wouldn't do anything but sleep and then go. He'd vouched for her and back up his actions with the law. He'd assured Ty that she'd behave, and to her that she'd be safe.

He wasn't sure who he'd betrayed. No, he did. He knew Trista hadn't done anything to provoke this violence. She wanted to live by the law and remain under the radar. Which meant he'd be going after Ty or one of the other bears in the clan.

Keen's inner-beast didn't give a damn who he'd have to tear apart. He just wanted her safe.

He slid around the last corner just as a wolf's howl joined the fray and then... The term "seeing red" had always seemed so unlikely, an exaggeration used in fiction, and yet it was a very real thing. The desire to see blood flow like a river overwhelmed him, destroyed any semblance of control he gripped, and his bear's instincts grasped power over his body.

Trista held a solid iron poker in her hands, wielding it like a bat before her, as she fought off two bears—*Ty and Van*—while a wolf seemed to be waiting in the wings. All the while her animal's sounds flew from her throat, battling her tormentors.

He recognized the bears, knew the wolf, and the only thing saving any of them was the fact she wasn't bleeding. Though it looked as if it was only a matter of time if the wolf had his way.

When it jumped at her, baring his teeth and snapping his jaws, Keen attacked.

He tore into the room, slicing and swiping at the males crowding the space, some strikes connecting while others did not. He distantly recognized the stinging pain of his own wounds, but they didn't matter. They were immaterial when compared to Trista's safety.

A large claw dug into his flesh and he turned his head, snapping at the leg of his assailant and sinking his teeth deep until he struck bone. That had the male backing off, but it left the way open for the wolf and Keen was quick to bat him aside. One wolf against a bear didn't have a chance. But against her, against a half-hyena, there was no contest. The wolf would tear her to shreds.

That's not fucking happening.

95

He glanced at Trista, noting her wide eyes and the stench of fear that flowed from her. Her attention flicked from him to just over his shoulder, cluing him in to another's approach. He swung his head around while pushing to his back legs, preparing to defend against attack. This bear was the bigger of the two, a hint larger than Keen, but not quite as strong.

Ty. His brother. His Itan.

He should concede to him, acquiesce to his dominance. Except another nervous, bestial chuckle came from Trista and it enraged his bear anew.

Without hesitation, he roared his displeasure and moved before her, blocking her from the other males completely. They would have to go through him to get near her and that would never, ever happen.

The smaller of the two bears curled his lips, baring his fangs, and took a step forward only to be shoved back by Ty. At least one of his brothers was smart. Even the wolf hung back, his hungry gaze pinging between them all.

Ty focused on him, black eyes meeting his own, and he refused to back down. Nothing—*no one*—would hurt her.

Finally, his eldest brother tore his gaze from Keen's and stared at Van for a moment before zeroing in on the wolf. A single growl from Ty preceded the males shifting, transforming in rapid cracks and snaps until three bloodied men stood before him.

They were vulnerable now, easily killed. It'd take one swipe to gut them all. One swipe and—

Trembling fingers dug into his fur, fisting his skin as her weight pressed against him. No, his first thoughts needed to be for Trista. Vengeance, more bloodshed, could come later. Right now both halves of his mind were in agreement. They needed to protect her. He couldn't care for her as a bear and even his animal accepted that fact.

96

With her touch, a peaceful calm overtook him, sliding through his veins and caressing him with a gentle touch. It soothed him now just as it'd calmed him when he'd held her last night. It started with a touch of fingers and he'd ended up with an armful of Trista. At least, until this morning when he woke alone. Alone and easily enraged.

His beast's power slithered to the back of his mind while nudging his human consciousness forward. In a breath, his transformation blew through him like a soft breeze. One moment he was a bloodied and battered bear and the next he was a stained and panting human.

Trista's hands hadn't left him, her touch remaining through his change as if she were afraid he'd disappear on her. He wouldn't. Not now, not ever. He'd made a commitment in his mind last night and it became a truth by standing against his brothers to ensure her safety. In that one instant, in that moment when he faced Ty and didn't relent, he'd set himself on a new path.

One that included her and not them.

His bear was not upset by that fact. It accepted that the walls standing between him and his brothers remained steadfast and now higher than before.

Reaching behind himself, he grasped one of Trista's shaking hands and gave it a gentle squeeze, doing his best to reassure her without words. When the shakes lessened, he assumed she'd gotten the point.

"Someone"—his voice was hoarse from his vibrating roars—"is going to explain why the Itan's guest, *my* guest, was assaulted in my home."

He didn't leave room for an argument and he sure as hell wasn't going to take blustering bullshit from any of the men before him.

"You're defending one of *them*." Van spat the word. "Do you know what her family did?"

At least he knew who'd started the fight.

"Did you try and stop it, Ty? Or were you both fighting to see who'd kill her first?" The answer would determine who he'd battle first. Now that he was faced with Van's words and not just his brother's actions, the bear's desire for blood returned.

"Of course I tried to stop him," Ty snapped.

"Uh-huh." Keen concentrated on the third male in the room. Not just a wolf, but the Redby Alpha. From all accounts, he was a crazed son of a bitch who sliced and diced and didn't bother asking questions later. He'd done that to the Boyne Falls Alpha as well as his own Beta. "Reid?"

The male shrugged. "I scented her before I even entered the house and I'm not opposed to finishing off my enemies." The wolf leaned to look past him. "We've been doing this dance for years now." He grinned, the evil smile lined with blood. Reid licked his lips. "His little sister—half-sister—has been escaping me for months, but don't you think it's time to end it?"

The body at his back stilled, frozen in place, and her hands no longer trembled.

"That's what the scent is." Ty's eyes darkened to midnight and fur sprouted along his arms. "I told you she smelled familiar. She's that bastard's sister. You brought the sister of the hyena's pack Alpha into my home."

Keen's bear reacted in kind, his own brown fur coating his arms and chest while his nails tingled in anticipation of his shift.

"She could be the devil herself, but she is here under the articles of visitation, under *my* protection"—he ignored Trista's surprised gasp—"which means she comes to no harm." He kept his voice firm, allowing them to hang over the room, and there was not a hint of recognition in Ty and Van's eyes. Reid, however, glared at him.

"What are—?"

Keen spoke over Van and rattled off the location of the law without hesitation. "Volume Three, Section Two, Paragraph Four, Subsection Three, Paragraph Seven." Not waiting for any of the males to question him further, he reached back and grasped Trista's hand. "And now, we're leaving." He stepped forward, heading toward the doorway, and Van moved to intercept him. Keeping his gaze settled on his brother, Keen spoke once again. "I forgave one attempt on her life due to your ignorance, but I won't tolerate another, Van."

"Do you know—?"

"I know you're breaking the law, that not two minutes ago you were ready to break the law!" His voice echoed off the walls and silence followed in its wake. "We're leaving." He looked to Ty. "I'll send someone to pack my things."

"Keen, be reasonable. There are plenty of women in the clan, you don't need to—"

"I would advise you to shut your mouth, Ty." His bear pushed against his flesh, stretching it until he felt as if he'd split wide if he didn't release the animal. "It's taking everything in me not to kill you three. And you know I can." Van snorted in disbelief, but Ty's eyes widened and it seemed reality finally dawned on his eldest brother. Adrenaline wasn't the only thing that'd fueled his stand against Ty. No, pure ability and dominance filled Keen from head to toe. "We're leaving."

Keen turned his back on the males and nudged Trista into action, pushing her from the room.

"Keen," she whispered and he shook his head, silencing her.

The next feminine voice he heard belonged to Mia and he turned his attention to the Itana. She stood framed in the kitchen entry, her hand lying protectively on her belly as she blocked their path. "Keen, it doesn't have to be this way."

He gave her a rueful smile and shrugged. "It was going to happen someday. You and I talked about that. It just happened sooner rather than later."

"But…"

Keen shook his head. "It doesn't matter now."

"But…"

"Isn't up for discussion. I'll call you later and we can talk more then. For now…" He checked his watch and noted the time. Trista's mention of the laws of visitation slammed into him and he realized they needed to get a move on if he wanted to keep her from ending up in trouble once again. He spoke to Trista. "Let's grab your things and I'll pack a bag. We need to get going."

Trista's twelve hours were almost up.

*

She…

And then they…

And he just…

Trista allowed Keen to push her farther down the hallway. Her shoe caught on the carpet, sending her stumbling forward, but his warm hands grasped her forearms and kept her upright.

"Easy." Keen's warm breath fanned her ear while his words reminded her once again of the pain her presence caused.

She jerked from her arms and forced herself to remain standing on her own. She didn't need him, she didn't need anyone. She was fine. *Fine.*

"I'm not going to fall apart." She forced herself to put one foot in front of the other, to feign a confidence she didn't feel. She was *not* going to rely on Keen Abrams. Last night had been an anomaly brought on by exhaustion and clouded by layers of muscles. "You think that's *not* the first time?" She glanced over her shoulder. "You think one of your bears or a wolf, or even a hyena, hasn't ever done that before?"

Trista ignored the warning growl from Keen, the audible hint that violence was on the horizon.

Instead of violence, he crowded her, herded her until he was aligned with her back while her front was plastered against the wall. It was a position of dominance, leaving her to accept whatever he desired, and yet she wasn't afraid of him.

"Never again." The words were barely audible, but she understood him. "No one will *ever* threaten you again."

Fur, not hair, tickled her exposed skin, teasing her and telling her exactly how close to the edge he currently lingered. He surrounded her, enveloped her in his strength, and she reveled in it just as she cursed her own weakness. She couldn't take comfort in anyone, in a man. It never turned out well and disappointment, even death, lurked on the horizon when a person lived with hope.

"Keen—"

A rolling growl vibrated through her, plucking her nerves and trembling through her blood. "Never."

Trista swallowed past the growing lump in her throat. She wanted to believe him so very, very much. And yet she couldn't allow herself that luxury. Deciding to avoid the topic, she focused on something else. Mainly, getting the hell out of Grayslake before it was too late, but not too early.

"Keen, I have to get out of here. Soon."

He breathed deep and released the air on a long sigh. His scent surrounded her, comforted her even when she knew taking that reassurance was a very bad idea. "You're right. We need to get moving. C'mon."

He stepped back, giving her space, and she nearly whined aloud at the loss of his touch. She wanted him close, wanted to rub all over her skin. She just didn't want to want him.

Turning toward him she squeaked and slapped a hand over her eyes. "You're naked."

Instead of immediately answering, he twined his fingers with hers and tugged her into motion. "It's kinda hard to become a half-ton bear and keep your clothes intact. I don't know why you're surprised. I'm sure you've had the same trouble in the past."

Trista kept her eyes covered, allowing him to lead her, and shook her head. "No. I can't shift."

He must have stopped because suddenly she was plastered to his front. "You can't shift?"

Disbelief filled his tone and she risked moving her hand so she could stare at him. "No. Half-hyena, remember? Don't you think I would have shifted and run if I could have? It wouldn't have been difficult to escape the bears. I don't have Reid's fighting knowledge, but a hyena," she shook her head. "It fears nothing. It'll fight everything. The animal is just flat out crazy. There's no real conscience. "

"Yeah," he murmured.

She sensed a sadness wrap around him like a cloak and squeezed her eyes shut. "But you know this already. I'm sorry."

He knew because her *half*-brother showed him the truth about her kind. She didn't know details. The fact that her brother's life touched theirs was enough.

"I guess I just thought... I've heard of half-shifter children shifting before. I forgot that it's not always the case." Keen cupped her cheeks and she reopened her eyes to stare at him. "It's fine. We're good and you being Heath Scott's half-sister doesn't matter. Go gather your things and I'll get dressed."

It didn't matter to *him*, but it sure as hell mattered to Keen's brothers and the Redby Alpha. It mattered a lot.

For now, she'd take him at his word and do as he desired. She needed to get gone and he wanted to help her with that. Win-win. When he turned right, she went left and dashed into the guestroom, gingerly stepping over the remnants of the broken door. It took seconds to slide the strap of her purse over her head to wear across her body. Holding the last of her cash, it was too important to risk losing. She was glad they'd been too exhausted to haul her measly bag of clothing into the house.

The moment she was ready, she retraced her steps and wasn't surprised to have Keen waiting for her, duffel in hand.

It hit her then. He was walking away from his family—his home— for her. "Keen, you should…" She shook her head, gaze intent on the bag dangling from his fingers. "You should stay."

It was his turn to shake his head. "No, I shouldn't." The distance between them disappeared as he crowded her, stepping close until their chests brushed. "This isn't just about you, it's about them. Like I told Mia, this was going to happen eventually. Your presence moved things along."

"Okay, but you don't have to rush off with me. I mean, thanks for not letting me get killed, but…" *I don't want to be why you're leaving. I don't want to be the reason you don't have a family.*

"Trista." He took a deep breath and released it slowly. "There's something between you and me. I don't know what it is, but it's there, and my bear is determined to keep you close. You felt it last night, didn't you?" She didn't want to answer that question and he didn't seem to be looking for a reply. "No matter what you say, no matter what anyone does, you're mine."

That sounded way too close to a declaration of claiming for her comfort. "You can't just say things like that."

"You know just as much as I do about the law. Do you need the formal words?"

"You can't just..." She shook her head, refusing to even let herself think about what he meant. Thinking about it could kindle hope and she had no room in her life for wishes and dreams.

"Amazingly enough, I can." He stepped away. "Now, c'mon. We have things to do today."

Yeah. They did. Without saying a word, she followed in his wake, down the hallway and through the kitchen. She turned her attention from the living room as they passed, forcing herself to breathe through her mouth so she wouldn't scent the blood that soaked the floor.

Before long, they stepped onto the front porch, the day's sun nearly blinding her with its brightness. She managed to thump down one step and then two before a familiar sound chilled her blood and froze her heart.

Beep-beep. Beep-beep.

The alarm on her watch repeated over and over again, reminding her that her time was up.

She was officially violating the laws of visitation.

She was officially free game to any shifter leader.

She was officially two steps from dead if the bears had any choice in the matter.

Instant awareness struck her, her senses kicking into overdrive as she evaluated her surroundings. Stupid, stupid, stupid. The fight fucked with her head and now she was in the middle of a hostile area. She

104

prayed the Abrams brothers would abide by Keen's wishes but this morning proved that Van's hatred was fierce.

Trista froze on the stairs, attention flitting across the open driveway. She tilted her head back, nostrils flaring as she brought the area's scents into her lungs. She couldn't shift, but she still had many of the animal's abilities. Bears—lots of them—but what did she expect in Grayslake. She identified Keen's and discarded it. Then there was Ty and Van's followed by Mia's. She didn't think they'd try anything, not with the stress between the brothers.

Then there was... Reid.

"Trista?" Keen stood below her, his brow furrowed and head tilted in question.

"We have to—"

"Stay exactly where you are." Reid's gravelly voice rolled over her, his words followed by the heavy thump of his booted feet on the aged wood porch.

The threat wouldn't come from the bears, then. It was the wolf she had to worry about.

Slowly, he came into view and she found him wearing his usual uniform of sorts. Black leather boots, dark jeans, black shirt, leather jacket. On the average male, people would assume he was trying too hard to appear menacing. Reid would scare the hell out of people even if he was nude. Clothes didn't do a damn thing but hide the ugly inside him.

A vibrating growl split the air between her and Reid and it got her into motion, had her stumbling down the remaining steps. She fell into Keen's arms and he immediately shoved her behind his back, hiding her from the Alpha's view.

It wouldn't do anything. It sure as hell wasn't going to save her from what was to come. He'd be violating the laws he held so dear if he kept her from Reid.

Still, the wolf approached, his steps measured and slow. She counted them as he tromped down the porch stairs, booted feet traveling over the gravel driveway until he stopped before Keen.

"Back off, *wolf*." Fur once again coated Keen's arms.

Staring at his back, she cursed herself for being a coward, for depending on the male before her to protect her from her own stupidity. She should have fought harder to be left alone, should have demanded he drop her at the hotel last night. Instead, she allowed him to drag her to the clan den. To her death if Reid had his way.

"Gladly, *bear*. Just as soon as you hand over Ms. Scott."

"She's not going anywhere with you." Keen's growls intensified.

"Hmm…" The sound was smug and condescending. "That's fine." Reid shrugged. "I brought her opponent with me anyway. Come along, Ms. Scott. I've finally caught you violating the law which means—as the Alpha of a pack—I can demand justice for the infraction. We can finish this. Let's go on the grass so we don't stain the Itan's white gravel while you die."

Trista didn't have to look toward the side yard to know what she'd find, that he had wolves lurking in wait.

The purge that made hyenas the bears' enemies may have only happened seven months ago but the hatred that lingered between Reid and her family had been going on for years. The wolf was constantly searching for a way to end her and now he had his opportunity.

Her mother's voice drifted across Trista's mind, the explanation so simple even a child could understand the words. When she was five, she *had* understood the law. Unfortunately, one look at Keen Abrams destroyed her good sense and any ability to think.

A leader can deny the right of visitation, but you don't need permission from anyone if you're not staying longer than twelve hours. So the trick, Trista-girl, is never being in one place for too long.

Staring at Keen's back as more and more dark brown fur covered his skin, she realized she was about to lose the best thing that had never happened to her.

All because she'd been in one place too long.

*

... stain the Itan's white gravel while you die.

Keen's skin went taut, muscles tight and bunching in preparation of his attack on Reid. The words, the inherent threat, enraged his beast.

"Never." He shoved the words past his gritted teeth. "You'll never touch her."

Reid, fucking *wolf* bastard, smirked and Keen's fingers itched with the need to rip that expression from his face. "No, my new Beta, Adrienne, will."

He flexed his hands, fisting them and then allowing part of his shift to flow through him as he relaxed. Hands became paws with that single movement, human nails giving way to blackened claws.

"No one is touching her." He tilted his head left then right, cracking his joints. "No one."

He drew air into his lungs, searching for any hint of Reid's true feelings, and found nothing. Psychopathic asshole couldn't give a damn about the strings he pulled.

"Oh, I disagree, *Keeper.*"

Keen didn't care for the wolf using his old title as a slur, a reminder of his duties, but it did bring forward a rush of knowledge. Ideas, ways to mold the laws to his bidding, filled him.

107

As he pieced together her defense, and his plan, Reid kept speaking. He had no doubt that the male goaded him, but Keen had a bigger play in mind.

"Ms. Scott has the Southeast Keeper's number on speed dial so my hands have been tied because the man's a stickler for the rules. He bitches to the wolf Alpha and he comes down on me. Not something I want. So, she's been rotating through my territory with that bitch mother of hers for years." When Trista's gasp reached him, he decided Reid would bleed for that remark. "Now, she stayed in Grayslake too long and, as you know, any shifter leader can exact justice for a true infraction whether she's in their own territory or not. She's mine, bear."

The wolf grinned like he'd won the lottery.

"Unless…" The idea twisted and turned through his mind and the bear was on board with Keen's thoughts. "… she is one of your allies. In which case, she's bound by that agreement."

He recognized that others appeared in a loose circle around them. Some he knew—Reid's wolves and a woman who he assumed was Adrienne—as well as his brothers and their mates. He let his gaze flick to Ty's and noted the remorse and pain etched in his brother's features. He was going to have to rely on Reid's knowledge of the laws and Ty's guilt.

Reid snorted. "An ally? A hyena? Heath Scott's *sister*? You gotta be fucking joking." He shook his head. "Pass over the bitch and let us end this. She knows this reckoning has been coming for a while. My ex-Beta caught the mother and *took care* of her before a true agreement for leniency was established. But this whelp—"

Suddenly Keen had a hissing and spitting woman attempting to crawl her way over his back. Fully human hands reached around him, clawing and scratching at the air as she fought to reach Reid. "You fucking killed her. You fucking bastard, asshole, son-of-a-whore! *You* violated the law, you *asshole!*" Keen spun and caught her, holding her against his chest and still she battled to get to the wolf. "Fuck you and your *fucking* laws!"

"It was a purge," Reid growled in return, but Keen heard the doubt hidden beneath the outrage.

"For *hyenas* fuck-hole, she was *human*," she hissed.

Dear God, he didn't even want to follow the lure Trista placed before him with those words. Reid had been trying to catch Trista and her mother for years as they skirted the laws of visitation which meant he knew they weren't part of the Boyne Falls hyena pack. Which also meant Trista's mother had been eliminated without cause since Ty's order addressed the pack. And if Trista was the half-sister of Heath Scott and only a half-shifter herself... Her mother *was* human.

He held her close, quieting her struggles until she sobbed against his chest, her face pressed along her neck as tears soaked his skin. So strong and so fragile at the same time. She'd been running and it was going to stop. Now.

"Through the law of claiming, I Keen Lincoln Abrams, fourth son of Jeremiah Abrams and youngest brother to Ty Abrams, Grayslake Itan, claim Trista Scott as my own. She is my mate, she will bear my young, and she will serve at my side." Trista met his gaze, red-rimmed eyes wide and filled with horror and hope and he didn't falter as he repeated the words that would tie them together. "I have said it and so it is done."

Then the air filled with howls battled by growls, but Keen didn't care. For the first time in his life, his bear was truly at peace, truly relaxed, and it was all because of the woman in his arms.

He had her. Now he refused to let her go. Ever.

chapter eight

Trista had to leave, had to get away. She was desperate to run and flee the moment Keen turned his back just as much as she craved being in his presence.

He'd claimed her before one and all. Claimed. Period. Done. No backsies.

And she'd stood there and let it happen. No. She'd fought to get to Reid, fought to scratch out his eyes and claw out his heart.

Her mother was gone. Morgan, the now-dead pack Beta, had killed her and Reid *gloated* about it. Gloated. Held tight in Keen's arms, her anger rushed forward anew, anxious to be unleashed on the wolf Alpha.

She wanted to kill him, to watch him squirm and cry out as she tortured him. Had it been quick for her mother? Or slow? What did they do to her?

Trista ignored the fight that surrounded them, voices raised as the men yelled at each other. They didn't matter. Nothing mattered.

Another sob raced up her throat and it escaped before she could swallow it once again. She couldn't let the emotion overtake her, not while Keen still held her. It would be another step, another shuffle toward depending on him wholly and that couldn't happen.

"Shh…" His large hand traced her spine as he hugged her closer. "I've got you now."

He did and she didn't want him and she refused to listen to the voice in her head that called her a liar.

"Keen." Another choked sob, another gasping breath as she battled for calm. She pressed against him, molding her body to his, and promised herself she'd allow him to hold her for one more minute. One more second and then she'd pull away.

The fight continued, the coppery tang of blood filling the air as the roars and snarls of the two groups went after each other.

Trista wasn't sure how long it continued—seconds? minutes? hours?—but it ended with one feminine shout.

"*Enough!*" Damn, the Itana had one set of lungs on her, and she was effective. All growls ceased and the sounds of battle quieted in an instant. As soon as peace reigned, she spoke again. "Now, I don't know the laws like Keen, but I know he wouldn't make a claim without being one hundred percent right." A snort shot through the air and it was immediately followed by a low grunt. "I said *enough*," Mia snapped. "I don't hesitate to believe him and that means it would be best if the wolves left our territory for the time being."

It was a prettied up order, plain and simple, and the low shuffle and crunch of wolves stomping past them filled Trista's ears. She kept her gaze averted, remained locked in Keen's embrace, as they moved along. She didn't want to look at them, didn't want to acknowledge that she cowered before them in another's arms.

She'd lean on him… just this once. Except, based on the tightening of his embrace and the rumbling growl coming from his chest, she didn't think he'd accept "once."

He wanted forever. His claim said forever.

And that scared the hell out of her.

112

The thunk of vehicle doors closing preceded the roar of engines and the scattering of gravel as the wolves departed. She stretched her senses, verifying the pack members no longer lingered, and then she allowed herself to relax a little. Not completely because Van still stood nearby, but some of her tension eased.

The sounds of the SUVs and cars departing slowly lessened until only the nervous shuffle of Keen's family reached her. An increase in volume and a rhythmic crunch announced someone's approach and the chest against her cheek expanded as a threatening growl escaped him.

Trista wasn't comfortable around Keen's family, but she figured none of them were ready to put her down. At least, not at the moment.

She wiggled a hand free and stroked him, rubbing her hand across his chest in a soothing motion. "Shh…"

The snarl lowered to a rumbling purr and he rubbed his cheek over the top of her head.

A low cough was followed by someone clearing their voice, and finally Ty spoke. "Keen? We have things to discuss." It was phrased as a statement yet sounded like a question.

Part of her was thrilled that her… something… was strong enough to make the Itan nervous. The other half of her didn't want Keen as her anything.

Keen slowly slid his arms from around her, easing his touch as he stepped away and then presented her with his back. Once again she leaned into him, taking comfort in his strength and power. He was her concrete and steel wall against the world.

"I think I said enough not two minutes ago." His voice vibrated through her, stroking her in a gentle wave.

113

Ty hesitated and unease filled his words. "I heard what you said, but I still think there are things to talk about."

Trista rubbed her cheek along his shoulder, transferring her scent to his clothes. It seemed to soothe him and she knew they were in the middle of a delicate situation. She'd do just about anything to keep the peace and get them out alive.

Keen reached for her hand and she quickly grasped his while allowing him to pull her to his side as he turned around. His fur-speckled arm draped over her shoulders and she leaned into him.

Ty looked at her and amended his statement. "Alone."

"Nope."

"Keen," Ty tried again, but this time he was silenced by the Itana.

"Ty, enough. I am so over this. I am five hundred months pregnant, Lauren is hardly showing in her fourth month, which *inhales rapidly*. I'd really like to say 'it sucks' but brilliant me decided the family shouldn't use that word." Mia harrumphed. "But that's beside the point. It's hot as huckleberry outside. I'm going in the house. I'm getting something cool to drink from Gigi, and then I'm going to try to not look like a beached whale while I collapse on the couch." Mia glared at her mate and then let her furious stare travel to Van. "You can join me or you can pout about being outmaneuvered. Either way, Lauren, Keen, and Trista are coming with me."

"Mia…"

Blatantly ignoring her mate, Mia stomped toward her and Keen and snatched Trista's hand. "Both of you, let's go."

"Mia, you can't do this. There are things to discuss. Her *family* caused the deaths of our own bears. Think about Isaac," the Itan growled.

There was no disputing the truth. Trista didn't know the details, but it sounded like something Heath and the pack would have done.

The Itana whirled on her mate. "Our bears? Isaac?" Mia shuddered and drew in a shaky breath. "I would like to think our clan was smarter, had more sense, than to rain the sins of others on an innocent's head. I would like to think that Isaac could easily see the truth about Trista *and* Keen and he would welcome her into this family. Keen was *shot* in the *chest* by hyenas while protecting me. He has done nothing but fight to protect this clan, and has acted as the clan's Keeper even though you men haven't given a flying fig about it. So maybe you all should take a good, hard look at yourselves before you condemn Keen and his decision to mate Trista. Because, I'm telling you now, Trista is one of us. Period. Even if Keen were to sever their mating right this second, I *would not* let her walk away."

Anger and hurt suffused Ty's features and Trista wished she could curl into a small ball and hide like she did when a child. Arguments, yelling, always ended in pain. She'd like to think Ty wouldn't harm his mate, but there was no telling.

"You can't just—"

Mia snapped her fingers and whirled on them, pointing at Keen. "I'm allowed to make decisions about clan membership, right? I can do that as the Itana?"

Keen furrowed his brow and nodded.

"Good. Quote the appropriate law"—the Itana snatched Trista's wrist and tugged her out of Keen's embrace as she waved her hand toward Ty—"to this cornnut and tell him what's what. I'll be with my new sister-in-law."

As she was dragged across the lawn behind the Itana, she wasn't sure what the hell just happened. She'd stepped outside the house an outsider and suddenly she was a hyena in a clan of bears and being personally welcomed by the Itana even though the Itan looked like he was ready to blow a gasket.

Oh. And she was mated.

115

She followed Mia, allowing herself to be hauled away from Keen. The farther away they got, the less she could hear of Keen and Ty's conversation.

"Just ignore them." Mia tugged. "Ty, God love him, is an idiot sometimes. Especially when it comes to Keen. Hopefully they'll work out a truce before one of them ends up bloodied."

The Itana didn't seem too broken up about the prospect.

She glanced at Lauren trailing in their wake, smiling wide as she rested her hand atop the small baby bump. She looked as if she couldn't care less about the unfolding drama.

"I'm sorry about all this. For Van getting hurt." Trista frowned and Lauren waved away her apology.

"Don't. I understand my mate and," Lauren shook her head, "he just wants to protect the clan."

They thumped up the front steps and Trista paused long enough to give Lauren her full focus. "And I'm a threat to that?"

"My mate seems to think so. He's not a bad male, but as the Enforcer, he's very, very devoted to the clan's safety. Hyenas threatened that, he lost some of his guards in the battle, so there's some animosity." Lauren reached out and squeezed Trista's hand. "But there's none here with us. There won't be with the clan. Powerful bears feel stronger than most and their emotions run hotter and deeper than anyone's. Even after the attack and purge, no one gave you trouble in Grayslake. They didn't even report your presence."

Trista knew that but it was because of her mother, of the relationships they'd forged over the years with clan and pack members.

Lauren released her. "Give Keen, give the clan, a chance."

Trista let her attention drift to Keen, to the massive werebear male who argued hotly with his eldest brother while his gaze was intent on her. Emotions tumbled across his face at an ever increasing pace. He still roared at Ty, but the warmth in his features heated her from inside out. Part of her wondered if his claim was due to more than just her salvation.

That same part stomped on the idea and reminded her that she didn't need anyone, that attaching herself to a man and depending on him for anything was a mistake. Didn't she remember what happened after her father died?

Lauren nudged her toward the front door and she followed the two women. The scent of blood crawled from the den, carried by the gently blowing air.

Van's shout had them halting, had Lauren turning toward her mate. "I don't think so." His words were garbled by his bear's snout. "She's not stepping inside the house."

Now it was Lauren's turn to yell at her mate, her turn to defend Trista. "She can either safely go into the clan den, or our home, but as you heard your *Itana* she's part of the clan." The woman stepped up to her mate, grasped his hand, and brought it to her stomach, forcing the fierce male to splay his fingers over the mound. "You told me no one would ever talk bad about our child because it's half human, that you wouldn't tolerate prejudice in the Grayslake clan. Why can't you see that it should apply to Trista as well?"

Van's midnight gaze traveled from Lauren to Trista and back again. Indecision warred with hate-tinged anger and then, finally, he bent his head and rested his forehead against his mate's.

"You're asking too much." The words were raw, hoarse, and she knew the scraping syllables weren't due to his animal, but the emotion that shrouded him.

"Lauren," Trista whispered and stepped forward, gently laying a hand on the woman's arm. "It's okay." Being hated was nothing new for Trista. "Don't fight with your mate over me."

117

She wasn't worth it. At all. Ever.

Lauren gave her a sad smile, tears filling her eyes, but it was Van who spoke. "We're not fighting. My mate is simply showing me that I'm an ass."

Mia coughed and then released a muffled "Language."

*

Keen refused to listen to another word. Not a one. Period. Ty kept talking, kept arguing and snarling about Keen's choice, while he focused on his mate—*mate*—and her conversation with Van.

Van, who only minutes ago, tried to gut Trista.

When a ripple traveled over Van's skin, fur rising in its wake, Keen walked away. He didn't say a word, there was no "by your leave." He turned from Ty, his Itan, and strode toward the gathering within the entryway. His bear bristled at Van's closeness, mere inches separating his new mate from his violent family member, and he increased his pace when Trista reached for Lauren.

Keen focused on Trista, speaking to her in low tones, and he pushed his way between the couple and his mate. A growl formed in his chest, vibrating his body with the weight of his bear's anger. Van shouldn't be near Trista. Ever.

That thought led him to another, to the realization that he needed to get away from his family as soon as possible. He had a new family now, one made up of him and Trista. One he hoped to expand just as soon as they turned their connection into something solid and real.

Everything in him craved that, his bear desired Trista above all else. He just hoped they could find their way.

The rumbling snarl continued as she glared at his brother. "Get away from her."

Van's growl countered Keen's as Van shoved his pregnant mate behind him. "Back off, Keen."

The sounds battled, his beast determined to dominate Van's. His animal pushed against him from the inside, stretching his muscles and pressing his bones almost to the point of breaking. It ached to shift, to destroy all threats to Trista.

She was his now—*his*—and he wouldn't allow any harm to come to her.

"Keen." Trista's hand fluttered over his back, fingertips stroking his ever expanding body. "I'm fine."

His beast calmed the tiniest bit, allowing him to speak more clearly. "Get back."

Van was too close to what the bear considered his. Deep inside himself, he recognized that his human half felt the same. From the moment he'd seen her, he wanted her. Hyena or not, he wanted Trista Scott.

He calmed even further when Van shuffled back. Anger still filled his brother's features, but he imagined Lauren's grip on Van's arm had something to do with the minor retreat.

Ty approached and he scented another bear nearing from inside the clan den.

Too many people, werebears, for his comfort. Threats surrounded them and his animal urged him to drag Trista from the hostile environment.

Keen was in full agreement.

Without another word, he took Van's slight opening and dragged Trista back down the steps and past Ty. He made sure his body blocked hers as they strode across the gravel. He paused long enough to gather his bag once again, and drew her to his truck.

"Keen!" His eldest brother called after him, but he refused to slow or halt his progress.

The rapid crunch of his brother's jog over the small rocks announced Ty's approach and Keen stood guard beside the passenger door. "We're leaving, Ty. You knew this was coming. I don't understand why this is so difficult to accept."

"Over her?"

Keen shook his head. "Over it all." He noted Ty's confusion and hurt, but couldn't do a damned thing about it. "I'm not your brother, I'm just another bear to you and that's fine. But I want to be more and I can't do that here. I definitely can't do that with Trista under your roof while you and Van are intent on destroying the best thing that's ever happened to me."

Shocking to his mind, yet his bear assured him it was true. Less than twenty-four hours in her company and he couldn't deny that Trista was now a necessity.

"But you're the Kee—"

"No." He shook his head. "Just another bear." He sighed. "I'll send someone for my stuff. Otherwise, I'll see you at the next run."

Ty looked torn, the anguish on his face plain to see, but it was beyond time for Keen to grow the fuck up and get the hell out. It was time for him to build a life of his own, one that didn't hinge on his brother's generosity and station.

The Itan stepped back, slowly retreating to where the rest of the family gathered twenty feet away. The moment Ty was far enough away for his bear to calm, Keen rounded his truck and climbed behind the wheel.

Trista didn't speak as he turned the key and got the engine rumbling. Nor did she say a word as they drove down the long driveway that led to the main road.

No, all she did was reach across the space separating them and stroke the hand resting loosely on his thigh. She ran her fingers along his fingers and then gathered them in hers, giving him a gentle squeeze.

He rolled to a stop when he reached the end of the drive and checked for traffic, resting for a moment as several cars sped past.

"You can go back to them, Keen. I won't hold you to your claim and you can—"

"No."

"I'm not worth destroying your life."

Without hesitation, he turned to her, giving her his full attention, and spoke from deep in his heart. "Unless you tell me you don't want me, I'm keeping you. Can you say that? Even if it's just a spark. Can you tell me you don't feel anything for me?"

She swallowed hard, tears filling her eyes. "No, I can't."

That's all he needed to hear.

chapter nine

Keen took her to the bed-and-breakfast on the other side of the lake, almost directly opposite the clan den. The Grayslake lake separated them by over ten miles, but they were still there, still close.

Trista stood on their room's balcony, staring across the water at the small dot that was the den. It looked so tiny now, so inconsequential, and yet the happenings in that home forged her future.

Keen moved around in the room they'd rented for the next week. She recommended the small hotel—it was cheaper—but he refused to listen. He wasn't having his mate stay in some rundown place. His words, not hers.

She'd become used to rundown. In some ways, it suited her more than the fine furnishings the bed-and-breakfast sported. The bed frame was intricately carved hardwood. The surface gleamed in the soft lighting, the evidence of recent polishing easily visible. The comforter was down with an honest to goodness duvet cover, silky and smooth to the touch.

Delicate chairs that had to be antiques and cost more than what she made in a *year* made up a small sitting area.

And then the bathroom… Traditional—probably original to the 1800s house—tile along with granite countertops on the vanity and a gorgeous pedestal sink. But the centerpiece that called to her was the massive, claw-foot tub. She wanted to sink into the slipper tub and relax, let the fears she'd carried her entire life be washed away by the warm water.

Instead, she stood on the back balcony and stared across the lake at the home that held Keen's past. Part of her felt like it held his future, too.

A future without her.

Keen's voice rumbled, blunted by the space and walls between them, but she was still reassured by his presence. Then she cursed herself for feeling better because he was near.

She shouldn't depend on him or crave his nearness. But she did.

Trista leaned over and placed her forearms on the banister, letting the solid wood take some of her weight. His words reached out to her, her tiny bit of animal allowing her to grasp more of his conversation.

"Helena? Yeah, I need... I'd appreciate... Thank you so much... Yeah, you too." His words were short, but held a tone that said he and the speaker were more than simple friends.

Jealousy, hot and searing, burned through her body from head to toe. It scorched her from inside out as her hint of beast cackled an objection. She wasn't sure why since they weren't mates, not really. They were hardly more than acquaintances.

She swallowed her emotions, shoving them away with a deep, determined breath. Moments later, Keen appeared, his steps light and some of the tension he'd carried was gone. She followed his movement through their room, his heavy tread carrying him past the double doors and on to the bathroom. Shortly after, the noisy flush of the toilet was followed by his steps on the porch, announcing his appearance.

Trista knew he was there, but didn't turn toward him or even acknowledge his presence. If she did, she'd become a jealous shrew

124

and ask him about Helena. So, she continued her sightless stare at the wilderness around them.

The sound of his deep breath reached her and he held it a moment before he released the air. He approached with slow, steady steps. His heat drifted to her even though his body remained apart.

"Tris?"

Tris. Her mother called her Tris. And now she knew what'd happened to her mom. It was done. She was no longer missing, but dead.

Because of a wolf. She wanted to call the Southeast Keeper, to have Reid brought up on charges and hauled away to confinement for violating the law. She'd helped the bear Keeper so many times over the years and he'd helped her a little in return, but she could still ask for a favor.

Except it hadn't been Reid, had it? No, Morgan did the deed.

Bastard.

His heat neared her and she knew his hands approached. Keen's touch was timid at first, palm sliding across her back as he stepped up beside her. "I can't get a handle on your emotions, so you need to talk to me."

She didn't, not really. Talking, sharing, and exploring… it'd all end in a fiery ball of broken dreams. So, she said nothing.

"Nothing to say?"

She didn't respond.

"I scent attraction, fear, and unease." He traced her spine and she fought not to shiver with the pleasure of his touch. "There's jealousy, too. There's no reason for it, Tris. Helena is…"

125

The name again. That name. More grief attacked her, new grief now that she knew the truth.

"Aw, don't fall apart on me now," he murmured and she didn't have a choice. He tugged her into his embrace. He held her tight, snug against him, and she fought the urge to lean on him.

"Keen..." She didn't know what she wanted to say. He'd destroyed her well-ordered, perfectly timed life in less than a day.

"I'm gonna hold you for a while and you're gonna let me. Then we'll get something to eat, and *then* we're going to find a place to live. The bed-and-breakfast is nice, but we need a home."

The feel of his lips on her temple was unmistakable, as was the feeling of rightness that settled over her as she finally relaxed against him.

Gathering her courage, she tilted her head back to stare into his eyes, to lock onto his gaze. "I don't know how to do this."

"What?" he whispered. Slowly he brought his hand up and tucked strands of her hair behind her ear.

Depend on you. She kept the words in her head and figured, screw it, he'd have to learn about her broken bits at some point.

"Be with someone, depend on them."

He squeezed her lightly. "You leaned on your mother."

Tears burned her eyes and she swallowed past the growing lump in her throat. "We depended on each other. We helped each other, but we were still alone."

His next words told her that he already knew her too well. "And now you're not. Not ever again, Tris. You're mine and I will *always* take care of what belongs to me. Always."

Her father never claimed her as his and she suffered for it. Day after day, she and her mother battled for their measly lives because she was fair game. They might have made a better life for themselves outside of the tri-cities, but her father kept a tight rein on their travels. He didn't want Trista, but he didn't want her to leave either.

This bear who could battle the clan's Itan and win had announced his claim and was more than able to put his strength behind his words.

For the first time in her life, she felt safe. And maybe, just maybe, she could lean on him a little.

"Okay." She whispered the word, trying very, very hard to believe Keen.

Slowly, treating her as if she were a frightened deer, he lowered his head. She read his intent, his desire written clearly in his gaze, and couldn't find it in herself to object. No, truly, she looked forward to the connection of a kiss.

His lips brushed hers, soft as butterfly wings, and he repeated the action, slightly more pressure than before. Gentle and soothing, the meeting of their mouths continued, growing more insistent. Her animal stirred, purring and reaching for more from Keen, and Trista's human half responded to its urging.

She slowly ran her hands along his arms, traveling to his shoulders and finally crossed them around his neck. She pressed to her tiptoes, increasing their connection further. He hummed with the slight deepening and she traced his lower lip with her tongue on the next pass. That earned her a moan along with a slight tightening of his arms.

The kiss grew more heated, his tongue meeting hers in a seductive tangle. He delved into her mouth and she did the same to him. She sought out his tastes, his delicious flavors that teased her from the moment they'd met. His warmth sunk into her, her curves flush with the hard planes of his muscles. While they discovered each other, her body reacted to him.

127

Arousal thrummed through her and her inner-hyena chuffed in response to his nearness. Her nipples tightened and hardened to firm points within her bra while the very center of her warmed and grew damp with her desire.

Keen's thick, hard length pressed against her hip, showing her that he was just as affected by their kiss. His reaction spurred her to continue, to keep tasting him. She swallowed his moans as he absorbed hers. The heavy pants of their breathy groans warred with the soft lap of water against the rocky shore below them. It provided nature's song as they explored one another.

Gradually he lessened their kiss, pulling his lips from her while continuing to hold her captive. With a low whimper, she tried for one last press and his mouth met hers in a gentle reunion. He was so fierce, so deadly, and yet he treated her as if she were glass.

Then it was at an end, his mouth no longer meeting hers. She nuzzled his chest, her hyena urging her to rub against him, stake her claim with her touch and scent. She was surprised when Keen did the same and stilled for a moment as his cheek brushed the top of her head before moving on to stroke her face and neck. Seconds ticked past and she didn't stop—nor did he—until she was satisfied he smelled like her.

Eventually they ceased, all attempts at defining their connection ceasing, and the sounds of the world surrounding them intruded. The warbling cries of the birds countered the gentle sway of the water to the shore and the wind whooshing through the trees. It was peaceful and soothing. The rush and race she'd lived with her entire life ceased to exist here. Here amongst her enemy's territory, she found tranquility.

Funny how life worked.

"You ready to get something to eat?" he whispered, hardly making a ripple in the quiet.

Truly, she didn't want to move, didn't want to break the soothing spell that'd woven its way around them. Yet, she knew it was necessary. The moment she pressed her lips to his, their future had been decided. Their lives were entwined, tied together by words and sealed by a kiss.

She was ready to shrug off her past and get on with her new life. Not all of it—she'd never forgive or forget so many things—but she could put aside some of her fear for him.

Trista cleared her throat. "Yeah, I'm ready."

* * *

Keen climbed from his truck and was quick to make his way to the passenger door. He caught it as Trista swung it open and immediately reached for her hand. "You need to lemme help you."

That earned him a glare, but she placed her palm in his and allowed him to help her slide to the ground. She was tiny, short, and small. Just a little bit of nothing.

His little bit of nothing.

Damn, it felt good to say that. It felt even better when he'd slanted his mouth over hers and tasted her for the first time. He couldn't wait to do it again.

"I'm perfectly capable of getting out of your truck."

Holding her hand captive, he used his grip to give her a sharp tug until she was pressed against him once again.

"Yeah, but then I wouldn't be able to do this," he murmured. Slow, as slow as before, he lowered his head and brushed his mouth across hers. The kiss was gentle, swift, and not nearly enough. But it flustered his little mate, making her cheeks flush red and her heart race. A vein in her neck pulsed and he wondered if her skin would be as sweet as her mouth.

Hopefully she'd let him find out someday. He didn't have any illusions that it'd be today. There was so much to learn and so many walls to climb. He hoped it was soon.

Keen's cock throbbed.

Yeah, soon, like 12:01 a.m. Then it'd officially be tomorrow. That sounded good to him *and* his bear.

Twining his fingers with hers, he gently pulled her toward the diner. It was the only one in their small town so it catered to humans and bears alike. The owners, Nellie and Edward, were sweet as could be and beyond nice to Lauren to this day. It was the perfect place to bring his mate and help her feel comfortable. It was also the central hub of any and all gossip in town. He'd be able to introduce Trista as his mate, get Nellie and Edward's approval, and get something to eat all in one shot.

The moment they stepped through the door, the scents of grilling burgers and french fries cloaked them. The rumbling buzz of conversations flowed around them and Edward's yell of "order up" lived above it all.

A waitress bustled by, racing to the window to snag the plates Edward had dropped onto the metal surface. Then she was racing away again, and Keen could see why Van was giving Lauren a hard time about working there. The moment the woman turned up pregnant, she'd resigned. Well, Van resigned on her behalf. That'd been one hell of a fight.

"Trista Ann, is that you?" Nellie's voice reached them and he spied the woman at the end of the long counter. She tossed her rag to the smooth top and then she was hustling toward them. She nudged one customer and then another aside. "Oh, it *is* you."

Nothing but happiness radiated from his mate as well as from Nellie. Then his mate was gone, encased in the woman's massive hug. "I haven't seen you in *forever*, sweet girl." Nellie hadn't even glanced at him. She simply commandeered his mate and dragged her through the diner, shooing the approaching waitress away as she settled Trista into a booth. "Now," she sighed and smiled wide. "The regular?"

"Sure," he drawled. "That'd be great, Nellie."

The older woman froze and finally looked at him, shock plain on her features. The look transformed to a narrow-eyed glare. Hints of anger dominated her scent and her face flushed red. "She's allowed to be here. I've been serving her and her mother for years. Sweet as can be and they never caused an ounce of trouble. Them laws of visitation say that—"

He loved Nellie for being so protective of his mate and any annoyance at her ignoring him was banished in that instant. He reached over and squeezed her hand.

"I know that. I'm not giving you a hard time about her." He tilted his head toward Trista. "Trista's my mate. I'm the last person you need to worry about."

"Oh." Her eyes widened. "*Oh*." Nellie sighed, shoulders relaxing as if she'd been carrying the world. "You'll take care of her then? No one bothers her here, I don't tolerate any of that, but…"

Yeah, he bet, and that thought sent his bear pacing and grumbling inside his mind. "But she's mine now." He let his gaze travel over the occupants of the diner, let it linger on the men and women— bears and wolves—and directed his next statement at them. "And she's under my protection. Nothing, and no one, will bother her again."

That earned him a glare or two, mostly from the females, but several of them bared their throats in acknowledgment as well. They may not know exactly *who* Trista was when it came to the problems with hyenas, but they now knew he wouldn't allow *anyone* to harm her.

That earned him a big, wet kiss from Nellie, along with a reminder to change his relationship status on the WereWeb, the shifter social network he'd developed. Then the woman was gone, bustling her way between tables as she headed toward the kitchen. With a smile on his lips and a shake of his head, he slid into the booth opposite Trista.

Trista met his smile with a grin of her own.

It felt right, being across from Tris as they sat down to a meal… it felt right. For the first time in his life, he relished in his calm bear and the beautiful woman near him.

Keen placed his hand on the table and reached toward her. Trista met him halfway, placing her palm on his and his beast relaxed further, practically purring from her touch. He had no doubt the animal would rise hot and hard if they were threatened, but now he wasn't fighting his inner-animal every second.

"Relationship status? WereWeb?" She raised her eyebrows.

He shrugged. Truly, it was one of his favorite projects plus it made a little bit of money on the side. He earned plenty from his regular job—developing software and testing company vulnerabilities—but the extra cash was always welcome. Now that he had a mate and a goal in mind, he was glad he had the money. He'd flag it for his cubs' college. Let the social network put their children through school.

Thoughts of children brought about thoughts of sex. With Trista. A lot.

Clearing his throat, he focused on her question.

"It's like Facebook but for weres. I mean, it does a lot more than Facebook and it's entirely locked down with several layers of security. It took me a while to implement the protocols and then coordinate various hacks and attacks against the site. But," he shrugged, "it's something that helped bring everyone together. We even have an Android and Apple app so you can post status updates whenever."

"You designed it?" Shock filled her features while pride filled his chest.

Finally someone thought it was a big deal.

Because, really, it was a big fucking deal.

Which had him launching into the whys and hows and did she know how hard it was to get were-children to remember *not* to use passwords like "god" or "1234." He lost her when he got to the best server configurations and surviving DDoS attacks.

Trista stared at him with glazed eyes and a blank look on her face. It wasn't until Nellie placed food before them that Keen shut up and his mate shook her head and snapped out of her stupor.

"Uh, that's interesting."

He kicked up the right side of his mouth in a rueful grin. "It's not for everyone and I tend to get lost in code sometimes." He shrugged. "You have to tell me to be quiet or change the subject."

"But it's important to you which makes it important to me, even if I don't understand what you're saying. I'm not going to cut you off."

"I get carried away."

Trista rolled her eyes. "It's obviously your passion, Keen."

Code and computers weren't his only passion, but he didn't think he could say that in the middle of the diner when anyone could hear them. Later was a different story.

"So, technology is my thing. I code, do some graphic design. Other companies pay me to hack into their systems and then pay me to fix their security vulnerabilities. What keeps you busy?"

Trista frowned and he immediately regretted the question. She'd been on the run for most of her life and he doubted there was much time for school when she was worried about staying alive.

"I worked at Jerry's, then at the bar, and then spent time in my shithole apartment. I mean, I once wanted to paint and go to college and major in art, but…" She grimaced. "You didn't mate the sharpest tool in the shed, Keen. I'm not even sure this whole thing is a good idea."

His bear growled low, annoyed that they'd rolled back to her doubting herself and doubting their mating.

"Trista, look at me." His voice held more than a hint of his bear and he couldn't fight the animal into submission. It was *not* going to be denied.

It took several seconds, but she finally raised her gaze. Extra moisture poised on her lower lids, waiting for a few more tears to gather before spilling down her cheeks. "Staying safe, keeping ahead of the wolves, bears, and even hyenas, takes a lot of knowledge, strength, and cold hard stubbornness. I bet you could quote me any law I asked without hesitation. I bet you know which counter others and when the most recent law should give way to the oldest. And I bet you could outmaneuver any shifter you come across based on the laws alone."

She didn't dispute any of his claims. He hadn't expected her to. Did she know everything there was to know about the world? Did she go to college? Probably not. But his woman was a genius when it came to survival.

He replayed Reid's words, melded them with what he knew of Trista, and came to a conclusion that was utterly the opposite the wolf Alpha's. "I also think you have the Southeast Keeper's number because he gets help from you, not the other way around."

Again, she kept quiet on the idea. She merely slipped another french fry into her mouth, chewing quietly as the world continued to swirl around them. The clink and clank of dishes peppered through the soft roar of the other patrons, giving them a raucous song to go along with their meal.

Keen remained silent, content to simply be near his mate as they shared a meal.

134

Minutes passed and Trista cleared her throat, snaring his attention. "He made sure the hyenas knew *he* knew about what I was doing and he does the same thing with the wolves and threatened them with going to their territory leaders if they bothered us."

He nodded. "That's the deal? You help him and he tells others to abide by the law? A little blackmail?"

With Trista's answering nod, he fought to keep control of his bear. The fucking bastard. He could have done something to help Trista and instead, used her to his benefit while leaving her to struggle.

He swallowed the roar building in his throat, pushed it down and beat the bear back. The shifters in the area around them fell silent as they eased away from them, him. He had no doubt they scented his towering rage and he was never more thankful that his mate wasn't a full hyena.

"There's no reason to be angry, Keen." Her voice was soft and a slight tremble filled the words.

"I'm fine." He managed not to snap at her.

Tris shook her head and tapped her nose. "No, you're not."

He narrowed his eyes. "You're only a half-were. You can't shift."

"No, I can't shift, but that doesn't mean I can't do things. I can smell scents and my hearing is better than others'. I have an animal here." She pressed a hand to her chest. "You just can't see it."

Rolling her words through his mind, he realized he'd let her distract him. Damn it. He went back to being pissed at the Southeast Keeper and decided the Southeast Itan was going to get a call from him as soon as they got back to the bed-and-breakfast.

"You're mad again," she murmured, her gaze flicking to the booth behind him and the now empty table nearby.

Keen took a deep breath, drawing Trista's scent into his lungs, and the bear lowered its rage to a manageable level. Instead of wanting to kill everyone, he only wanted to have the Keeper's blood on his hands. There, that was better.

"You won't be helping the Southeast Keeper any longer."

"But he—"

He shook his head. "No, he used you and didn't give you anything in return. He could have brought you and your mother to their compound. He could have actually paid you for your services. He could have done more than simply make a phone call." The fury threatened to overtake him once again. "I don't want to be a caveman mate, but in this instance, I'm telling you I don't want you helping him. I refuse to have you taken advantage of. He's disrespecting you, Trista, and that is not something I'll tolerate. Ever."

Trista's brow puckered, her lips doing the same thing, as she stared at the battered tabletop between them. The look of confusion was unmistakable and it broke his heart. She'd become so familiar with being used that she no longer realized she *was* being used.

It made him furious on her behalf and he resolved to keep her sheltered from those types of people. His mate should be a shining light safe from the bastards of the world. From now on, she would be.

She still wore that confused expression and he redirected her thoughts. The level of asshole-ishness of the Southeast Keeper could be explored later.

"Eat up. We've got an appointment with Helena in half an hour."

chapter **ten**

If Trista had claws, she'd scratch out Helena's eyes. She hadn't met the woman yet, didn't know her from Adam, but the hint of caring that entered Keen's eyes when he spoke of her was enough for Trista. She wasn't going to address the fact that she'd tried, more than once, to cut Keen free. The thing was, she decided to keep him and she wanted Helena far, far away. Maybe across the ocean.

While they rolled through the streets of Grayslake, Trista allowed her thoughts to drift to Keen's words. They were flat, a base pronouncement that allowed no wiggle room.

I don't want to be a caveman mate, but in this instance, I'm telling you I don't want you helping him. I refuse to have you taken advantage of. He's disrespecting you, Trista, and that is not something I'll tolerate. Ever.

She was glad in a way. She didn't want wiggle room, she didn't want to speak to the Keeper ever again. She'd always secretly harbored the same thoughts, but fear kept her calling him once a week, kept her checking in and solving his problems while her father's decree kept her in town.

Every Wednesday for years and years, she'd made that call.

… I don't want you helping him.

She wondered how the Keeper would react when she didn't call. With a mental shrug, she realized it wasn't her problem anymore.

They rounded another corner and traveled down a small, quiet side street. The homes were neat and cute with their throwback architecture and manicured lawns. Large trees shadowed the asphalt, sprinkling their path with flowers and leaves. Most of the driveways were empty and she assumed their occupants were off at work while their perfect 2.5 children were in school. That's what it was. This block, this area, epitomized the perfect American neighborhood.

She wondered if June Cleaver was going to walk out of a home and wave in welcome.

They traveled a little farther and finally pulled into the cracked driveway of one of the homes. It was an enormous, two-story house with gorgeous flowers lining the walkway and a massive oak tree in the middle of the front yard. A tire swing hung from one of the larger branches and she could imagine taking a swing. Or rather, their cubs.

Trista's heart fluttered at the thought of having cubs with Keen. Having cubs meant sex and... her breath caught, body liking that idea way too much.

Keen shifted the SUV into park and turned toward her. "Ready?"

That's when she tore her mind from thinking about sex with Keen and focused on the For Sale sign stuck in the ground near the sidewalk. She also noticed the vehicle in front of them that sported one of those magnetic signs. It was splashed with an image of Helena Montgomery along with the woman's contact information.

She glared at the sign. The woman was way too pretty. And skinny. And all around Miss America type sugary sweetness.

Movement near the front door caught her eye and she spied the woman waving at them, a wide smile in place.

Strike that, she wasn't pretty, was way too gorgeous.

138

"Stay put, I'll come around." With that, Keen climbed from the vehicle.

Unfortunately, Helena got to him before he got to *her*. The skinny woman with the perfect hair and the perfect makeup and the perfect body launched herself at *her* mate. She wrapped her arms around Keen's neck and gave him a tight hug followed by a smacking kiss to his cheek.

Wow. Just… wow.

The bit of animal inside her snarled and growled, urging her to claim her man.

Reaching for the handle, she kept her gaze focused on Keen and Helena as she hopped from the truck and then thumped the door closed. The two didn't even look at her. Helena kept chattering like a fucking *bird* even though one sniff told Trista she was a bear.

The woman was still prattling on when she stopped beside the couple; Keen listening, Helena blah, blah, blah-ing.

Trista wasn't one for hating people in general, but Helena had officially flipped her "I hate you with the strength of a gajillion suns, you evil whore" switch.

Standing beside the couple, Trista did notice that Keen seemed to be fighting Helena's touches, easing her hands away when the woman reached for him and brushing her off when she managed to make contact. That didn't satisfy her inner-animal though. No, it was still pissed as hell and even more pissed that she couldn't do anything furry about it.

"Ahem."

"And this house is *so* gorgeous. You're going to love this place. But it's so big you should think about finding a mate—"

"*Ahem.*" She even coughed that time. All to no avail.

139

"Finally settling do—"

"A. *Fucking*. Hem."

Two sets of eyes focused on her, one set filled with apology and a hint of shame as well as sincere thanks. The other was decidedly cool along with a "WTF, bitch."

Nice.

Keen immediately slipped his arm around her waist and tugged her close until she was plastered to his side. He dropped a kiss on the top of her head and lingered for a moment, drawing in an audible breath as he rubbed his cheek against her hair.

"Helena, you're right, it is time to settle down. I'd like you to meet my mate, Trista." His rumble vibrated through her, plucking her nerves and adding a new awareness.

"Mate?" The woman practically screeched and Trista winced. "You mated this—the... ew, a hyen—"

Now it was Keen with the frozen stare.

"Excuse me?" His voice was deceptively quiet, but Trista sensed the suppressed rage in his body.

Helena swallowed hard, her eyes suddenly wide. "I was just saying that, uh, you and I seemed... you know, I thought that..."

Trista's own jealous and anger swirled together until she was nearly overcome with the urge to go after the woman.

"I'm sorry if you looked at our time together as anything but friendship, but that's what it was."

"I let you sleep in my bed," she snapped.

Keen tightened his hold on Trista, not allowing her to go after the perfect Ms. Montgomery.

"As friends, Helena. Now, are you going to show us the house or do you need to call another Realtor to assist us?"

The werebear woman breathed deep, tossed Trista one last glare, and finally spoke through gritted teeth. "No, I'll open it for you. I'm sure you can tour the home on your own with your new *mate*."

Keen led her around Helena and across the lawn, leaving the furious werebear on the driveway. By the time they reached the door, Trista couldn't figure out what angered her more. The fact that the woman spent time in Keen's bed or the fact that... Okay, no, it was all about Helena the Whore being that close to her mate.

Feelings of possessiveness and ownership bombarded her and she didn't even try to suppress them. Keen was *hers*. He'd said the words and she'd finally settled on the idea of belonging to him in return.

They stepped into the dim home, the interior empty of any furniture. The wood floors gleamed, reflecting the hints of sunshine that peeked through the windows. The walls were painted muted hues of beige and cream. Part of her itched to throw bright paint on every surface and breathe life into the place. It was plain and simple, generic like every hotel room and apartment she'd lived in. Ideas about decorating and brightening up the place came crashing down with the thump of the heavy front door swinging closed.

Then she was reminded of Keen and ultimately Helena.

He reached for her and she stepped away, not allowing the connection. Whatever happened between him and the woman was in the past, she knew that. She also knew the moment they fully mated, he would never, ever cheat. But right now, the hyena thought of his hands on her. Those same hands that stroked her and held her hand.

"Tris..." He sighed and leapt for her in a single, blurring move.

One moment he was five feet away and the next he had her captured, bracketing her body as her back collided with the wall. He surrounded her, held her prisoner with his presence. With him so close, his scent filling her lungs, some of her jealousy drifted away. Keen was a fierce, strong, gorgeous hunk of werebear. Any woman would be pissed about losing him.

"Listen for a minute." His voice was deep and husky.

She nodded, waiting for him to speak.

"I…" He dropped his head forward, pressing their foreheads together. "I know what my reputation is in town."

Trista did, too. He was a womanizer. A man whore. There'd been more than one instance of him stumbling out of some female's home in the early morning hours. Then he'd be in someone else's that night. When she'd decided to accept him as hers, she'd also tossed that knowledge aside. Stupid on her part.

"I have never had sex with Helena or ninety percent of the women who claim otherwise." He pulled back, placed a fingertip beneath her chin, and urged her to tilt her head back. She allowed him to move her. "When we're alone, when I don't have to suffer through having her scent on me instead of yours, I'll tell you more. But I can count the women I've been with on one hand and Helena is not one of them. I swear to you, Tris."

He paused for a moment, indecision coating his features, and then spoke again. "She wanted to be a notch on my belt and she *told* people she was, but I'm discerning when it comes to sex. And yeah, it's weird, right? A guy sleeping with a woman, but not *sleeping* with her. I get that it's hard to believe, but when the bear rides me hard, it takes everything inside me to keep it contained. It'd difficult to think of sex when my animal is aching to go on a bloody rampage. So, no, I didn't."

Her eyes burned, tears gathering, and she didn't know why the hell his heartfelt promise had her crying. She'd become a basket case since meeting Keen Abrams and she prayed she'd get her emotions under control. Soon.

"If you say you haven't, then I believe you."

"I haven't." His gaze searched hers, his eyes entirely too intent.

"Okay."

"Okay?" He sounded skeptical and she nodded to assure him she told the truth. "Okay then. Let's see the house. It meets all of my wants, but we need to see if you'll be happy here."

Her. Trista Ann Scott. Happy. It was such a foreign concept that she feared she'd wake up any moment.

But she didn't as they moved through the family room that sported a large fireplace to warm them on winter nights. Or even when she described the type of rug she'd love to have spread across the floor.

Keen told her it was a good idea since they didn't want their cubs banging against the hard floor while they learned to walk. That made her heart stutter and she pretended the next room was more interesting than the last.

That'd been the kitchen with its six-burner gas stove, double ovens, and island with two sinks. The counters were polished granite and smooth to the touch. She imagined herself preparing dinner for Keen and their cubs and maybe, someday, the rest of his family.

That had tears springing forward once again and the stairs became the most interesting part of the home.

He didn't object to her random dashes for other parts of the house. No, he simply followed her, adding his own comments, making her fall a tiny bit in love with him. Which… which was not fair. She didn't want to love him, didn't want to think about a future where she depended on him for everything. But he wasn't going to let her imagine a time when he wasn't at her side, holding her up when she leaned close.

They emerged onto the second floor landing and the view had her freezing in place. Keen's warmth surrounded her and still she stared at the backyard, at the trimmed grass, and the lush tree that held a massive treehouse. The area was a young child's dream, her dream of years and years ago.

"Tris?" he murmured, his heated breath fanning her face.

"I—It's beautiful." It was.

He wrapped his arms around her waist and tugged her back to mold to his front. His chin rested atop her head, gently resting there. They stared at the backyard, watching the gentle sway of the trees and the rustling of the flowers that lined the back patio. There was even an area for a grill, and she wondered how many nights they'd spend out there, cooking and chatting and enjoying life.

"It's gorgeous, Tris." He leaned down and pressed a soft kiss to the side of her neck. "Come see the rest of it."

*

Keen changed his hold, catching her hand and leading her down the hallway. The home was everything Helena had said it would be. Better than the pictures that accompanied the listing online.

They came to the regular bedrooms first, four in all and each exactly the same as the others. They had different views, two of the front yard and two of the back, but that was the only thing that separated them.

He took a moment to imagine them filled with their cubs. He figured four was a good number. They'd have four and each one would be taught control and would be loved and treated equally. Unlike him.

"The master bedroom is this way." He eased her to the last bedroom. Until the moment she was fully in the hallway, her gaze remained intent on a pattern of pale baby animals that decorated the walls. It'd obviously been a nursery at one time. Was she excited by

144

the prospect of cubs or did she loathe the idea? He quietly took a deep breath and was relieved that anticipation filled her scent.

He didn't hesitate to draw her into the last space. It was large, as wide as the house was deep and it almost felt as if it took up half of the upper floor. He imagined his large bed dominating the center along with new matching furniture peppering the space. To the left was their bathroom and closets while the right boasted a large, bay window and welcoming window seat. It was uncommon for a house with this design, but the notes on the listing stated certain upgrades were made for comfort. He assumed this was one of the changes.

Trista immediately drifted toward the window, her gaze focused on the backyard.

He went to her slowly, gently gathering her in his arms and then sitting. He drew her into his lap and held her close. It felt right, perfect even. He knew holding her would never get old.

"What are you thinking?"

"That this house is gorgeous."

Keen smiled and his bear chuffed, pleased they'd found a good home.

"Do I hear a 'but' in there?" He hoped not yet. Her hesitation said otherwise.

"I'm sure it's expensive." She shook her head and turned to look at him. "It's too much and I can't contribute right away. I'm sure there are smaller—"

He silenced her with a kiss, a sweet meeting of their mouths despite the fact he wanted to deepen the connection. "I'm *very* good at my job and this house won't begin to touch my savings. If you like it, it's ours."

She swallowed hard and he saw the emotions flit across her face. Worry, hope, unease, happiness, anxiousness...

145 *anxiety*

"I want you to be happy, Tris. This place? We're gonna make it ours. We're going to fill it with cubs someday and I want to wake up to your smiles right here in his room."

Trista grimaced. "Not Helena? She's so beautiful."

His bear snarled at him, pissed that he hadn't told her about his past already. She could help him, but not if he didn't trust her with the truth.

He hated when the bastard animal was right.

Keen traced the back of her hand, fingers gliding over the pale blue veins that lingered beneath her skin. "Do you remember how I reacted in the living room this morning?"

God, had his life changed so quickly? He went from destroying his brothers to claiming Trista, and possibly buying a house all in one day.

"Yes."

"That is my normal self. It's how I feel twenty-four hours a day, seven days a week. The urge to tear through anyone who hints at opposing me is a constant in my life." He breathed deeply and let it out slowly. The bear didn't want to reveal his vulnerability, but she needed to understand what she was getting herself into. "Except when I'm with a woman. The touch of a female soothes me and quiets the animal. It allows me to get through another day as the bear slowly wakes from that feeling of euphoria and calm."

"Helena," she murmured.

"Yes. I slept in her bed, but it was only sleeping. Just like a lot of the other women in town. People joke that I have a girlfriend on every street, but it's not like that." Trista turned into him and rubbed her cheek against his. "The problem is the serenity wears off. The bear gets tired of the female and I'm forced to find someone else."

She stiffened, tensing in his arms. "I don't think I can go through that, Keen."

He shook his head, rubbing his scruff against her smooth cheek and enjoying the small shiver that traveled through her. "You won't have to. He wants you and only you, which is new for him. He's possessive as hell and the mere scent of Helena nearly sent him into a rage."

She harrumphed. "You didn't look too rage-y to me. You looked—"

Keen captured her lips in a quick, bruising kiss. "I was a man trying very hard not to tear through her to get to you." This time the kiss was softer. "Believe me, if I could hole up in a room with you for a week and bathe in your scent, I would." Another gentle meeting of lips. "If I could take your mark right this second, I would. You wouldn't have to let me claim you in return, but knowing that I belonged to you…" He knew what he wanted, but he also knew it was too fast. Especially for someone like Trista. "When you're ready, when you trust me, I'll bare my throat to you."

"I…" Her whispered words faltered, but he kept hope close to his heart.

Unwilling to let her finish her sentence, he eased her from his lap. "Let's check out this bathroom and then we can talk about whether we wanna buy it or not."

Trista shook her head, but allowed him to draw her to her feet and snug against him. One more cuddle before he had to release her. Her curves clung to his hardened body and he savored the softness of her form. So sweet and welcoming even if her insides were prickly and snappy. He was slowly breaking down her defenses and he couldn't wait for her to welcome him into her heart.

Hopefully, buying this house was a good start. He'd admit, if only to himself, he wasn't above buying her affections. With luck, her feelings would shift from appreciation and gratitude to something deeper and lasting.

The bathroom was like the rest of the house, a combination of modern design with historical touches. The Jacuzzi tub beckoned and foreshadowed long nights of relaxation. Hopefully with Trista. While the tile and sinks remained original, the standup shower had clear glass doors and he couldn't wait to happen upon Trista as water ran over her lush form, washing away the remnants of soap that clung to her. He'd pause and watch her for a moment, drawing out his need, before finally joining her.

Yeah, he couldn't wait.

"What do you think of the house?" His voice drew her attention and he smiled at the wide-eyed wonder gracing her face.

"It's gorgeous."

He nodded. It was. Beautiful and perfect and the home he'd dreamed of for longer than he could remember. The bear didn't like sharing its den, even if the other people were family members.

"So, we'll buy it."

Trista scoffed. "There's no 'we' here, Keen. I'm ninety-nine percent sure I've lost both my jobs by now. Definitely the one at Jerry's. How am *I* exactly helping *you* with the cost?"

He couldn't resist the urge to touch her and his boots echoed in the tiled room as he strode to her. He cupped her cheek, forcing her gaze to meet his. "You are the greatest thing that's ever happened to me in my entire life, Trista Scott. If this house brings a smile to your face, then you've done your part. Let me do mine."

His heart cracked when he noticed the moisture gathering in her eyes. He wondered if the woman cried all the time or if he was the lucky one who made her teary whenever he spoke.

"You're sure?" It was so fast, she'd spun from running for her life to verbally mated and buying a house in hours.

He bent down, pressed his forehead to hers, and rubbed their noses together. "I've never been so sure of anything in my life."

chapter **eleven**

Trista stared at the boxes piled in a haphazard fashion and scattered throughout the first floor of their new house.

Their. New. House.

It'd taken two days for the sale to be completed. One for the paperwork to be drawn up for signature and then anther for Keen to wire the money. Now it was Thursday night, and they had keys and were moving his furniture and belongings into the house. Their new furnishings and decorations also showed up this morning.

At 10 a.m., when Trista stood in the middle of the family room, gawking as movers brought the new things into the home, Keen gathered her into his arms and smiled down at her. *This is what money can do and this is how it will be for you.*

Now, four hours later, and she was still seeing man after man enter the house, carrying things she didn't even remember ordering.

"Tris?" Keen's yell rose above the heavy tread of the men carrying their couch through the front door.

"Yeah, coming." Still shell-shocked, she made her way to the stairs and thumped up them, hunting her mate.

Just as she reached the landing, he stuck his head out of a doorway. "There you are. Come see."

She'd been "coming and seeing" all day. The man was like a kid in a candy store and had to show her everything that moved through the home. She was exhausted from the constant running and hunting, but the fatigue couldn't destroy her happiness.

"What'd you do now?" She grinned and went to him, allowed him to draw her into the space. It was one of the rooms that faced the backyard and she noticed he'd had a window seat installed, as well as a drawing desk and an area that featured a painting easel. The light was perfect for early morning sessions. She remembered saying something about wanting to paint and draw, that'd she'd loved it in middle school but the idea had been pushed aside with Mr. Scott's death. Living became more important than paints. She froze in the doorway, unable to breathe. "Oh, Keen…"

"I'm guessing I did good." He approached her, wide smile in place. He captured her hand and drew her deeper into the room. "Come see."

He showed her everything. The paints he'd purchased, the brushes and pencils and everything she'd ever need. Plus he had a schedule of art classes at the local community college. "This is too much."

He shook his head and kissed her, hard and fast and not nearly enough. They'd done nothing but hold each other in the night and kiss during the day. He hadn't pushed for more and neither had she. It'd happen someday, they'd eventually solidify their mating, but it didn't seem like he was in a hurry. At the moment, she wasn't either, but each morning, each minute, he showed her he was dependable. He was worthy to be leaned upon and he'd never destroy her trust.

"It's not too much, and I'm not done yet." He pulled her to the single picture decorating the wall. Or rather, the lone framed document. "It's a copy of the original. I've got that one locked in our safety deposit box."

She still hadn't looked at the form, not closely, she was too surprised by the "our" safety deposit box. "Ours?"

Keen shrugged. He did a lot of that, especially when he was caught doing something that added her name to yet another part of his life. "It was one of the things you signed."

She glared at him. "You put that in there with the house paperwork, didn't you?"

By the time they'd finished reviewing and signing things, she didn't know what the hell she'd done. The house was free and clear, he hadn't taken out a loan, and it wasn't like she had credit or much of an identity he could steal. He'd assured her that she signed nothing that would negatively impact her in any way. When the attorney representing them reinforced Keen's statement and reminded her he was ethically and legally bound to tell her the truth, she'd finally scrawled her name on each page.

"Maybe." He grinned. "Now, look at the first bit of art you've got."

Glare still in place, he turned her attention to the frame on the wall, focused on its contents, and gasped. There, in black and white, was the deed to the house and it held one name. Hers.

"Keen…" She read it again, skipping over the legalese and simply hunting for any hint of Keen's name. And she found none. "You…"

He nudged her until she fully faced the wall and plastered himself to her back, enveloping her in a warm hug. "The house is yours. Completely. If something happens to me, if you realize I'm a bad bet, you'll always have a home."

"But…"

"You'll also have your own bank account that has enough to cover the taxes, utilities, and cost of upkeep for the house for twenty years. Longer if we invest it right. But it's yours."

Trista nudged him back and turned toward him, staring into his midnight black eyes and noticing the new hint of brown scruff on his cheeks. The bear was out, peering at her, and both of them were waiting for her reaction. Not hesitating, she cupped his face and held him steady as she pushed to her tiptoes. She brushed her lips across his, enjoying the first kiss she'd initiated.

When she felt him give in, she wrapped her arms around his neck and held him in place. She savored his innate flavors, the smoky sweetness specific to him. One gentle kiss turned into a simmering passionate tangle of tongues and nipping teeth. The familiar heat, the well-known rush of arousal that came with their kisses, assaulted her. It overtook her body in a blinding rush, filling her from head to toe. It urged her to wriggle closer to him, to press against him until their bodies were like one. She wanted to trace every dip and curve of muscle, learn the taste of his skin and the feel of him beneath her hands.

She wanted Keen Abrams plain and simple.

Keen moaned against her lips and wrapped his arms around her waist, hands coming to rest at the top curve of her ass. That was as forceful as he'd become, as if he were simply waiting for her to break free and shy away from him. She had to admit, it'd been a very near thing several times, but now...

Now he knew her, knew what she needed, and had handed over the answer without question. The old house, even in the middle of a tiny town like Grayslake, went for easily over two hundred grand and he'd paid cash. Then there was the value of her new account. She couldn't imagine how much he thought she'd need. Trista was sure it was way too much, but he just... gave it to her.

God, she needed more than these passionate kisses. She lifted her leg and wrapped it around Keen's thigh, pulling him even closer than before. She wasn't tall enough to rest it on his hip, but a gal worked with what she had.

That drew a deep moan from him followed by the rumbling growl of his bear. She wasn't afraid of the sound. No, she recognized his bear's response for what it was: pure need. For her.

She broke the kiss long enough to beg for him. "Please, Keen…"

She knew she wasn't ready for sex, but she sure as hell was prepared for more than what they'd shared. It'd taken one piece of paper and she realized he knew her better than she knew herself. One of the final walls protecting her heart crumbled beneath him.

Keen bent his legs, shifted his hands to her ass and then her feet no longer touched the floor. He lifted her until her pussy met his hardened cock and the only thing separating them was the cloth of their jeans. She wrapped her legs around his waist, welcoming him without hesitation. He stumbled forward until her back met the wall, her head coming to rest beside the frame that'd started their desirous frenzy.

She dove into their kiss, welcoming the heat and pleasure that came from their new position. He rocked his hips ever so slightly, as if testing her willingness, and she moaned in approval. Yes, she wanted this closeness more than she wanted anything in the world and she wanted it now.

Her heat throbbed while her clit twitched, and warmth enveloped her in an aroused wave. Her nipples hardened, pressing against the fabric of her bra and thin T-shirt as if they wanted to break free of the cloth. She wanted skin on skin, mouths on flesh, and bodies meeting in a rhythm as old as time.

Yes. Yes. Yes.

What she got was a masculine throat clearing followed by a loud cough. The sound had Keen yanking away from her, dropping her to her feet while he spun and faced the interloper. On unsteady legs, she stared at her mate's back, noting the way his shoulders expanded and stretched his shirt to almost tearing. His legs were doing the same, pushing against his jeans. That's when she noticed the rolling, threatening growl. Keen wasn't just annoyed, he was furious and was ready to take out his anger on their unfortunate visitor.

Taking him at his word, trusting in her ability to calm the raging beast, she eased her arms around his waist. When he didn't pull away, she allowed her front to align with his back until she touched him from shoulders to knees.

"Keen." She whispered his name and his reaction was instantaneous.

Beneath her touch, he deflated, his size shrinking the tiniest bit while his sounds were swallowed. One of his hands rested atop hers while he reached back, his palm sliding along her arm in reassurance. When he finally spoke, his bear imbued the syllables, but Trista was too thankful for the animal's retreat to care.

"What?"

"Uh... I... Um..." The man seemed unable to get his message out.

Peering around Keen, she spoke instead. It was one of the movers, she couldn't remember his name, but he'd been all smiles as he'd worked downstairs. She smiled, attempting to calm him. "Is there something you needed?"

"There's a woman downstairs who—"

Trista's heart stilled and the blood in her veins froze. A woman. She'd met a few of Keen's women over the past several days and while she was grateful they'd helped him through the years, she was jealous as hell. Which was stupid, but it was what it was.

Keen's snarl had the man snapping his mouth closed and she shoved a placating smile to her lips. "Thank you. We'll be right down."

The man took his chance to escape and his race down the stairs thundered through the house. The second he was gone, she prodded Keen's back. "C'mon, let's see what this one wants."

Would there be no end to the women? Gah. She had to take comfort in the fact he hadn't had sex with them all. That was reassuring. But they'd still touched his body, slept in his arms, and woken coated in his scent.

Now her jealousy was rearing its ugly head while her inner-animal snarled and chuckled in her mind. Damn it, she needed to get a handle on this.

He tugged her around until they faced one another again. "You know they didn't mean anything to me. They were a means to an end."

She nodded. She knew, she did. "But not all of them realize that. And they still held a piece of you. I know it was nothing to you, but it was something to them."

Sadness and regret overtook his features. "Will we always have this between us?"

"A little, not like it is today, but as I get to know you, it'll lessen." She smiled, hoping to reassure him. "I mean, I don't want to bludgeon Helena to death anymore. That's progress."

No, she just wanted to bury her alive, but she didn't say that out loud.

Raised voices reached them, muffled by the distance, but still audible. The anger circulating downstairs was unmistakable and it caused Keen to sigh in resignation.

"C'mon. Let's send this one on her way, too."

The annoyance in his expression and the slump in his shoulders almost made her happy. He looked forward to the confrontation as much as she did. That is to say, not at all.

They trudged down the stairs, the voices growing louder the closer they got. By the time they neared the bottom step, Trista was ready to kick the people to the curb. A man and a woman argued somewhere on the first floor. It annoyed her that they'd gained access to the deeper parts of the house. It was her place, *their* place, and they'd intruded.

At the bottom, Keen froze and she smacked into his back, not realizing he was gonna come to a sudden stop in the middle of their travels. It wasn't hard to see past him, her position on a higher step making it a simple thing to tilt sideways and look at their intruders.

Intruders that looked surprisingly like...

"Mom? Dad? What are you doing here?" Keen's voice cracked and Trista opened her eyes wide in shock.

She couldn't have suppressed her next words had she tried. "Oh fuck."

Keen's mother smiled wide at her while his father glared at him.

*

Oh fuck. Yeah, that pretty much echoed Keen's thoughts.

His parents were here. In his house. In his family room amongst boxes and random furniture that still needed positioning. Trista's rug hadn't been delivered so they were waiting to place everything until it showed.

And why the hell was he wondering about the rug when his parents were standing before him? In his house. In his family room.

Now he was repeating himself.

His mom bustled forward, arms spread and her smile wide. She looked like she did when he was five, all energy and happiness. She was the bright light in Keen's world, the first woman to soothe his bear. Trista was his last.

Trista.

Oh fuck.

He wasn't ready to expose her to any more bears. Least of all ones who might hold the same opinions as Ty and Keen.

"There's my boy. Look at you." She yanked him down the last step and then wrapped her arms around him in a tight hug. She was like that; a hugger while his dad was more about grunts. "You look good and I *love* this house." His mom looked around him and reached for his mate. "You must be Trista. Oh, honey, you're beautiful. George, isn't she beautiful? You're going to make such pretty babies."

Trista stared at him with wide, fearful eyes and his mother kept chattering away as if she didn't scent his mate's unease and anxiety. That was his mom. She sorta bulldozed everyone.

Before his mom could make off with Trista, he snatched his mate's hand and yanked her close. He wrapped an arm around her shoulders, keeping her captive.

"Oh, George, do you see that? He's already protective. That's so sweet." His mom pinched his cheek. Pinched it! "I knew he'd find the perfect woman."

His dad grunted in agreement. That was one thing he'd learned over the years. He could tell one grunt from another better than anyone. Surprising, since he hardly spent any time in his dad's company. Not when his father was consumed with teaching Ty everything about being Itan.

At the same time, he taught Keen how not to be a father.

"Mom, what are you guys doing here?" He shoved the words passed panicked lips.

"Well, you knew we were coming. Mia's about to give birth and Lauren is pregnant and—"

"After the birth, Ma. You weren't supposed to be here for a few weeks." It was what he'd counted on. It was going to give him time

159

to get to know Trista before his parents descended. They hadn't been the greatest parents, but they were the only ones he had, so Trista would have to meet them. Then, not now. *Then*.

"Oh, well." She waved her hand. "Ty called and he was in a tizzy—"

His dad grunted again, telling Keen his father was disgusted with his eldest brother.

"And then Van was being bothersome."

Another grunt. Okay, Dad was furious with Van.

"So we came a little early to visit a little longer." His mother finished with a wide smile as if all was right in the world.

Dad's latest grunt told him they were there to meddle.

Great.

"Plus, Isaac is on his way. He wasn't going to come home for Mia, but I told him she'd feel better if the clan's Healer was here." Dad actually broke away from grunts for a snort which earned him a glare from Mom. "So he'll be here tomorrow along with Mia's father."

Isaac was supposed to be in Cutler, helping Mia's father keep the town under control and lead the clan. It was one that Mia's dad had once upon a time belonged to, but the old—now dead—Itan had been a dick and ran Mia and her parents out of town.

"Won't Cutler need them?" He wasn't sure he could deal with Isaac if his brother's hatred ran as deep as Van's.

"Oh, no, they have things fairly settled and calm."

Keen looked to his dad and noticed the eye roll. Wow, the old man had become rather demonstrative in his old age. "Okay, so everyone will be hanging around?"

"Of course, dear." His mother patted his chest. "Now, let me meet my new daughter-in-law and then we can tour the house. I love these old homes, all big and beautiful. Did I spy a treehouse in the backyard?" Mom tried to reach around him and he cut her off.

He loved his mother, but he wasn't about to inflict her on Trista. "Not without me."

His mom sniffed. "That's rude."

"We can see it together. Dad, you want to come?" His father stuffed his hands in his pockets and gave a grunt Keen didn't recognize.

"No, you stay here with your father. I'll keep—Trista is it?—company." She stepped left and hopped up a stair before he could stop her.

"*Mom,*" he murmured and that earned him another pat.

"You talk with your father. I promise not to scare your mate away."

Keen flicked his gaze from his mom to his father and back again. "Mom…"

"Show him the yard. Talk to him. You two haven't ever done enough of that and you need to." She reached down and actually swatted his ass as if he were a five-year-old being sent away. "Now, go."

With that, she snatched Trista's hand and half-dragged his mate up the stairs. The last thing he saw was her fearful, panicked expression. If he wasn't faced with having to speak with his father, he would have rescued her. As it was, he couldn't exactly turn his back on the man who could—even at over sixty—kick his ass without trying. Ty wasn't a match for Keen, but Dad… that was a different story.

He stared at his father, trying his best to read the older man's expression, and came up with nothing. It was a look he'd never seen on his dad's face, one of guilt and sadness? Nah, it had to be indigestion or something.

161

With a jerk of his chin, his dad urged him to the backyard and Keen took the silent order. They wove their way past the crooked piles of boxes and he pushed the back double doors open with a gentle nudge. They'd been left unlatched after bringing the massive couch into the house.

Keen padded over the worn wood of the back porch and strode to the railing. He gripped the bar, using it for support as well as a reminder that he was human, that he had hands not claws and they needed to stay that way. He couldn't let go of the banister, not for anything.

"What really brought you here, Dad?"

He got the usual sound, the one that told Keen he was being impatient and it annoyed his father. Fine, he'd keep his mouth shut then.

With a sigh, his father took up position beside him, mirroring Keen's stance.

Then his dad spoke. It was only two words, but they would forever change Keen's life.

"I'm sorry."

He cleared his throat, stalling for time as he rolled those two words through his mind. His dad was sorry? *Sorry?*

"For what?" Keen rasped, surprise still clouding his throat. He hadn't heard of his father apologizing. To anyone. Ever.

Dad coughed and he gripped the railing as hard as Keen, his knuckles white against the tan hue of his skin. "For Quinn."

Keen grimaced and turned his head, not wanting his dad to see the tears gathering in his eyes.

"For Jessa," he rasped.

162

A shudder wracked his body and he fought to remain upright.

"For it all," his dad whispered. "For it all."

Keen pushed away from the railing, fighting his bear with every flex of muscle and shift of bone. The animal wanted to rage at his father. The man was apologizing too little, too late. He couldn't change and suddenly become a normal bear who could keep his cool. A bear who wouldn't shift and attack with the hint of disrespect.

"I can't do this." Not today. Not now. Maybe not ever. His father's voice followed him as he strode through the house, the familiar bass yelling for him to come back.

It wasn't happening.

He raised his voice, loud enough to be heard through the whole home. "Trista!" He needed her, needed her skin beneath his palms and heat sinking into his soul. The bear was restless, nearing closer and closer to the edge of his control. "Trista!"

The rapid thump of her feet on the old wood preceded her appearance. Eyes wide, a hint of panic in her gaze, and the animal was immediately focused on her. It wanted to destroy whatever scared her while soothing her as well. Convenient that he could handle both since he was the one that frightened her with his bellow.

"Keen? Wha—?"

He reached out and tugged her into his arms, breathing in her sweet scent and letting it soothe his heart. His father's words tormented him, poked and prodded at old memories. Thankfully Trista was able to calm the raging beast.

"I didn't mean to scare you." He pressed a kiss to the top of her head, long and lingering as he brought in more of her flavors. "Grab your purse, we're leaving."

"But—"

"Please, Tris. I'll explain, but I gotta get out of here right now."

Keen allowed her to pull away and he focused on her upturned face. Her eyes stroked him and she must have seen something that swayed her to listen to him. The next thing he knew, his mate was racing away, intent on doing as he asked. While she'd disappeared for a moment, his father entered the house as his mother delicately made her way down the stairs.

"Keen Lincoln, what are you doing?" His mom's voice was chiding and filled with love.

"Trista and I are getting out of here." He sighed. "I can't do this, Mom."

She'd always acted as an intermediary. When she was available. The thought made him sound ungrateful, but the fact was, he still held a lot of bitterness where his parents were concerned. If it were simply a matter of them not being as attentive as he would have liked, it would have been fine. But their disinterest led to something far more dangerous, far more deadly. For which Quinn and Jessa paid the price.

"I'm sorry." Dad should have said that to Quinn's and Jessa's parents, not him.

A hint of sadness and remorse filled her gaze and she reached for him, her thin aged hand trembling, and he stepped out of reach. "I can't." With Trista not at his side, he wasn't sure how he'd react. Then his mate was with him, her hand in his, trust filling the connection. "Ask me to dinner, to visit, but don't ask for forgiveness and don't ask me to relive it."

Tears clouded his mother's eyes. "And what about the family? Your brothers?"

Keen gently squeezed Trista, welcoming the warmth her body emitted. "They made their choices and I made mine. This is my mate and we'll make our own family."

"Don't—Don't run away like this, Keen, sweetheart, please. We don't have to talk about— Let's go out and—"

He shook his head. "Not now, not today. I'm taking Trista shopping." Anywhere they weren't. "I'd appreciate it if you were gone when we returned." He swallowed his heart cracking and healing in equal measure. Part of him ached for the approval and love of his parents. The other part, his bear, reminded him of the pain they'd caused. What made today any different from yesterday or the day before? Nothing. No, it was Trista. Trista who he'd defended with his life while his brothers were so intent on ending hers.

For once in Keen's life, he'd stood up for himself and what he believed. For the first time in his life, *he'd* been the source of conflict within the family. He hadn't been the crazy boy who was overlooked in favor of his brothers and he wasn't the child that'd decimated... If he wouldn't let his father talk about it, he'd be damned if he let those memories surface.

He had to focus. They were here because he wasn't acting like the Keen they knew. He didn't look like the Keen they were familiar with because he *wasn't* the Keen they'd grown up with. He was better. He had Trista.

chapter **twelve**

Keen's emotions were palpable, flowing from his hand to hers as he led her toward his SUV. She sensed his unease, his anger, and frustration. As well as his vulnerability.

Trista wasn't sure what'd happened when he went to the porch with his father, but it had obviously not ended well. Judging by the blank mask covering his expression, she knew it'd been more than unsettling. He attempted to appear unaffected, but she knew him now.

He helped her into the vehicle and then moved to his side, climbing behind the steering wheel. It didn't take him long to get underway and racing along the streets of Grayslake.

Instead of heading to the center of town where the stores were located, he picked a road out of Grayslake. He steered them toward the open fields that led to forests that led to... the lake.

With his speed, it didn't take long to arrive at their destination. The SUV bounced over the rise and fall of the earth, bumping over fallen trees and dipping into natural ditches, before he finally drew the vehicle to a sudden, dust-stirring stop.

As the dirt cleared, she found herself staring at the smooth, placid surface of the lake, its soothing waves lapping at the rough shore.

"Keen?" She reached out for him, gently laying her hand atop his forearm and brushing his smooth, fur-lined skin.

"C'mon. I wanna show you something." He pushed from the SUV, leaving her to scramble after him.

And she hurried to catch up with his long-legged stride as he made his way along the rock-strewn ground. He strode over small patches of gravel and large clumps of stones, never slowing his pace.

She wanted to stop and enjoy the view, marvel at nature's painting and the fresh air that surrounded Grayslake. Instead, she raced after him. Normally she'd whine and cower, unwilling for a gorgeous man like Keen to see her jiggle. But there were more important things than vanity, weren't there?

Staring at the stiff line of Keen's spine, the way his hands trembled even though he'd fisted them to prevent the shakes, the brown fur coating his arms and the tautness of his clothes…

Yes, there were more important things in the world. Mainly: Keen.

How long did they travel before his pace finally slowed? A half hour? A full hour? How about two? Trista didn't know. All she did was keep her attention fully focused on his back, watching the shift of muscles while he kept his determined stride steady. She was exhausted, beyond exhausted, but hadn't said a word. Not when his bear so obviously rode him hard. She didn't want to set off the animal. He wanted her with him so she did her best to keep pace.

It hadn't been easy and by the time he stopped, by the time he crumpled to the ground just inside the mouth of a small cave and leaned against the roughhewn wall, she was ready to collapse. Hell, she did collapse into an undignified, roughly panting heap. There was no grace in sprawling spread-eagle on the ground. There was only relief at the fact the man wasn't forcing her to take another step.

A low, masculine whimper flowed into a gentle, rolling growl and suddenly Keen's hands were on her, pulling her from the earth and into his lap.

168

"Oh, Tris. I'm sorry, baby." He made another whining sound, his hands sliding over her skin, massaging her muscles. "I'm so sorry. I shouldn't have dragged you out here."

Yes, he should have, because he obviously needed her.

"I'm..." She drew more air into her lungs. She couldn't lie to the man. He was a shifter, he would have scented her deception. Instead, she went for the shined up truth. "Fine-ish."

His furred arms wrapped around her waist and he buried his face against her neck, breathing deep and stirring her hair with every exhale. They sat there, she trying to catch her breath while he seemed intent on drawing in as much of her scent as he could.

Like at the bed-and-breakfast, the soft lapping of the lake lulled her, encouraged her heart to resume its normal beat as her breathing calmed. Her body matched the ebb and flow of the water, forcing her to relax into Keen's embrace. As the tension inside her drained, so did her mate's until they moved as one.

Slowly his tanned skin was revealed and then his body deflated in a heaving rush as if he were a popped balloon.

"Keen," she whispered, unwilling to break nature's spell. "Are you okay?"

He nuzzled her neck, tickling her skin, but she resisted the need to pull away from his touch. It was obvious he needed to lean on *her*. Her entire life, she'd fought to be independent, living with her mother and without the need to depend on another. Especially after Mr. Scott. Funny how she never referred to him as "Dad."

And now... now the future rested on her shoulders. A mating was give and take. It was time for her to give.

A soft breeze brought the scents of the forest to them, the crisp water of the lake and the gently blooming flowers that swayed in the wind. The low song of the birds filled the air, soothing her further, and she hoped it did the same to Keen.

Are you okay? It'd been the wrong question to ask him, the wrong direction to travel. He'd been taking care of her from the moment they'd met. It was her turn now.

"Keen, what do you *need?*"

Keen lifted his head and stared at her with midnight black eyes swirling with a hint of brown. The bear lurked, the color telling her without words that he battled with the animal and neither was coming out on the winning side.

"Tris…" The word was a growl, but still she recognized his nickname for her.

"What can I do? What's wrong?" She couldn't fix him if she wasn't sure what was broken.

Keen stared into the darkness of the cave.

"I don't want to go inside." The admission was hoarse and strangled.

She brushed strands of his hair from his eyes, fingers ghosting over his skin. "Then we won't."

"But we have to." This was a whisper almost carried away by the breeze.

He gently lifted her from his lap and then rolled to his feet, steadying her. He twined their fingers together and he led her into the cave. The bright light of day ceded to the dim interior of the cavern until shadows enveloped them.

Still they walked a few more feet, sliding around a boulder hardly visible in the darkness. Despite the gloom, Trista noted a patch of rock and earth that seemed darker than their surroundings. As if the ground had been stained by… what?

170

He pulled her before him, encouraging her to lean against his chest as he wrapped his arms around her waist. His body curled around her, protecting and supporting her.

She ran her hands over his forearms, grimacing when fur once again coated his flesh. Not because she disliked the bear, but because she hated the war he waged within himself. She hated that her presence wasn't calming him like so many times before.

Trista longed to get him talking again, wanted him to release whatever torment seemed trapped inside him. Instead, she remained silent, waiting for him to let the emotions free.

She waited one minute and then two and after what seemed like an eternity, he spoke.

"You asked me what was wrong. Why I…" He sighed, breath stirring her hair with the exhalation. He swallowed hard and then did it once again. "I lost everything here, Tris. I lost my soul."

*

Keen stared at the stain, the darkness still present after all these years. Then again, he'd forbidden anyone from coming here, from destroying the evidence of his sins. After they'd removed the bodies… *The bodies.* Then he'd demanded that his father issue the order to make the cave off limits. It was the only time he'd ever roared at his dad, but it wasn't a son speaking with his father. It was a fierce bear bellowing at his Itan.

Thankfully, he'd listened.

I lost my soul.

Yes, it disappeared that day. Gone in a flurry of fang, claw, and fur.

Quinn hadn't had a chance. Neither had Jessa.

171

Trista struggled against his grip and his bear allowed him to release her. They wouldn't hold her captive, not when his control was nearly shattered and his sanity lingered by a thread.

Only... she didn't leave. No, she wrapped her arms around him, hands going to his back as she urged him to resume his position. Only now she could touch him, stroke him, and soothe his animal. He needed that. He couldn't push the words past a bear's snout.

"Tell me, Keen. Tell me," she whispered and he shuddered.

Old pain rose hot and fast, burning his blood and squeezing his heart.

He drew in a painful breath, pulling it into collapsed lungs, and forced himself to let the past rush forward.

Even after he spoke the words, after he began the story, the events of that day shrouded him and he imagined himself traipsing through the forest.

"I was coming here to see Jessa..."

Keen, fourteen and a little bit gangly, but still strong as heck, strode through the forest. He kept to the trees that lined the bank of the lake. No sense in letting his dad catch him sneaking off to see Jessa. Dad didn't like her, but what did he know anyway? His father didn't even like *him*. So, whatever.

He tripped over a rock, skinning his knee, but by the time he brushed off the dirt and grass, he was healed. Kinda cool since his older brothers couldn't get better that quickly. But they would be the next Itan, Enforcer, and Healer. Not Keen though. He was just... Keen. Bratty brother, ignored son, and wicked strong. He could probably take on Ty. Maybe even win. Definitely could when he grew up and finished this puberty crap.

Whatever. Again.

He pushed to his feet and was more careful. Getting slowed by falls and injuries meant less time he'd spend with Jessa.

Man, she was so beautiful. Her hair was long and shiny when the sun hit it. And she was sexy and curvy. Her boobs were huge! His thing—his brothers called theirs dicks—got hard whenever he was around her. He felt more like them when he thought of it that way. Then he remembered they didn't think of *him* at all.

Jerks.

Jessa thought of him. She always spent time with him, sat with him near the cave and it sorta calmed his bear. She made it not wanna take on his dad or fight his brothers. The animal liked the sight of blood and it freaked Keen out a little. Okay, a lot.

Which brought him back to Jessa and how she made it not want so much.

He smiled and jumped over a fallen log. He liked her a lot and he'd tried to kiss her a couple of times but she said she wanted to take things slow. She also didn't want to be his girlfriend, but that was okay, he guessed. She liked him enough to meet him out here. It'd happen eventually.

The birds sang, filling the air with their sounds. They knew he was happy and stuck around. Usually they shut up when he passed, like they knew his bear was angry all the time. Today he wasn't because he was going to see her.

Part of him wondered if he should be traipsing out here. She hadn't called or texted him, but he'd seen her car shoot down the side road that led here. Well, it wasn't much of a road, really. Sort of a path people made over the years.

He would have missed her if he hadn't been outside, watching Ty and Van train with their dad. Yeah, *their* dad, not really his.

Anyway, she went by and Keen managed to wander off when no one was looking. Not that they did all that often anyway.

He neared the mouth of the cave and he knew he'd have to leave the camouflage of the trees soon. He paused near the opening and slid behind the trunk of a tree. He peered out, looking toward his house and saw his brothers and Dad training. Two on one and still his father was winning. With the fur flying, they wouldn't see him.

He raced over the damp ground, feet slipping when he hit a really soft patch, but he still made it inside. They wouldn't be able to see him now. Not really.

The air in the cave stank a little. Stale and wet even though it hadn't rained. He supposed that was because of the lake being so close. He shrugged. Not that it mattered. Jessa never complained about the smell and still visited him.

Keen took a step deeper into the space and then another, gravel and rocks crunching under his shoes. He managed a total of four steps before he heard the first sound. It was kinda low, a deep moan. It was followed by a quick gasp and then a groan.

But then… then there was a whimper and another moan and he thought there was a sound kinda like a slap. Maybe? He was only used to hearing punches and this didn't seem quite like that, but close.

Was someone fighting? Here? Nah. He didn't scent any blood.

Another groan followed by a low whine then a softly murmured "Oh, God."

That he knew. He'd know Jessa's voice anywhere. He'd never heard it like that, breathy and moan-y, but when it was followed by a few more slaps, his bear reacted.

Shit. It reacted a lot.

Shifting still hurt, mostly because he didn't let it out too often, and it burned like hell now. His fingers snapped and stretched until claws formed while his muzzle pushed into place, teeth replaced by long fangs. It didn't come out completely, the space was small, but it shoved forward to attack and defend.

More slaps came, Jessa's cries, audible and bouncing off the cave walls.

He was hurting her. *Her.* His Jessa.

Using his bear's enhanced eyesight, he navigated the cavern with ease. Even after the sun no longer filled the space, he could see without a problem. The larger boulders that littered the ground hardly hindered him. The sounds of Jessa's struggle intensified as he neared her, filling his ears and spurring the beast's rage. His human half cried out as the bear snatched more of his control.

It was jealously protective of Jessa. It'd claimed her as his. At least for now. It knew she wasn't their mate, but she was still theirs. And she was being hurt.

He finally rounded the last massive rock. The one that hid them from view day after day when they met. Even if his family looked, they wouldn't find them.

So, yeah, he went around the last one and then froze mid-snarl. The sound echoed and bounced against the walls, causing the two people to freeze which gave him a chance to see…

Only her head was visible, a man's nude body covering her from shoulders to hips and her legs were wrapped around his waist. Shock coated her face and then anger. At the same moment, the guy on top of her rolled to the side. They were both naked, both stinking of, of… sex. That was it. He remembered the smell now. It'd filled his brother's car once. His dad had talked to Ty and Keen hadn't ever smelled it again.

Until now. Until he saw all of Jessa and all of—he squinted and tried to figure out who the guy was—Quinn. That was it. Quinn Foster. He was a werebear and just turned seventeen. He'd already asked his dad to train him as a guard when he was old enough.

But… but he was here in the cave, in his and Jessa's secret place, and, and… *fucking* her.

Fucking. They were fucking. Quinn sticking his dick inside his Jessa.

But she'd been moaning and groaning and maybe she hadn't wanted…

"What the fuck, Abrams?" Quinn's yell bounced inside Keen's head.

"Keen, what the hell are you *doing*?" Jessa's shout followed on the heel of Quinn's.

What was he doing? What was he doing? The bear wanted to know what the fuck his woman was doing here with Quinn's dick inside her. She was his.

"Me?" He glared at her. "You're mine." He turned to Quinn. "She's *mine*."

Quinn laughed and climbed to his feet, brushing dirt off as he rose. Keen barely held onto the bear, barely kept it from leaping at Quinn and wiping the smile from his face.

"Yours?" Quinn chuckled. "My cum is filling her pussy, not yours, *cub*."

Jessa said something, called Quinn an asshole. Then Keen looked at her—looked *there* even though he shouldn't because it wasn't right to stare at a girl like that—he saw what Quinn was talking about.

"You…"

Jessa snatched a blanket and covered herself. "It wasn't like that. Quinn… He…"

She hesitated and he took a deep breath to try and calm his animal. Only, it didn't work because he also smelled her blood. Just a little, but enough to know she *had* bled. Maybe was still bleeding.

He turned back to Quinn, rage filling him. "She's mine! You hurt mine!"

Keen leapt, the shift rolling over him in a blinding rush to the point where his human half didn't exist any longer. No, he was all bear, a half-ton of rage, anguish, and hate.

Keen was snapped back to the present by small hands gently stroking his back, petting him with soothing strokes and he noticed the soft murmurs escaping Trista's lips. Trista, not Jessa.

Trista Scott.

"It was…" He cleared his throat, voice hoarse from retelling his story. How long had he been speaking? "I don't remember much after that. The bear… I was all bear then, Tris. All of it." He shuddered, new memories rushing forward as if the animal was finally ready to release them to the human's care.

He didn't want them. Not a single one. But that didn't keep them from overwhelming him and dragging him into an abyss of blood, fur, and pain.

"I'll listen to whatever you have buried inside, Keen. Let me carry it for you," she murmured against the base of his throat, her lips grazing his skin.

And so… so he released the new memories as the bear handed them over.

Really, it was Quinn's laugh that set him off. The boy made fun of him, talked bad about Jessa. He was mad at her, too. She let Quinn… do things to her even though she wouldn't let Keen kiss her. He didn't understand, didn't get it, but he did know Quinn was a jerk and the bear didn't want any other male touching the girl who belonged to him.

Keen shifted in mid-leap, skin abandoned and discarded beneath his fur. It hurt like hell, but the animal refused to be denied. It played along and let him suppress the beast, but not now. As the change rippled through him, so did the pain, angering his beast even further. Now the bear was pissed at Keen the human in addition to the asshole Quinn.

He saw Quinn trying to change too, but he wasn't fast enough, he wasn't as fast or as strong as Keen. There was no one like him and this proved it.

A scream echoed and bounced off the rock walls. Jessa's? He wasn't sure he cared all that much. Not when Quinn snapped at Keen, teeth coming close to his neck.

Blood splattered on the wall, followed by a chunk of flesh and fur. It slowly coated Keen, Quinn's blood changing his fur from brown to deep black. The large boulder at his back kept him from drawing Quinn into the larger parts of the cave, limiting his strikes and bites. The space was small and the bears were big, not giving them much room to battle. Yet they made do.

A streak of a pale body broke into the darkness, flying past Keen just as he reached for Quinn once again. Somewhere in there, amongst Quinn protecting himself while Keen sought more flesh, Jessa disappeared and quieted. Good, he could deal with her later. After he handled Quinn. Quinn the bastard who, even through the pain, looked at him with laughing eyes.

Keen kept going, the bear pulling on every ounce of strength and cunning. He wasn't hindered by teachings on how to fight. That knowledge truly limited a bear. Without those lessons, he reacted on instinct, attacking when another would retreat, slashing when another would dodge. Rules of conduct and engagement didn't apply. Not to Keen's werebear, who was more wild than tame.

That meant when Quinn went down, when he panted and fought for breath and looked near dying, Keen still raised his paw. In his mind, he saw Quinn atop the girl who belonged to him, at his cum dripping out of her and the scent of their sex filling the air. Yes, he was ready to destroy the male who threatened his happiness.

He flexed his claws, spreading them wide as he brought them toward the prone body. That familiar flash of pale skin dashed before him, a shout on her lips, but it was too late.

Too, too late.

He couldn't stop mid-swing, couldn't end the blow before it connected. So Quinn and Jessa died beneath his claw, staining the ground and rocks with their blood. If remorse hadn't suddenly filled him, he would have thought their final resting place was fitting. They'd perished where they'd fucked.

Panting, sucking in blood-tainted air as he fought for calm, he stared down at them. Quinn's destroyed body slowly changed into his human shape, chunks of flesh missing from his arms and legs. A massive gash was carved down his stomach and a matching one stained Jessa's body. Parts of her were crushed, buried beneath Quinn when he'd still held his animal's form. Other parts of her were shattered due to the power of his hit that sent her careening into the cave wall.

They'd fallen with one last strike.

The animal stared at the carnage, satisfaction filling him at the conclusion. The beast relaxed and stumbled backwards until it too pressed against the rock. He glanced at the exit, realizing he couldn't leave while so large. That's when he ceded control to his human half, allowed fur to be drawn from skin and paws to transform into hands. The change back was just as painful as the shift to his inner-animal.

The moment he could balance on two legs, he stumbled toward the light, uncaring of his nudity and the blood coating his skin. He needed to run and shy away from the afternoon's events, was desperate to wash the blood from his body.

Keen stumbled past the boulder, using the stone to steady himself before moving on. His hand slipped on the wet surface and he realized blood had been flung so far.

His feet finally carried him to the mouth of the cave, to the light of day and the shining sun. It was bright, cheery almost, the birds picking up their song as he emerged. It was clean and pure and held no hint of what'd transpired deep within the darkness.

Someone's rapid approach reached his ears, yet exhaustion pulled at him. No, it wasn't just exhaustion, but hate and disgust as well. He hadn't loved Jessa, and yet he'd destroyed her just as easily as he ended Quinn's life.

Gone, gone, gone.

He shuffled to the edge of the lake and dipped his hands into the cool water. He cupped his palms and brought the liquid to his face, washing away some of the red fluid. He wasn't trying to hide his crimes, he merely wanted to be able to see when his sentence was passed.

His arms and legs twinged with a sting of pain, but that disappeared as quickly as the thought filled his mind. His body worked double-time to repair itself. Still a neat trick.

People finally emerged from the trees. No, not people. His parents. He drew in a breath of clean air. His parents and... the Enforcer? Dad's Healer came along as well.

"Keen?" His mother's voice trembled, wavering.

Keen turned his head and stared at his mother, finally noticing the fear and unease that coated the men's faces. Even his father seemed afraid. And his dad was holding his mom back, her entire body shaking as she pushed against his father's arm.

So, Mom wasn't afraid. That was... good, right?

"What happened?" Mom asked the question that rolled through everyone's mind.

Keen focused on his dad, on the combination of rage and unease, two emotions he'd never seen warring across his features.

"I'm sorry."

Two meaningless words, but they were all he had.

chapter thirteen

Trista sensed when he came back to himself, when his memories released him into her care. She hugged him tighter, squeezing him as if her touch could banish the pain that lingered.

Her mate, her Keen… She wanted to cry for him, to cry for the victims of that horrible nightmare.

"Oh, Keen…" She nuzzled his chest, rubbing her scent on his shirt, trying to soothe him with her presence. She couldn't even imagine the horror he'd visited on those two teenagers and the hell he'd lived in ever since.

He whispered a handful of words yet they were garbled by the bear's presence. He coughed, the warmth of his breath sliding down her neck, and tried again.

"They didn't die. I thought I did… then. At first…" His heart skipped a beat, her ear against his chest picking up the stutter. "But I didn't kill them. Jessa is… And Quinn…"

A tear slid from her eye, followed by another and another. He'd lost control, but she was grateful he hadn't ended anyone's life. So very, very grateful. Her heart still broke for him and shattered for Jessa and Quinn, but the relief was palpable.

"I'm glad."

"She wasn't a strong bear. She's scarred."

"But she's alive?"

"Yes." He choked out the word. "Quinn left with his family. I think Dad paid off Jessa's. She..." He shuddered and squeezed tighter almost to the point of pain. Almost, but not. "She's had a lot of plastic surgery, but looks better since... then. It hurts, Tris."

"What?" Trista placed her hands on his upper back, tightening her hold.

"Knowing, feeling. They sent me away for retraining." He shook his head. "It doesn't mean what everyone thinks it means." He sighed. "If I hadn't lost myself here, they would have beat it out of me."

Trista had no heart left. It'd crumpled to dust and been scattered by the wind. She was lost to him now, her very center cracking and breaking for him. "What about your parents? Your family?"

Keen barked out a laugh, the sound harsh and grating. "If they hadn't cared before, there was no reason to care then. No," he shook his head. "I was alone, I figured things out myself, and then returned when I was 'discharged.' That means I discovered a way to live without their brand of help. I came home two years later, done with puberty and stronger than before. But I had my trick, my answer."

"The women," she murmured and he nodded.

"I need them, but I can't become attached. Not like Jessa... And then there's you, Tris." Shaking overtook him, barely perceptible trembles that filled his body. "If you ever..."

"I won't." She couldn't imagine even touching another male let alone having sex with one. Why would she when she had Keen?

"I lost my soul here, Tris, and destroyed lives in the process. If you were to..." He shook his head. "I don't know if I'd survive."

"You know you have me." But he didn't. He'd said the words of claiming and she hadn't repeated them in return. They'd lain side by side in bed, exchanging kisses, and yet hadn't shared the one thing that would tie them together forever.

Words were what he'd had with Jessa and they'd been betrayed.

Keen needed more than that, he needed a leap of faith and a bond that could never be severed by anything but death. And even then, she wouldn't betray him.

Trista traced the stiff line of his spine, letting her hands glide over his cloth covered muscles until she reached his waist. She slowly withdrew her touch, ignoring the needy whimper that escaped him as she pulled away. But she wasn't leaving him. No, she wouldn't ever do that.

Instead, she gently took his hand, cradling it in one of her own. It was so large, so deadly when it needed to be. It seemed his inner-bear felt that way pretty often. Except when a woman held him close. She'd prove to him that she was all he needed.

And it'd start with a bite.

"Come on." She lightly tugged, drawing him forward with light steps.

"What are you doing?"

She smiled at him, a small curve of her lips as she anticipated what was to come and prayed this would help him. "Giving you back your soul."

Keen stumbled for a moment, tripping on his own feet, and she waited for him to right himself before drawing him forward further. "Tris, you can't—"

"I can." She wouldn't allow herself to believe that she couldn't heal him. It was the only hope she had left if they wanted to have a true mating.

It was time to be his, wholly and without hesitation. When she glanced over her shoulder at him, at the large male who stared at her with swirling black eyes, she looked forward to what was to come.

Sunlight burned through the darkness, welcoming them with an ever increasing glow until it bathed them in warmth. She let nature soothe her as she snuggled into Keen's arms and pressed against him. Anticipating the coming mating, her body grew heated, her nipples hardening while her pussy became slick with her burgeoning desire. Yes, her body wanted him and after hearing his staggering confession, her heart wanted him as well.

Deep inside him, he was a good bear and an even better man. She was sure other stories about that time in his past lingered. She'd heard about retraining, about the consequences of losing control like that. She could quote a half-dozen laws about what occurred and how Keen should have been handled. Being sent away for retraining was the worst punishment. She wondered who protected Keen at the time, who represented him before the Southeast Itan, and she hated how much they failed a young boy. At fourteen, he'd been very, very young.

But then those thoughts vanished because Keen was staring at her, gazing into her eyes. She was overwhelmed with the urge to calm the deadly midnight storm.

Trista ran her hand over his chest, tracing the muscles hidden beneath his shirt, memorizing every dip and curve. His body was hard and cut like any other male's. Unlike the others, this one belonged to her and her alone.

Her travels took her to the snap on his jeans, the zipper keeping her from her destination.

"Keen?"

The black of his irises was blacker than midnight. "Tris…"

186

Taking his hoarse whisper as permission, she flicked the snap and carefully lowered the zip. The slide of metal against metal warred with the soft sounds of the lake.

"We shouldn't—"

"We should," she countered. "We're going to make love, Keen Abrams. Right here, right now." She pressed to her tiptoes and brushed a soft kiss across his lips. "I told you. You lost your soul here, part of you was broken and it overflowed to others. I can't help them, only their loved ones can, but I *can* help you if you let me." She pulled back, hand still resting on the ridge of his hardness as she stared at him. "Will you let me, Keen?"

"Yes." The word was choked and rough, but it burst into the air as if it had wings.

It echoed and flew past the trees before sinking into the earth itself. This coming together, this mating, would heal Keen and the earth as well. He just had to take what she offered. Staring at him with expectant eyes, she waited. Moments ticked past, their focus remaining intent, and then finally he blinked. He blinked and a single tear slid down his cheek, traveling over his whiskered skin to drop to her arm.

His agreement made her heart soar. She was filled with hope and a good dose of affection for Keen. Affection… No, a feeling akin to love yet one step shy of that giant leap.

Before she could move, shift her attention to his body and bringing him pleasure, he rasped a final plea, one she wished to fulfill.

"Please."

*

Keen had never wanted something so much in his life. He'd never craved anything like he burned for Trista. And she was giving herself to him with no reservations and no hesitation. He scented the air, hunting for any aroma that would prove her statements were a lie and found nothing.

Her flavors were pure and sweet and painted with her arousal. It was a familiar scent now, one she carried to bed with her each night and woke with each morning. Their kisses were passionate and their bodies' responses just as heated.

He wouldn't have to stop today. She'd give herself to him, he'd claim her as his own and he'd never…

Keen shuddered, those memories threatening to push forward once again and draw him into the depths of hatred and despair. "Tris…"

"Right here. Always here."

Then her small hand slipped inside his boxers, her fingers curling around his length and stroking his cock. This time the shudder was one of pleasure, of his rising desire and need for his mate.

"God…" He gasped out the word, her delicate palm causing wave after wave of bliss to course through his veins.

She slid over his length, squeezing into his jeans and reaching to the base of his shaft. Then she rose again, rubbing the tip of his cock. She repeated the motion, slow and unhurried as she pleasured him.

Him.

No, the bear snarled. It shouldn't be one-sided. She was his mate. *Mate.* And deserved to find as much joy in their touches as he.

"Tris." He wrapped his fingers around her wrist, stilling her movements.

"Keen?" His name came from her lips with a breathless whisper.

"This is for us. Together." He encouraged her to release him and then he drew her to the spot they'd shared before venturing into the cavern of pain and blood. He stared at the ground, noticing the small rocks and twigs that littered the area. With a growl, he led her toward the path they'd used before, back into the woods. He wouldn't mate her on the rocky forest floor. He wouldn't.

It was only Trista's refusal that had him halting in his tracks. She froze and tugged on his hold. "Where are we going?"

"Home." He shook his head. "I won't mate with you on the hard ground." He gathered her in his arms. "You're worth more than that. You deserve a soft bed and sweet words and…"

She deserved more than him.

Trista looked over her shoulder and then back at him. "We can heal both of us, Keen." She stepped out of his embrace and shuffled backwards. "Let's let the lake wash away our pasts. It bathed your face when you were younger, let it take away the rest."

He stared at the placid water, remembering that day, the red stain that lingered before being washed away by the gentle lapping caused by the rising wind.

"How"—he swallowed hard and tore his mind back to Trista—"how will it help you, Tris?"

A grin teased her lips, one that surprised him while brightening his heart. "I have to depend on you to not let me drown."

Drowning. He wanted to drown in her, sink into her and let her cradle him. He was shattered on the inside, shattered and damaged and broken and… For the first time, he felt a hint of hope, a glimmer that he could almost be normal. Almost. He had no delusions that he would suddenly be perfect and calm like his brothers. But with Trista's help, he could be less inclined to strike out. He was sure of it.

So, he let her draw him toward the shore, feet stopping when they approached the very edge of the water, and then her hands were on him, tugging on his T-shirt and encouraging him to whip it over his head. Just as she undressed him, he did the same to her. He slipped button after button free until their arms were a tangle and one of them would have to stop. He voted for Trista. He wanted to unwrap his mate, expose every inch of her pale, curved body to his gaze.

"Let me…" He brushed her hands away and reached for the last button that held her hidden. The moment it gave way, he urged the fabric to part. "Damn."

A blush coated her skin, starting in her cheeks and slowly making its way down her body, stroking her plump breasts and sweet stomach. He followed its travels until the pinkness ventured beneath her shorts. Then he returned his attention to her breasts, to the lacy fabric that covered her. Focus shifting from her chest to eyes and back again, he reached for her. There was no catch between her breasts, but that didn't deter him. With a whispered request to his bear, his animal gave one hand claws. His human hand eased the cloth away while the bear's paw sliced through the silken material.

Trista gasped, but no scent of fear drifted to him. No, it was all sweet and musky arousal. He wanted to feast on her, take his time and taste every inch of her body. Next time. Definitely next time. This place, right now, it was perfect for them.

The cups parted beneath the weight of her mounds, exposing berry hued nipples that seemed to call for his lips and tongue. His mouth watered and a strangled moan escaped his lips.

"Tris…" He ignored the whimper of need that escaped him as he cupped them, weighed them in his hands and brushed his thumbs over the hardened nubs.

Thankfully his sound was echoed by hers and more of her heated scent reached out to him. Her hands slid over his, encouraging him to knead her flesh and tease her nipples. He wanted more than that, wanted to taste and nibble as well.

Nibble… He'd do more than nibble soon.

That thought spurred him to move on, encouraged him to nudge her touch aside as he drew the tattered remains of her bra and soft shirt from her shoulders, leaving her bare to the waist. A sudden gust sent a scattering of goose bumps over her skin, but they disappeared almost as soon as they'd arrived.

Next he reached for her shorts, flicking the button with practiced ease. He hooked his fingers over the cloth, ready to push them past her hips and down her legs, but he paused and looked to her again.

"Trista?" It was her call, her choice. Always.

"Please, Keen." The plea was evident in her eyes.

Without another word, he nudged the material and it fell to the ground with a soft whoosh, exposing her fully to his gaze.

"Gorgeous. So goddamned pretty." That blush resurged, and she really did pinken from head to toe. "Do you know how beautiful you are? All sweet and sin?"

"Keen," she whispered and he yanked his attention from the juncture of her thighs, from the patch of closely cropped curls that begged to be discovered, teased, and tasted. "Your turn."

She gave him the same treatment, to the tug and push of his jeans, to the sound of his clothing falling to the ground until he stood nude before her. He hoped he didn't disappoint her, hoped she was satisfied with him as her mate. He wasn't normally so fucking self-conscious, but she was his and above all, he wanted her happy.

Women wanted him, but he wanted *her* to want him. The flare of pleasure in her gaze told him that she was more than content with what she saw.

"C'mon, Tris. Lemme make you mine."

"Please."

*

191

Trista begged. Plain and simple, she begged. He was gorgeous, all cut muscles and smooth skin. His body rippled with every movement, with every contraction and release as he stepped out of his flip-flops and jeans. He helped her do the same, pausing to lick and press his lips to her skin. He growled and moaned, tasting his way down her legs and then back up as he assisted her. One particularly long, sweet kiss to her mound had her whimpering as her knees went weak.

Later. Later she'd beg him to lick and taste her there, beg for that pleasure. For now, they needed to heal, needed to repair the damage life had wrought and come together as mates.

Slowly he retraced his path with his lips, moving beyond her pussy and over her hips. He paused, flicking first one nipple and then the other, with his tongue. A bolt of pleasure zipped through her and she gasped. She wanted more of that, more of everything.

His lips continued higher, pressing against her collarbone, ghosting over her neck, and then finally settling over her lips. His kisses were like wine, sweet and drugging. Over the days she'd come to love each one they shared.

Standing now, his full length brushed her hip. He was aroused and on edge... because of her. Plump, sometimes plain, Trista. She rejoiced in his attraction and desire, internally dancing because her need was returned.

Finally he pulled his mouth away and stared down at her with midnight eyes. His breathing came in heavy pants as he fought for air. No, he wasn't unaffected at all.

"C'mon." She snagged his hand and tugged. She took a step into the cool water, toes curling, and winced when the ball of her foot connected with a sharp rock.

Before she could even voice her pain with a low "ouch," Keen swung her up into his arms. She released a high-pitched squeak at the sudden move while he just chuckled and shook his head.

"I've got you. Trust, remember?" His voice was a deep, bone-melting purr.

"I remember." She twined her arms around his neck. "How far out are we going?"

"Deep enough for water to cover you. I shouldn't have let you strip on the beach." He growled, flashing his teeth. "I don't want anyone looking at you."

"So, you like me a little bit?" She grinned and he narrowed his eyes.

"More than a little."

Leaning forward, she rubbed their noses together. "I like you more than a little, too. Now, why don't you show me?"

With a snarl that didn't scare her in the least, he increased his pace, striding further into the water until it met his chest. That meant there was no way her toes would touch the bottom.

"Keen," she murmured and he smiled.

"I won't let you drown. You're too important to me." His eyes caressed her. "Trust me. Just a little. I won't let anything happen to you."

Trista released her deathly hold and cupped his cheek. "I do. I wouldn't mate with you if I didn't."

"Good." He brushed his mouth across hers as he relaxed his hold, moved her body as he desired and then her legs wrapped around his waist.

His long, thick hardness was nestled against her pussy, the cool water of the lake doing nothing to diminish her heated need for him. He cupped her ass, his large hands covering her globes as he kneaded and squeezed her flesh. Each press transferring sensation to her center, arousing her further.

Then he… Trista shuddered as he lifted and then lowered her in a gentle rise and fall. His length stroked her clit, nudged her hole, and then repeated the process. Shards of bliss assaulted her, forcing gasp after gasp to pass her lips.

"Keen."

"I've got you," he grunted. "Take what you need."

She squeezed his shoulders, fingernails digging into his flesh, but he didn't seem to care. No, he was intent on her, entirely focused, which only served to increase her desperation.

How much time passed? Seconds? Minutes? She had no idea and didn't really care. Not when wave after wave of joy filled her veins and consumed her. Her pussy clenched and quietly begged to be filled while her clit rejoiced in the spears of lightning his touch created.

But, but, but… she needed more, needed him.

"*Keen.*"

"What do you need, Tris?" he grunted, his face tightening further and further with every slip and slide.

"You, only you." She gasped and arched, depending on him to keep her from floating away. And he did. He tightened his hold, shifting one arm to brace her back, but still her pace didn't slow.

Then his hold changed, his grip tightened, her body was raised… Keen brought her down on his cock, his thick length filling her in one thrust and a scream tore from her throat. Not one of pain, never of pain with Keen, but one of pure undiluted pleasure. His dick stroked her inner walls, ignited nerve endings that'd lain dormant and sent a rolling wave of ecstasy through her.

With the rapid penetration, she arched her back and stared at the sky, the sensations of his possession overwhelming her. The hand between her shoulders moved to wrap around the back of her neck.

Gentle pressure had her attention dropping to focus on Keen, on his black eyes and the brown fur that lined his cheeks.

"Oh, Keen…" She mirrored his hold, pressing one palm to his neck while the other cupped his cheek. They remained frozen, stares locked as he encouraged her to ride his cock.

She catalogued his expressions, each emotion that flitted across his face. One after another battled for supremacy, but she latched onto the one that so closely mirrored her own. One that hinted of love even if the feelings hadn't settled into the lasting emotion.

Its presence encouraged her and she let her body fall into the whirlwind of sensations his shaft gifted her.

Each glide up stroked her while each fall had her clit nestling against him. The pleasure pinged through her, lighting her blood on fire.

"Yes. Yes…"

He grunted and snarled, flashing a slowly elongating fang. Yes, the bear was with them as they sought their mating. She wouldn't have it any other way.

The next rise was slower, slower than any others, but her descent was anything but. It was a fierce, rapid tug that tore another scream from her throat as pleasure fell upon her in a tumble of bliss. "Yes."

He did it again, slow ascension and fierce descent.

"Yes."

Again.

"Yes."

And again.

"*Yes.*"

Trista was going out of her mind, lost in the pleasure and need, but she wanted more and more and more.

No matter his rough pulls and jagged pushes, she craved more of him. And she wasn't afraid to beg.

"Please."

He opened his mouth wide, saliva dripping from his bear's fangs. In a threat? Was he trying to scare her away from the beast? That wasn't going to happen. Ever.

"*Please.*"

*

Keen couldn't resist the temptation she presented. She was slick skin and plump seduction and he wanted more of her, he wanted everything.

This connection, this meeting of bodies, wasn't enough for him, not nearly enough. He needed them tied together tighter than anything before.

Which made him sound like a stalker, like he was crazed, but he didn't care. Not when it came to Trista.

Her pussy milked his shaft, squeezing him in rhythmic tightening that seemed to beckon his release. But he held off by sheer force of will. He wanted her to come with him, to scream as he sank his teeth into her shoulder and mated her. He wished she could do the same to him, bite him and claim him just as he claimed her.

Then she smiled at him, gasping and whimpering while he continued to slide her along his shaft, and he didn't give a damn about who bit whom and when.

"Will you come with me?" He hardly recognized his own voice, the bear having pushed forward so hard that the human had ceded some control. The bear had endured his half-life just as much as the man.

196

They should both claim the female who would live at their sides until the day they died.

"Yes," she gasped as he yanked harder, slammed her down on his dick. "Oh God, yes."

He did it again, loving how she rippled around him, how her eyes darkened and the way pleasure transformed her face from beautiful to luminous. He didn't think he deserved her, but he'd take her anyway.

"I'm gonna…" A low mewl escaped her throat.

Keen didn't slow, didn't alter his pace or the strength of his movements. Not when she was so near the edge. He didn't want her pleasure to float out of reach, not when her glazed eyes shone with the promise of ecstasy.

His own body reacted to her responses, his balls hard and tight against him while his cock twitched and throbbed inside her sheath. Yes, he wanted to come, to fill her as he sank his teeth into her flesh.

Soon. Soon. Soon.

As her gasps and moans increased in volume, as her chest heaved even harder, her release neared. He fed off her pleasure, drank her desire, and allowed her enjoyment to drag him in her wake.

She opened her mouth, fighting for air, and flashed her teeth. She licked the blunted white fangs that filled her mouth. Without an animal, they weren't sharp and fierce like his, yet he still wanted them in his flesh.

"I want you to be mine," he snarled, his bear taking over as he squeezed the back of her neck. "*Mine.*" The aggression he normally carried was directed at her, but instead of anger and rage, it was pure need and desire that spurred his animal into action. "Belong to *me.*"

He opened his mouth wide, exposing his fangs fully, and she didn't shy from the threat. No, she released him long enough to brush her hair aside as she tilted her head. His goal was exposed, pale and glistening beneath the bright warmth of the sun and the coolness of the wind.

"Yes." She licked her lips. "Now." Her grip tightened, spears of pain adding to the bear's thirst for her.

The first scream from her throat, filled with pleasure and need, had him striking. He sank his teeth deep into her, savoring the sweet flow of her blood over his tongue. His cock pulsed, reacted to the sudden tightening of her pussy, and then she cried out again as she came. Keen's body overrode his desires then as pure bliss consumed him. The coppery heat of her blood filled his mouth while his release overtook his control.

Ecstasy like he'd never known overwhelmed him, stole all thought from his mind until he was nothing but pure animal emotion.

Suddenly, pain seared his shoulder—harsher than the sting of Trista's nails— and it added to the bliss of his orgasm. It forced his body to continue shuddering with the joy. His bear rejoiced, seeming to know something Keen's human mind did not, but he couldn't focus on the animal's happiness. Not when he filled his mate, not when he'd finally, truly made her his mate.

Mate. Mate. Mate.

Trista's tremors finally slowed to shadowy shudders and then she lay heavily against him, giving him her weight. Trust. Something they hadn't had and now they did. Maybe not entirely, but more than she'd shown others. And he'd take what he could get.

Gently, he slid his fangs free of her shoulder, softly licking and kissing her abused flesh. It was purple and bruised, blood welling to the wound and escaping her flesh. He hated that he'd hurt her, but he was thrilled that it was done.

A stinging ache scratched at his shoulder and he turned his head enough to spy Trista in his periphery. To spy her licking a wound that now marred his own shoulder. It wasn't as deep and damaging as the one he'd caused, but it was hers. Hers.

She gave him one last lap and then met his gaze, blood still staining her lips. Her eyes seemed more copper than gold, as if her animal had pushed forward as hard as it could in order to join their mating.

Trista's irises flashed even brighter, and her voice was hoarse and raspy when she spoke. "Mine."

Keen captured her lips, tongues tangling, teeth colliding as they kissed. He tasted his own blood on her tongue and remembering how it'd gotten there had his cock twitching and fighting to come back to life.

For the first time in his battered and unsteady life, his bear was at peace, damn near happy. It sighed in contentment, relaxed now that she was theirs and they belonged to her. He moaned against her mouth, holding her tighter, wanting to consume her with his need. His. His. His.

Trista tore her mouth from his and bracketed his face with her hands. Her gaze was still coppery tinged, but it was intent on him. "You're mine now. I didn't think…"

He hadn't either, and the bear was damned pleased. "And you're mine."

Tears sprung to her eyes and he was quick to kiss them away. "Hush."

She shook her head. "I didn't think I'd ever— And you're—" She wrapped her arms around his neck and buried her face against his shoulder. "I didn't think I'd ever feel safe."

His heart broke for her, shattered there on the rocks of Grayslake, as he thought about the fear and worry she'd lived with her entire life. "I won't ever let anything happen to you, Tris. Ever."

She nodded and with a final shudder, stilled in his arms. He welcomed the weight of her, the feel of her curves against his body, and the thought that someday she'd be full and her stomach stretched by their cub.

Much like… the very pregnant woman on the shore not fifty feet from them.

Mia shaded her eyes with the flat of her hand while waving at them with the other. "Are you two done? Even better, do you know how unsanitary that is? I mean"—the Itana shuddered—"really icky."

Trista squeaked, Keen snarled, and Mia just laughed. If she hadn't had some weird, uncanny ability to know when someone cursed *inside their head* he would have said something. Instead, he settled for gritting his teeth and glaring at her for ruining his mating. His mate—*mate*—trembled in his arms and then he truly was tempted to tell the Itana what he thought. But then Tris raised her head and he looked into mirth-filled eyes and she flashed him a wide, blinding smile.

That saved the Itana, but he still wanted to hit something.

The rustle and snap of branches reached him, the sounds so loud they overrode the giggles from Trista. "Who else is out there, Mia?"

Mia sighed and rolled her eyes before turning toward the tree line. "You might as well come out. Hiding will just get his dander up and then where will we be?"

A glaring Ty emerged from the forest, followed closely by Keen's— he sighed—father.

"Have everyone turn their backs." He nearly growled when Ty rolled his eyes, but that snarl turned into a chuckle when his dad whacked his brother in the back of his head. That was immediately followed by a muffled "language" from Mia.

But the moment they averted their gaze, he changed his grip on Trista. "I'm sorry we had to cut this short."

200

She nuzzled his neck, pressing a kiss to his skin and then licking his flesh with a soft moan. "We have the rest of our lives. This was… perfect."

Water sluiced from their bodies, doing exactly what Trista had predicted; it washed away the pain he held. The guilt remained, it probably always would, but the agony that tormented his bear was soothed by the lake… and Trista.

Dressing took little time, their clothes stuck to their wet skin, but they managed to pull everything on. Once done, he focused on his father. Not his Itan—or even his Itana—his father.

"Dad." The word was a croak so Keen coughed and swallowed, trying again. "Dad."

His father looked to him, hope accompanying his raised eyebrows. "Yes?"

Keen focused on the mouth of the cave and then turned his attention to Trista, seeing his emotions mirrored in her gaze. Without looking away, he spoke again. It was time to lay the past to rest and move on from this moment. It was a blank slate and he welcomed it with open arms.

"I'd like someone to clean the cave."

Ty's words were right on the heels of Keen's "The cave? What about the—"

Another smack cut off his eldest brother and Keen smiled, imagining Ty rubbing the back of his head. Trista's smile was just as wide and just as warm as his own.

Yes, it was time.

chapter fourteen

Trista hadn't even thought that the Itan and Itana along with Keen's father would come looking for them for a reason. It just... hadn't registered that there was a purpose or a goal to their search.

Unfortunately, the reason became blatantly clear the moment Keen drew the SUV to a stop before the clan house. Cars littered the graveled driveway, all lined in a pretty row off to one side. A sense of foreboding fluttered in her stomach and a hint of unease snaked down her spine.

Her mate reached for her, his hand grasping hers and giving her a soft squeeze. "We'll be fine."

"You don't know that. We really should have listened to Ty."

"I couldn't stand around and hear what Ty had to say."

Trista could understand Keen's feelings after what they'd shared, the events of the last few days, and she could empathize with her mate. "Okay. And we didn't hear out your dad because..."

He didn't answer and instead released her and climbed from the SUV, narrowing his eyes at her before he slammed the door shut. If she wasn't so nervous, she'd smile over the fact that they were having their first mini-tiff.

She waited for him to come around to her side of the vehicle and allowed him to help her down. Her shoulder stung, aching from Keen's bite, but there wasn't much to be done now. It'd heal at its own pace. At least she had her half-shifter abilities to hasten the process.

Just after he pushed the door shut, she reached for him. She managed to tug him close and wrap her arms around his waist before he could stride away. "Keen?"

He grunted, much like his father. She wondered if he realized they were very much alike.

"No matter what, I'm not leaving you. I..." She looked at the house, watching Mia, Ty, and his father George file inside. "They came looking for you, for us, and no matter what waits for me and you, you need to remember I'm yours and you're mine."

Some of the tension drifted from his body with his heaving sigh. "Okay." He dropped a kiss to her head. "Let's see what the fuss is about. I'm guessing it's some sort of intervention. Mom's gotten into those shows lately."

That did not reassure her.

Keen eased her arms from him and grasped her hand, using his hold to urge her toward the house. Dread filled her with every step, memories of the last time she'd stepped over the threshold assaulting her. Blood, she remembered the blood and fear, and Keen's eruptive shift followed by his fierce protection.

"Keen... What if..." What if Van suddenly decided he didn't need to listen to Ty—or even George—any longer?

He paused, brought her hand to his lips. "Tris?" She raised her gaze to his and he continued speaking. "I may not be as unstable any longer, but I will allow *nothing* to happen to you. Nothing."

Right. She knew that. Instead of pushing words past her lips, she merely nodded and allowed him to draw her forward.

She had a feeling of déjà vu as her steps echoed on the worn stairs, and over the wood of the front porch. The screen door opened easily when Keen twisted the knob and then they were inside the home. The musk of bear invaded the space with no hint of blood. Whoever had cleaned the mess in the living room did a good job.

The low murmur of voices floated toward them, several males along with the high tinklings of women. A female stepped into the entry way from one of the rooms down the hall, and slowly came nearer. Trista immediately recognized Keen's mother... Anna. Before things had gone downhill at their house, she'd introduced herself as Anna. The woman had left before them, intent on returning to their guests.

"Keen," Anna murmured and held out her arms for her son. Keen didn't release Trista, but did give his mother a one-armed hug.

"Mom. What's going on?"

"Oh, well." Anna released him and stepped back. Even without the ability to scent the air like a full shifter, Trista could tell that unease and worry filled the woman from head to toe. Anna breathed deep and the anxiety worsened. "That's going to complicate things, isn't it?" she murmured.

"Mom?"

"Well, someone came by looking for Trista, but he's also—"

"Anna? Keen?" George, Keen's father, followed Anna's path. "He's waiting."

"He who?" Keen voiced Trista's question.

George's gaze shifted from Keen to Trista and back again. "Southeast Keeper Foster."

The dread filling Trista's stomach tripled and sweat sprung from her pores. It coated her skin in a sudden wave and sank into her clothing. It stung her new wound, making it ache and throb, but it also reminded her of Keen—of his promise.

George cleared his throat and then spoke again. "Quinn Foster."

A new tension thrummed through her mate, pulsing through his body and transferring to his grip on her hand. He tightened his hold, as if his body were looping in on itself, and she grasped their joined hands with her other one.

She knew why the Keeper scared her; she'd lived and nearly died by his word alone through the years in exchange for her help. She wasn't sure why Quinn Foster would...

Oh, dear God, no.

"It's *that* Quinn, isn't it?" She didn't have to explain more, not when George focused on her and gave a quick, brisk nod.

"It's going to cause problems. Originally, the charges were due to extenuating circumstances and your relationship, but with Trista..." His father's voice trailed off and she wanted to curse at him to continue.

Before she could demand an answer, Ty joined their impromptu, anxiety-laden party. "They're waiting."

"They?" Keen's voice was a rough croak. Some would consider his actions as ones of fear, but Trista knew the truth. It was remorse and worry. She didn't think her mate feared anything.

"Reid." Ty snapped the wolf Alpha's name.

The change in Keen was blatantly visible. He shrugged off the shakes and rose to his full height, chest swelling, and she realized that in truth, her mate was larger than Ty. It was obvious he'd spent years attempting to appear smaller than the Grayslake clan leader when, in fact, he was much bigger. "Sounds like you've created a great party. Is Van in there too? Anyone else who'd like to see my mate broken and bloody?"

It was rough and grating and downright aggressive, but Trista couldn't fault Keen for his abrasive words. Especially since they crowded her throat as well.

"Keen," Ty sighed and opened his mouth to speak again, but her mate didn't give the man a chance. No, he merely pushed past his family and dragged her toward the room the trio exited.

Then she was more than happy to turn her happy butt right around.

Because yes, Van was there along with Lauren. And yes, Reid had arrived as well with Adrienne at his side. The she-wolf wiped away a droplet of drool as she stared at Trista and she suppressed the desire to cower behind her mate.

Another male stood nearby, one that rivaled Ty in size yet was nowhere near the Itan's strength. Oh, she had no doubt he could hold his own in a fight, but he didn't hold the innate power that seemed to flow from Ty and… Keen.

Was this Keeper Foster? Or was it the thinner, older man at his side? The younger, and larger, of the two had scars that lined his arms and he directed a hate-filled, revenge-seeking gaze at Keen. The other seemed like he would happily murder everyone in the room without a moment's hesitation.

Nice.

"Well? Who wants to go first?" Keen's tone was antagonizing and abrasive, but Trista couldn't blame him. Not when they were faced by someone from the Southeast inner-circle, Reid, and Van at the same time.

Trista prayed they could figure things out before it got bloody.

*

It was about to get bloody. Keen was sure of it. Reid's yellow-eyed gaze was centered on Trista as were Van's midnight orbs. Then there was Quinn Foster. He was older now, age giving him an increased size while his position gave him a haughty attitude. Keen would beat it out of him if the male thought he'd speak to Tris again. The bear was more possessive and protective than ever now that he'd sunk his teeth into her flesh. He'd claimed her and he *refused* to let her go.

Ty eased past him, moving until he stood slightly before Keen and to the right. It was a position of dominance without being protective. One that said Keen was his bear, but he could stand on his own paws. At least his eldest brother gave him that much. Van still looked like he wanted to go after Trista.

He'd really hate to have to kill one of his brothers. It'd piss off his mom.

"Anyone?" He tried again and the men in the room exchanged glances, his enemies looking for a sign from the others before stepping forward. It was like that, then. They were working together somehow.

His dad pushed past him and Trista, taking up a stance that mirrored Ty's. It surprised him, this protection and assistance. What was his father playing at?

"Van?" Dad's voice cut through the tense silence.

Van shook his head, blazing glare focused on Keen for a moment before shifting to Trista. "It's better this way. He'll be free of her. You have to see how that's better for him. It will mess up some things, but…"

Lauren reacted before Keen had a chance to let his brother's words sink into his heart. The pregnant woman yanked her arm from Van's grasp and spun on him, shoving his shoulder until they faced one another.

"What do you mean 'free'? You said we were here to support Keen. That you still had an issue with her being a hyena, but that you wanted to help your brother," Lauren snapped and snarled. Very threatening considering she was a human.

"Quiet, *human*. What place does she have in this room?" That came from the older male beside Quinn. He wasn't sure what the man had to do with the proceedings, but Keen didn't like him already.

"Oh, bite me," Lauren growled, curling her lip. Pregnancy had made the woman scary.

"Female…" The older man took a step forward, his eyes darkening to black, and that had Van shoving Lauren behind him, answering the male's rumble.

Keen spared a glance for Reid, noting the smirk that graced his features. He really wanted to neuter that wolf.

"Enough." Ty's voice was quiet, but firm, and everyone fell into silence.

Except for Lauren. No, the woman stomped from Van's side and came straight toward their small gathering, pushing her way behind Ty. He glanced over his shoulder and found her with one arm wrapped around his mother's waist while the other was circling Mia's.

He turned his attention back to Van, narrowing his eyes. "How will I suddenly find myself 'rid' of Trista, Van? Do you hate her, hate me, so much that you'd betray your brother and his mate?"

"She's not your real mate, Keen." Van shook his head. "She's bad news and it's good that you haven't—"

"*She's mine!*" he roared, shaking the entire home with the strength of the sound. "Bound by claim and bite, she's *mine*."

Trista's grip tightened but he didn't scent fear from her, only pride.

Van's face paled, skin lightening until it was nearly white. "You…" He swallowed hard, Adam's apple bobbing along his neck, and Keen's bear was tempted to rip out the flesh. Van was involved in something, a plan to separate him and Trista. That wasn't going to happen. "You bit her, you're fully mated?"

"Yes," he hissed, daring his brother to comment further.

"Oh, shit." Van's gaze shifted to Reid's and then Quinn's. "You can't do this."

"Oh," Quinn smirked. "I definitely can."

Keen gave Quinn his full focus, noting the excitement filling his gaze as well as the fur that covered the man's scarred arms. The male at his side was similarly eager for what was to come.

"Ty? Do the introductions." He didn't blink twice at giving his brother an order and Ty was smart enough not to comment on the lapse. Keen was too close to the edge to beg and scrape for anyone, not even the clan's Itan.

Ty raised his arm and pointed around the room, repeating names as his focus changed. "Reid, Redby Alpha. Adrienne, Redby wolf."

"Beta," Reid put in. "I made her my Beta."

"Right. Beta," Ty added.

"Progressive of you." Keen raised an eyebrow.

Reid returned the expression. "Convenient."

"Hmm..." Keen hummed.

When he said nothing else, Ty continued. "Quinn Foster, Southeast Keeper."

Keen knew who he was. He was more interested in the other male.

"And Malcolm Porter, Second-in-Command to the Southeast Itan."

Malcolm tilted his head in acknowledgment. Keen didn't bother returning the gesture. He hadn't recalled meeting the male during the Southeast Itan's visit almost seven months ago, but the clan had been in an uproar.

Every opponent in the room was part of a puzzle and he was anxious to fit the pieces together. It wasn't until they were aligned in a pretty row that he'd realize the shit storm that'd erupted around them.

"Any reason Terrence didn't want to tag along?" He kept his tone smooth and free of emotion beyond passing curiosity.

Ever since he'd spoken with the Southeast Itan months ago, he'd been on a first-name basis with the powerful male. They'd eventually moved from speaking about the laws broken by Mia's grandfather to their favorite sports teams and the antics of his growing and adult children. They weren't close friends, but they weren't strangers either. Terrence appreciated Keen's computer talents and knowledge while Keen appreciated talking with a man who took the time to know him as a worthy bear, not as an Abrams brother.

Malcolm bristled. "How dare you speak of—?"

Quinn placed a hand on the older man's arm, cutting off his posturing. "Unfortunately, Itan Jensen is otherwise occupied. We are here in his place."

"Uh-huh." Keen crossed his arms over his chest, uncaring if his aggressive stance annoyed the opposing males. "What's this about?"

Van approached him from his right and he looked to his brother. When Van opened his mouth as if to speak, he cut him off. "Oh, you're not talking right now. And depending on what happens next, you may never will."

He'd make sure of it. He'd lived with disinterest, survived the agony of his punishment only to be thrust back into the world of apathy. Now that he'd found something to live for, he refused to acknowledge anyone who threatened his new peace.

"So, who's first?"

Quinn stepped forward, the Second-in-Command at his back. Typical old male. Useless.

"When you were fourteen…"

Screw it. Keen would finish the story. Give a nice summary for everyone in the room. His father knew most of it, but he doubted many others did. "I fell in love with Jessa Clark, but she didn't want me. She wanted to be fucked by you. When I found you two together, I beat the ever living shit out of you and hurt her in the process. I thought you were dead. You weren't. I was punished and have lived with the guilt and remorse every day. Oh, and you were an asshole then. It seems like you still are now." He looked around the room, letting his gaze linger on the other males, shifting his attention from the Second-in-Command as he still cowered, to Reid and his she-bitch, then Van's still pale face. "Anyone got anything else they wanna know?"

Ty leaned in. "You were fourteen."

"Yup."

"He was—what—seventeen then?"

Keen nodded. "Not long after his birthday. A few months maybe."

"So, he had the beginnings of an adult's bulk and two years of training? And you kicked his ass?" The disbelief was easily heard in his brother's voice and Keen's bear didn't care for it at all.

Letting the bear rush forward, he increased in size, his teeth sliding free in a flash as fur rippled over his skin. He knew his abilities and knew how they compared to the others in the room. He was faster, larger, stronger… He just didn't want to do anything with all that power.

Keen stared at Ty. "Yes."

Quinn coughed, bringing everyone's attention back to him. "Your father and mine argued about your punishment and it was ultimately placed before my grandfather as he was the Southeast Keeper at that time."

Keen wasn't sure how that'd all gone down, but it seemed he was about to find out.

"Grandfather heard testimony, including Jessa's, and it was decided that, as a young male, you'd assumed more emotion was attached to your friendship than what truly existed and felt you were defending a mate. Your strength notwithstanding, he determined you were a child in need of retraining."

A child shouldn't have to endure daily beatings that merely enraged his animal rather than trained it.

"The thing about it is, Jessa has had... a change of heart."

Keen froze, tumbling the words through his mind. "What do you mean?"

"She has admitted that you two planned to assault me, kill me, because you were jealous of what I had."

He snorted, he couldn't help it. It was too funny for words. "What did you have that I didn't?"

Quinn's voice was filled with ice, his eyes holding nothing but malice and hate. "A loving family."

The words speared his heart and he sucked in a harsh breath. The pain dug into him, the truth making it ache even more, and he fought to appear unaffected. Anger flowed from his father, the scent tinged with regret while pure confusion floated from Ty's direction. Of course his brother wouldn't understand.

"No objection?" An evil smile played around Quinn's lips.

213

"We didn't plan anything. Jessa may have been..." He hesitated. The words "a slut" popped to his mouth, but he swallowed them back. "... free with her favors, but I doubt she'd fuck you just to lure you to your death."

The Keeper shrugged. "And yet she admitted she did."

"And what punishment did she suffer for her part?"

"Oh, her cooperation was rewarded with a suspended sentence. You, however, won't get so lucky." He clucked his tongue. "You should have shown more control. Now you'll have to pay for that."

Keen kept his gaze centered on the too cocky Keeper while rolling through the laws of the clan. God, he knew *today's* laws, but not those from years ago. Each year they were changed, tweaked, and refined. What was valid then might not be valid today and who knew what it'd be like ten years from now.

"What's the charge and how will I pay?" So many laws overlapped.

"Premeditated initiation of a Challenge outside a clan sanctioned gathering." Quinn laid the charge at his feet and Keen waited for the rest. The male gloated, happiness spreading with each passing second. "As for your sentence, I'm going to be merciful. My options are death or permanent marking of your disgrace and banishment." Quinn's eyes deepened to black. "I choose to dig my claws into your face and retroactive banishment."

"What...?" Keen furrowed his brow.

Malcolm cackled then, crazed joy overtaking him while the sounds echoed off the walls. "You won't be tainting the bears further, Abrams. Your brothers are destroying their lines, but you won't add to the destruction of Grayslake."

Trista fisted his shirt, her fear palpable in the room, overriding every other scent. "Keen, oh God."

His bear reacted to her panic, pushing forward, forcing his body to swell and prepare to shift. He wouldn't tolerate anyone scaring her. Not his family and sure as hell not the Southeast Second. He didn't give a fuck about the man's position when it came to Trista.

"What does that mean?"

"Oh, shit," she gasped.

"Trista?"

"She knows." Quinn's gaze shifted from him to Trista and Keen was quick to cut off the man's line of sight.

"Trista?" Keen tried again.

"He's right. The laws say he can do that. And banished retroactively means you haven't been part of the Grayslake clan since you were fourteen. Which is fine, because a banishment strips your clan association, but not your family. You were still allowed on clan land as long as your family is in power. But," she faltered, her breathing audible and harsh in the room. "But because you're not part of the Grayslake clan, it means I'm not either. So…"

"My objection and ruling regarding her presence stands." Reid's voice rang out, booming and loud as it overrode Trista's. "And Trista Scott, bastard daughter to Brigham Scott and half-sister to Heath Scott, will face Adrienne in a Challenge to the death. She's either strong enough to hold her place in the territories or she dies."

Reid's shrug gave off the appearance that he didn't care either way, but the flare in his eyes, the hunger, told a different story.

Ty stepped forward even further and put his growing body between Keen and Reid. "I claim her now as part of my clan. You're not touching her, Reid."

"Ty? What are you doing?" Keen didn't need Ty to fight his battles.

215

His brother looked back at him over his shoulder, a hint of regret etched in his features. "I may not understand, and part of me may not like it, but she's yours and you're my brother even if I've been a shitty one."

With that, Ty looked at Reid and they waited for the wolf's response.

It was another feral, crazed grin. "The thing about today's laws is the timing. You can't save another by making broad claims after the fact any longer. She was violating the laws by staying on your land for too long. As a leader of my own pack, upon finding a shifter in violation of the law, I made a ruling and sought to enforce the law."

Trista's hands twisted and knotted his shirt, her body pressed firmly against his. Any other time, he'd be aroused by the nearness. Right now, it fueled his rage.

His words tickled Keen's brain, had him sifting the words and picking them apart. "But you didn't press the issue earlier in the front yard when I claimed her because..." Deep red filled the man's features and Reid's attention flicked to Quinn for the barest of moments. "I see. Because you didn't know that my claiming her didn't negate your ruling. You didn't know that whatever I did— claiming her—couldn't save her from the Challenge. You were ignorant about the intricacies then and Quinn helped you out with that when he came into the area."

Reid snarled and stepped forward, fur sprouting and coating his face as his lips and jaw half-transformed to his wolf. "I'm not stupid, asshole."

"Ignorant means uninformed, not stupid. And that response was ignorant, asshole," Keen volleyed back.

Panic had him lashing out, fear had him panting, and Trista's terror had his bear scraping for release. If only... For now, he had to step back, had to regroup and figure out a way to keep Trista safe. He didn't care about his punishment, about Quinn marking him and being banished from the clan. Nothing mattered but Tris and her safety.

"If everyone is done yelling," Quinn spoke up. "We can go to the side yard and—"

"The Right of Preparation!" Trista blurted out and Keen sighed with relief.

There was his answer. A stall tactic, sure, but it gave them time. "As the mate of the accused, I claim the Right of Preparation on her behalf."

Quinn sputtered. "You-you can't do that. It's not— You can't—"

"He can." Trista stepped to the side, revealing herself, but still clutching his shirt. "When a Challenge, or sentence, could result in death"—her voice wavered and he heard the hint of tears clogging her throat—"the Challenged's mate is able to require the Right of Preparation." She swallowed hard and he wrapped his arm around her shoulders, giving her his support. "It is the mate's choice and *cannot* be denied."

Quinn narrowed his eyes, glaring at him, and then centered his rage on her. He felt Reid's simmering anger as well and he wondered if his brother Van held the same emotions. Battered on three sides and supported on one. At least, he hoped.

"And how long does this '*right*,'" Quinn spat, "last?"

Trista was firm and clear in her response. "Twenty-four hours."

Twenty-four hours. He had twenty-four hours to figure a way out of this cluster-fuck and if all else failed, they'd run. He'd run far and fast and with Trista at his side.

chapter **fifteen**

Trista stared at the people surrounding the table, Ty and Mia, Van—
Van—and Lauren, George and Anna. Even Parker had grudgingly
apologized for trying to eat her, which was news to Keen and she'd
winced at his glare. Then there was Gigi, the clan house cook, who
cuddled her close, told her she was a precious little thing.

They welcomed her with open arms, if not open hearts in Van's case.

George had gruffly, and roughly, escorted the wolves along with
Quinn and Malcolm from the clan house despite their protests.
Quinn spouted something about being welcomed to reside at the
host house. At that point, the ex-Itan reminded him that Keen was
the accused and didn't have a clan anymore and Trista's relatives
were dead, there was no host. The motel was fifteen minutes away
and he and Malcolm wouldn't be welcome until five p.m. tomorrow
evening.

The subsequent slam of the door shook the house and the heavy
stomps of the retreating males vibrated the floor.

And still, Keen's father hadn't appeared the least bit upset at having
thrown part of the Southeast inner-circle into the cold. Well, heat.

Now they surrounded the large kitchen table, mates sitting on laps to
give room to the others. Trista even ended up snuggled against
Keen, uncaring if parts of his family didn't like her presence. Van's

gaze landed on them for a bare moment, but he quickly shifted his attention away. Amazingly, enveloped in Keen's embrace, his dislike didn't affect her. She didn't need Van's approval, or love, just Keen's.

Oh, shit. Love. She'd thought of the word, let it blossom in her head, and she realized she really, truly wanted that with him. Even with their differences, the species ties that kept his family from liking her, she craved that.

"Well," George sighed. "What's our plan?"

We don't have one.

Keen voiced her thoughts aloud. "We don't have one."

The ex-Itan shook his head and pinched the bridge of his nose. Anna ran her hand down her husband's back and George sighed. "Okay, walk me through all the garbage he spouted."

Keen looked at her, nodding as if encouraging her to talk, so she cleared her throat and took them through the logic of the laws and how they would apply to her and Keen's situation.

The way the rules of over ten years ago applied today and then how it all rolled into her presence. When all was said and done, yes, Quinn could require Keen be marked and banished from a clan, and yes, Reid could force her into a deadly situation with Adrienne. The worst of it was, yes, Adrienne could shift for their fight and there were no clear instructions as to the fighter's forms during a Challenge in association with violations of the laws of visitation. Which sucked.

But what her recitation truly amounted to was a roomful of people staring at her with wide, pained eyes.

"And what's the Right of Preparation?" Van actually participated in their conversation and *of course* he had to ask about that, about the one thing that'd bring tears to her eyes and remind her of the timer counting down.

"After a sentence is passed down, and if it involves a punishment that may result in death, the mate of the offender can demand the Right of Preparation." She fell silent, the words writhing inside her like a thousand snakes, twisting and turning in her gut.

"But I don't know what that means," Van tried again and the snakes rose, snapping at her stomach.

"It means that my punishment is delayed for twenty-four hours to give Keen a chance to say goodbye," she murmured and Keen cupped her cheek, brushing away her tears. She hadn't even realized she'd begun crying, but she supposed it was fitting. She'd sobbed when her mother disappeared, had begged Quinn—Keeper Foster—for assistance, but he said there were casualties in war. Now she was devastated at the prospect of being without Keen.

No one else said a word, the oppressive silence capturing them in a bubble of dread and heartbreak. Her emotions were mirrored in the others' faces. Varying degrees, and yet the same.

Regret was the most prevalent, the one that overrode grief and sorrow.

"There has to be something..." Van again, disbelief filling his voice.

"What do you *care*?" Keen spat, new tension filling her mate, and Trista laid her head on his shoulder, hoping her touch would help calm him. "You tried to kill her when she was under the Itan's roof, when she was under his protection. What the fuck do you care now? Suddenly she's part of the family? Suddenly she's welcome because *Dad and Mom* are supporting us? Fuck you very much, Van."

The quiet was oppressive, charged with emotions, and her mate's body vibrated with renewed tension. They didn't need this, didn't need the anxiety driven squabbling between siblings when so much more hung in the balance.

Van shoved to his feet, dislodging Lauren. "I care—"

221

"That's enough." George spoke with a firm tone that brooked no argument. He might be the ex-Itan, but Trista saw a hint of the man's strength. He stared at Van. "Sit down."

Van faltered, but finally lowered back to his seat and reached for Lauren except this time, she stepped out of reach. "Lauren?"

"Van…" Tears swam in the woman's eyes. "It's all…"

It was all too much. Too much heartache and drama and pain all in one. She couldn't do this *kum ba yah* work together and figure shit out bullshit.

Trista shrugged off Keen's hands and pushed to her feet, unwilling to be at the center of this cluster of madness. "George, Anna, Mia, Lauren." She tilted her head slightly. "Thank you for welcoming me into your lives. Now, if you'll excuse me, I'd like to spend some time with my mate."

With that, she reached for Keen and sighed when he slid his hand into hers.

"So, what, you're just going to give up?" It seemed Van had become the spokesperson for the group.

Trista, plagued with heartache and tears brimming in her eyes, turned to face him. "I'm going home to the first real home I've ever had, and I'm going to spend time with my mate. Tomorrow will bring what it brings, but right now I'm going to revel in the gifts I've been given. I earned them, I fought hard my entire life and it may all be taken from me tomorrow. So, tonight, I'm going to enjoy what I have."

Anna grasped Trista's hand and gave it a gentle squeeze. She found answering moisture in the woman's gaze. Part of her pined for what could have been if she had spent time with the Abrams family. She'd lost her mother seven months ago and she had a feeling Anna Abrams would have been happy to add Trista to her family.

Too late…

Releasing Anna, she continued her way down the table, forcing herself not to look at others in the room. She took strength from Keen's touch, from the power he held inside himself. She knew it looked like she was giving up, that she was lying beneath a blade and simply waiting for it to be thrust home. But she wasn't.

No, she needed a minute to breathe, time to simply restore a tiny bit of peace with Keen, and then she'd think about the hell of tomorrow. She just was desperate for a hint of heaven today.

They made it to the kitchen doorway before someone spoke, before George rose from his chair and took a step toward them. His brow was furrowed, eyebrows scrunched.

"Trista, something has been pricking my mind. Your mother was human and your father was a hyena, right?"

She internally winced. The family didn't need a reminder about her parentage. "Yes."

"So, if you had nothing to do with the bears, why did you turn to *them* for help when your father died? Why did they keep a leash on the wolves? Why didn't you appeal to another hyena pack?"

Memory Lane. Joy.

Trista went back to that time, to when she was scared and bleeding as they raced home, as her body fought to heal itself and she couldn't see past her blood-soaked tears. She remembered her mother screaming into a cell phone, begging, desperate for help from… someone.

"I don't know. Mom was begging for help and…"

"You have your father's last name, but what was your mother's? Maybe she was known to a clan. I don't remember her from when I was Itan, but perhaps we can appeal to—"

223

"She was human. She didn't shift. She was just normal and ordinary and…" Her mother. That's all she was and Trista's heart clenched as the loss hit home.

"Humor me." George's eyes were soft and sweet like a big teddy bear.

"Her name was Debra, Debra Cleary."

"Oh, fuck." That came from Keen and she looked at her mate, noting his wide eyes and pale face.

"That's right." George was just as pale and Ty looked like he was about to be sick.

"What do you know that I don't?" Trista's attention continued to swing around the room and then she focused on the man beside her. "Keen?"

"Cleary? You're sure?"

Trista huffed. "Yes, Cleary. I know my mother's last name."

"Shit. We need to call Terrence. Dad?"

"I-I-I," George stuttered and swallowed hard before speaking again. "Trista, I know you want to get out of here and spend time with Keen. I know this is hard and, dear Lord, this is one cluster fuck." He took a deep breath. "Ty, grab a notepad and pen. Trista, you need to write out everything you know about your mother and her family."

She was shaking her head before she registered the action. She didn't want to go there, didn't want to think about being alone and spending days hungry and nights cold. "I can't."

Large hands squeezed her shoulders and she was slowly turned until she was pressed chest to knees against Keen's front. "You can because I'm here. Right here and I'm not leaving. This is important,

224

Tris. I want you with me for a hundred years, and I think this will help. Please."

The please did her in. He asked, nearly begged, and it was such a simple thing to do. And if there was even a chance she could get out of tomorrow's confrontation without having to run with Keen and become fugitives, she'd take it.

Taking a deep breath, she spun to face the Abrams family. "What do you need to know? And why?"

Ty laid the pad and pen on the table then slid it across the wood surface. George intercepted the materials, focusing on her. "All of it and I'll tell you just as soon as I'm sure."

"I don't want to get my hopes up, George—"

"Dad," he interrupted.

God, she'd never had one of those, not really. "Dad. I don't want to let them rise only to have them shatter into a million pieces."

"Just jot everything down. Write it out and then you two can go. I won't hold you here while we work things out, but give us this much so we can try and save you both." He was so earnest and seemed to be holding enough hope for both of them.

So, Trista returned to their seat, settling on Keen's lap and leaning toward the table as she wrote out the answers to question after question.

When was her mother born? *June 19, 1952.*

What did she look like? *A little taller than Trista, maybe 5'5", with dark red hair and green eyes. She was curvy, Trista's size, but her mom always said baby weight was a bitch to drop, even after twenty years.*

Did she have any birthmarks or scars? *One long scar along the right side of her face from temple to chin. It followed her jaw and was old, so it was easy to cover up.*

225

Was there anyone from her past that she talked about? Any family?
Just Terry, but she didn't talk about him often. Trista wasn't sure who he was to her mom, but she loved him a lot.

What was her reason for staying in town? Trista's father wouldn't let her go. The law said...

George, Dad, knew about that law.

Dad gently eased the notepad from beneath her fingertips and nudged it toward Ty. "Take a picture of her and then get on the phone with him."

Ty dug into his pocket and grimaced at his father, obviously not liking the order. "Dad..."

"You're the Itan," his father growled.

"You're his friend." Ty was equally as annoyed. "He won't kill you if you're wrong."

George pushed to his feet, rising to his full six-plus feet, and she watched as his body expanded, pushing his clothes almost to the point of snapping. "I gave you this clan because I thought you were ready to lead. Do I need to take it back?"

A tense silence swirled around them, ghosting each occupant until the room was buzzing with the tension. Finally, Mia shattered the thickness with a low grunt.

She levered herself out of her chair, glaring at both George and Ty in equal measure. "I swear, you two are like big babies. He's hundreds of miles away. What's he gonna do, growl you to death?" She reached out and plucked Ty's cell phone from his hand while also snatching up the writing-covered pad. "Gimme that. I'll call the fire trucking man." She waddled away from the table, grumbling about stupid males and cursing and massive amounts of money in the swear jar because she'd been keeping track. It wasn't until she was standing on the opposite side of the kitchen near the secondary door

226

that she stopped and whirled on them. "I'm calling him. What am I telling him?"

Quiet. Nothing but the hum of the fridge and the gentle swoosh of the dishwashing cycle filling the air.

It took a moment, but George finally spoke. "Tell him we *might*, stress *might*, have found his niece and she needs his help."

Niece? Which meant she was part werebear? And her mother... No, she would have known. Wouldn't she?

Instead of following the line of questions, she echoed the men. Trista uttered the first words that came to mind. "Oh, fuck."

* * *

Keen held Trista's hand as they walked the edge of the lake. Neither of them said a word, simply allowing nature to welcome them. The quiet was comfortable and easy, as if they'd been together years instead of mere days.

The turmoil and anxiety still tainted the air, the emotions pushing a sharp tang into the wind, but there wasn't much to be done about the burning stench.

He allowed Trista to lead, to gently choose their path. Every once in a while she'd bend and snatch up a stone, tossing it into the water and watching as the delicate ripples marred the surface. It was like their short relationship, smooth one moment and trembling the next.

Minutes sped past and darkness eased closer, the sun casting a multi-hued glow over the lake.

"Trista?" he murmured, not wanting his voice to destroy the calming peace they'd established. "Talk to me."

She drew to a stop and turned to face the fading sun, drawing him closer until he wrapped his arms around her. He molded himself to her back, taking a bit of her weight when she leaned into him.

"I don't want him to be my uncle."

Keen leaned down and pressed his cheek to hers, enjoying the touch while hoping his nearness calmed her. "Why not?"

"Because it changes who I am. Because it means he didn't care enough *then* so why should he care *now?* It means that my mom and I scraped and fought and got our shit together without him when he could have made our lives easier." She turned her head slightly and nuzzled him. "Do you know what it's like to be hungry? To not have a place to live because you can't hold a job because you're forced by what seems like *everyone* to stay in this god-forsaken area?"

"No." His heart broke for the pain in her voice now and the agony she'd faced over the years without him. "No, I don't." He took a deep breath and released it slowly. "And I wish you could have had an easier life, Tris. But the fact is, I wouldn't want yours, or mine, to have been any different. If it'd been easy, if we'd sailed through our childhoods without rage, violence, and hunger, we wouldn't be here today. And I love where I'm at right now."

He loved her. After five days of stress and happiness, he refused to entertain the idea of not spending the rest of his life with her at his side.

Trista sighed and turned in his arms, cuddling close to him and rubbing her cheek across his chest; over his heart. "I love it, too."

He heard so much more in those few words and realized she felt the same as him. Or at least, close enough. Now wasn't the time, not with violence and the threats hanging above them, but as soon as they ended the dangers, they'd explore those feelings further. Hopefully naked.

"So we won't have regrets and we won't think of what-ifs. I don't care if you're a quarter werebear and you can hate him for abandoning your mother—his sister—and you. You don't have to ever speak to him again, if you'd like. But right now, if it's true, we need him to save you." God, they needed Terrence.

"I know."

The squeak of the back door opening and then the thud of it slamming closed broke their sweet peace and Keen focused on the clan house in the distance. It was the clan house, not his house, or his childhood home. He had a new place, a place he'd fill with love and cubs once this nightmare was at an end.

His enhanced eyesight allowed him to identify the interloper with ease. *Van.* What the hell did his brother want *now?*

Keen stepped away from Trista and nudged her behind him, creating a barrier between his mate and a dangerous male. A rolling growl formed in his chest and the closer Van came, the more it increased in volume. Trista rubbed his back as if trying to soothe and calm him, but it wasn't going to happen. With a mate, he was like a normal werebear and even a normal werebear would want to eliminate a threat to his other half.

Van had tried to kill Trista. Now Keen *would* kill Van. The bear thought it was a wonderful idea. It put brother against brother, but familial ties meant little when compared to Trista's position in his life. Hell, she was his whole world.

Van stopped twenty feet away, his hands outstretched, revealing human fingers and furless arms. "I just wanna talk, Keen."

Keen couldn't stop the rumble. His inner-animal wanted Van dead beneath his paws.

Unfortunately, his mate disagreed. "Keen…"

It was a plea and a reprimand in one.

Keen looked over his shoulder at his pale mate. "He tried to kill you. He conspired with Reid and Quinn, Trista."

"And I'm sorry about that."

229

Keen refocused on his brother and Van continued. "I *am* sorry, Keen. If I'd known about your mating... I thought I was doing a good thing, the *right* thing. I didn't mean..." His brother shook his head. "It doesn't matter what I thought or what I didn't mean to do. I came out here to apologize and to let you know that Ty left a message for Terrence. There's no news yet, but Dad doesn't think staying out here much longer is a good idea. Reid should adhere to clan laws simply because Trista is your mate and that places some restrictions on his behavior. He's just not sure if the wolf's control will endure the temptation you two out here alone presents."

Instead of snarling at his brother, attacking him for the havoc and pain he'd caused, Keen kept his mouth shut and jerked his head in a stiff nod. He couldn't speak, not yet and not now. Someday he might have a kind word for Van, but that wasn't today.

Van slowly turned and retraced his steps, retreating and finally disappearing into the house.

"You should forgive him." Trista's words were hesitant, but he caught them nonetheless. "He's your brother."

"Would you?" He couldn't keep the harshness from his voice, the disbelief.

Trista stepped around him, stopping once they faced one another. She reached for his hand, and he allowed her to direct his movements, to place his palm on her throat and his fingers to curl around her neck. "Do you feel them? The scars?"

He did. He'd seen them and kissed them and he prayed there weren't any others marring her body. "Yes."

"They were formed the day of my fath— Brigham Scott's funeral. Heath's claws were tainted with poison. He made sure they'd scar, that I'd always remember that day. If Heath had come to me and apologized, if he had welcomed me into his home and tried to love me as a brother should, I would have forgiven him. Even after *this*"—she squeezed his hand, encouraging him to feel the marred flesh—"I would have forgiven him."

230

Keen snatched his hand away and stared at her, reading the emotions cascading across her face. She pleaded with him to understand, to accept and relent his anger.

"He set this up. He is—was—trying to send you to your death." It hurt, dug into his heart and burrowed into his soul. His brother betrayed him and he wasn't sure he'd ever get over it.

Trista shook her head, a sad smile on her lips. "No, he contributed, but he didn't put this in motion. It's been coming for years. It's convoluted and twisted now, but Reid has been after my mother and me since I was a child and it was only a matter of time before Quinn came after you. It just so happened that the stars didn't only align, but folded and turned in on themselves to create what's happening now."

Keen ran a hand through his hair, accepting Trista's words as truth, but the bear still raged at his brother's behavior. "I can't forgive this, Tris."

"You can."

He shook his head, anger burning hotter at the suggestion. "No."

"You will because I'm asking you to."

The growing rage deflated, crashing back to Earth in a wheezing heap. "You can't."

"I can." She hooked a finger through his belt loop and tugged him closer. "Because if I... When... You'll need them and I don't want you to go through this alone."

A new shade of anger pulsed through him, one tinged with disgust and he even hated himself a little for that emotion. He cupped her cheeks, forcing her to focus on him. "Are you giving up? Already? Before the fight has begun, you're rolling over? I may talk about the possibility, because let's be honest, there's only one winner in a fight to the death, but it sounds like you're throwing in the towel. Is that the type of woman I mated?"

A wave of burning heat struck him, Trista's emotions searing him with their strength. "Fuck you, Keen." She brushed off his hold and stepped back. "It's not giving up, it's being a realist. We already know I'm not running because I've been running my entire life, but we also know that Adrienne is going to step into that yard on four feet, not two. I'm three-quarters some kind of shifter, but she's gonna have fangs and claws while I've got a fat ass and blunted teeth. So fuck you very much for me knowing that tomorrow will go one of two ways and wanting someone to be there for you."

Trista's hair was carried away and stroked by the wind, tendrils waving in the air. The waning sun made her pale skin glow and her eyes sparked with her anger. She was... beautiful. Pissed off or coming apart in his arms, she was gorgeous.

"God, I love you." The words escaped, slicing through her ranting and silencing her in an instant. That's when he realized what he'd said, what he'd admitted, and he held his breath. He was such a fucking girl, but he hoped she'd return his words, mirror his emotions. He knew it was new and fast and yet...

"You love me?" She raised her eyebrows high and he nodded. "You love me? After I said... And tomorrow..." He nodded again and she glared at him. "How am I supposed to stay mad and finish yelling at you if you say something like that?"

Keen shrugged. He kinda hoped she wouldn't.

Trista remained rooted in place, her attention locked on him, and he let his emotions shine through, allowed the bear to push forward and add his feelings to the moment. Right, wrong, or indifferent, he wouldn't call the words back for anything.

"I don't want you to love me." A tear trailed down her cheek. "And I don't want to love you."

"Why?" He managed to shove the word from his throat.

"Because then it won't hurt so much. Tomorrow…"

"C'mere."

Keen stepped forward and she eased back. He moved toward her again and this time she didn't move away from him. Instead, she stayed cemented in place and he reached for her hand and brought it to his mouth. He brushed a soft kiss across the back, breathing in her sweet scent. The smells of the lake still clung to her skin—they hadn't showered after their mating—but beneath that her true flavors lurked. He flipped her hand over and pressed a hard kiss to her palm.

"Tomorrow we're going to face Quinn, Malcolm, Reid, and Adrienne, and we're going to have this out once and for all. I have no doubt that my family is inside making every phone call they can and pulling every string available." He took a deep breath and held it a moment before letting it escape his lungs. "I have no doubt tomorrow will be difficult, I have no idea what's going to happen, but I will be with you and I will protect you with my dying breath." He tucked stray tendrils of her hair behind her ear. "I love you and I'm not about to lose you to some upstart bitch."

A woman's voice interrupted their moment, crashed and stomped on it as if it'd never existed, and Keen cursed Van for being right. "Upstart bitch?"

chapter sixteen

The words scraped down Trista's spine, the high voice digging its nails into her flesh and grating her nerves. She didn't recognize the speaker, but the tone was right, belligerent and aggressive and tinged with a hint of a growl.

Trista looked past Keen, focusing on the female behind him, and was unsurprised at what she saw. "Adrienne."

Keen tore away from her, blocking her from the she-wolf, but then Reid stepped out of the woods and into the rapidly lessening light. There was just enough glow to make the handgun sparkle in the sun. She didn't know anything about guns, but when it came to firearms, details weren't all that important, were they? No matter the size, it could still kill.

And right then, it was aimed at Keen's head.

No one moved. It was if they were frozen in time; no one breathed as decisions were made in a split second. Options, scenarios, pinged through Trista's mind. Should she rush Adrienne? Or run? Jump in front of Keen? Or try and shove him down?

She readily admitted that none of the options appealed to her. Each one ended in pain… or death.

"Step away from her." Reid waved his gun, the barrel wavering and sliding through the air.

Keen crossed his arms over his chest. "No."

With the weapon aimed at her mate, she wished he would do whatever the Alpha asked. She could live through pain, deal with what these two had in mind, but she couldn't abide Keen being injured.

Reid smirked, evil and wicked. "No?" The wolf raised his eyebrows. "We'll do this then." The man strode forward, stopping just outside of reaching distance, and extended his arm. "Trista, I'm going to count to five and if you don't step out from behind him and go to Adrienne, I'll pull this trigger. You can face the Challenge head on or you can watch your man die and then still have to fight your way free. Which is it?"

Nothing. She wanted nothing. She didn't want a choice, she didn't want the wolves on bear land. She wanted it to all disappear.

But she had to face this, face the fucking wolves with their fucking ultimatums and pain. She'd have to face pain.

Trista took a step toward the woman, easing half of her body from behind Keen.

"Trista…" Keen's voice rumbled in warning.

Her life didn't matter when it became a choice between her and Keen. She'd pick him every time. Just as she was doing now.

She took another step and her mate's arm shot out, hand reaching for her. She darted away again, bolting out of reach until she stood between the man she loved and the woman who'd gladly end her life.

"Trista, get your ass back here." Her mate's words were hard and commanding.

"Move and he dies." Reid was calm as could be, as if he couldn't care less. The male wanted her gone, wanted her to face the Challenge and disappear. The grudge he held for so long was finally culminating in this moment.

But why?

Fuck it, she was already losing, she might as well find out why. "Why this? What have you got against me? My family? Why'd my mother have to die and why did you chase me every day of my life?"

She kept her attention split between the three people occupying the small area. She was aware of the home looming behind them and just as aware of the fact that they were hidden—partially or fully—from the house's occupants.

"Why?" she tried again.

Red suffused Reid's face, anger and heartache overcoming him. The muscles in his arm bulged and skin strained, his hand tightening ever so slightly on the gun. Asking had obviously been a mistake.

"I'm older than you." He curled his lip and she nodded. He'd always been the big, bad wolf. Older than her by at least five years. "So you don't know what your *daddy*"—it was a slur and curse in one—"did to our pack."

Adrienne shifted, feet crunching and snapping the dried twigs and leaves beneath her. Trista shuffled back, still between her mate and the female, yet farther away.

"Your *daddy* caught my mother on his lands. She was there to pick up a few things for the pack since Redby's store was out of stock. Your *daddy* didn't listen to those laws of visitation. Instead, he took her." A ripple of fur slithered along Reid's arm, attesting to his wavering control. "He took her. And beat her. And raped her." The snap of bone cut through the air. "And when he was done, he kicked her over the border with a note pinned to her chest, *in her flesh*, that thanked my father for use of his whore."

237

The air rushed from Trista's lungs, stealing her breath and punching a whole in her chest. She'd hated Mr. Scott for as long as she could remember, he was a bastard, but she hadn't ever heard...

"You wanna know how your *daddy* died?" He didn't wait for an answer. "My father gutted him. Found the bastard close enough to the border that he dragged the asshole onto our territory and tore him apart. I did the same to your brother. Parker's kidnapping was the perfect reason to join the bears' fight and it gave me the chance I needed to go after that piece of shit." The Alpha focused on her fully, yellow eyes boring into hers. "And you're the last one, the last piece of shit in that family. But I don't kill women, I don't fight women. So, Adrienne is going to take care of that for me." Reid waved the gun between her and the she-wolf. "Get to it then."

The rest was a blur. Trista went from panicking on the inside, heart racing and pounding, to battling for her life.

Adrienne was on her, teeth exposed, hands curled like claws and aimed right for her. She heard Keen's roar, felt the sound vibrate through her bones, but she couldn't spare him a glance. If he was making noise, he was alive, and that's all that mattered as she fought for her own existence.

Since Heath's attack on her at thirteen, Trista had taken a few free self-defense classes at the various YMCA centers throughout the towns. They came in handy now. If only the lessons included ways to defend herself from teeth and claws.

Adrienne struck out, claws extended, and Trista jumped aside, tripping on her own feet as she scrambled away. Her shoes slid in the damp dirt, but she managed to clamber out of reach.

Then the woman pounced, flying through the air. Fur sprouted and the she-wolf's mouth formed a muzzle as she sailed toward Trista. Teeth lengthened and became more menacing, deadlier.

Roars and growls came from her right, Keen's animal battling Reid. The Alpha kept her mate occupied while giving Adrienne the chance to get the job done. She turned her head, worried for the man who'd become her whole world, but was only able to spare him the sparsest glance.

Because suddenly the woman was there, on top of Trista, claws aimed for her throat and open maw heading toward her head. Death lurked in Adrienne's eyes, the promise of a quick, painful demise.

That expression had Trista's inner-animal raging against the situation. It was stuck inside her, deep within her body and unable to emerge. She was a shifter, but not, and it enraged the beast in her heart.

But just because it couldn't appear didn't mean it couldn't help. She'd healed quickly her entire life due to the animal. Now it gave her strength and speed.

Trista caught Adrienne's hands, wrapping her fingers around the woman's wrists and keeping her at bay. She used her hold to halt the woman's progress, but the she-wolf leaned down and snapped at Trista's vulnerable throat. The wolf's heated, moist breath coated her neck and face, bathing her in the disgusting stench of wolf and rage.

She jerked her head aside, bolting left while pushing Adrienne right, attempting to buck the woman from her body.

But it didn't work. Even with her animal's strength. No, it allowed the wolf to snap her right arm free and scrape those deadly nails down Trista's arm. She dug deep furrows into her flesh, exposing muscle and releasing blood. She tried to suppress the scream that rose furiously, but it emerged anyway.

The sound soaked the area and Keen bellowed in return. She sensed his anger, his pure fury. Hopefully he'd take out his rage on Reid and then come to her before Adrienne got her way.

Then the she-wolf was there again, clawing and snapping, hunting for any hint of Trista's flesh. Her wounded arm throbbed and pulsed with agony, but she couldn't spare a thought for the damage. Not when Adrienne attacked anew.

When Adrienne swiped again she released the woman altogether. She blocked the strike with one arm while she formed a fist with her other hand. She'd been taught how to punch. She'd just never used it on a half-shifted woman before. Well, she used it now. She cocked her arm back, borrowed strength from her animal, and struck. Her bare fist collided with the woman's lower jaw and more pain vibrated down her arm. Knowing how to throw a punch and actually striking skin and bone were two entirely different things.

But while she recovered from the bolting ache, Adrienne rocked back. Her balance shifted, the bulk of her weight no longer crouched over Trista but on her ass as it rested on Trista's hips. This was another thing she'd been taught, how to lie passively beneath someone and then buck them before they had a chance to do any further damage.

She planted a foot and shoved, twisting her hips to dislodge the fierce woman. The moment she was free, she rolled in the opposite direction and sprang to her feet. Her left arm hung limply at her side, blood trickling over her skin to soak the ground.

It didn't matter, though. She was free and she had to survive. Survive long enough for Keen to get to her, to save her.

She was depending on him to save her, and her mind didn't balk at the idea. Sometimes leaning on someone was necessary and Keen was the first person, the first male, she'd ever put all of her faith in.

He *would* save her.

Survive. Survive. Survive.

And she did. When Adrienne came after her, pushing to her feet as she wiped blood from her cut maw, Trista ran. She ducked behind trees and wove through the forest. The heavy thump and crunch of Adrienne's pursuit filled her ears, but it also spurred her to go faster.

She skirted the area where the battle began, making sure she was still within Keen's reach.

Survive. Survive. Survive.

She was running and winning. Staying alive meant winning. Adrienne was there, she hadn't caught her, and she hadn't—

Claws scraped down her back, scoring her skin and snaring her shirt. The sudden tug jolted her and she went from racing away to falling back. She shouted in surprise, stumbling until she collided with a tree.

Blood dripping from her claws, a morbidly smiling she-wolf advanced on her. That was Trista's blood, Trista's life, coating the woman's paws. The pain of her new wound intensified, the nerves finally realizing that bare skin was pressed against rough bark.

Didn't matter though because Trista had to remain mobile, had to remain on her feet and out of the woman's clutches. She backed away, shuffling behind the tree and continuing her backward escape. Still the woman advanced, keeping pace.

"I'm going to win. I'm going to gut you and bathe in your blood, little bitch. I'll make it quick if you submit now."

No. She wouldn't submit. Not ever. Before Keen, she might have. She might have given up and let the woman end her rapidly worsening existence. But no more.

Trista spun and ran. Blood created a red trail across the leaf-strewn forest floor. She tripped and shuffled, but kept distance between her and the wolf. She flew over the ground, racing toward her original position by Keen.

She neared the tree line, clear sky in sight, and tripped before she could burst into the air. Once again Adrienne was on her, straddling her as she reached for Trista's hands.

"I'll tear out your throat, bitch." Adrienne's face was more wolf than woman. Yellow eyes, gray fur instead of skin. The head of a wolf on a female's body. The beast nightmares were made of captured her.

Or rather, her body, but not her hands. One, but not both.

Trista reached for a weapon, a rock, a branch, anything. And God, for fucking once, answered her prayers. Maybe he didn't hate her any longer.

Her hand closed over a rock, a stone larger than her palm, and she curled her fingers around her makeshift weapon. Adrienne still scrambled to capture her wrist, but Trista's animal was pissed. Pissed and angry and aching to taste the she-wolf's blood.

With all of her strength, with every ounce of power she had lingering in her body, she raised her arm. She heaved the stone at Adrienne's head, pushing through the motion, pretending she punched through the woman's skull. She imagined it sinking into bone and flesh and destroying the woman.

Once again, vibrations jarred her bones, sending a new ache along her frame. But her strike connected, landed on Adrienne's temple. Split the she-wolf's skin and a trail of blood snaked down her face. It also stunned the woman, freezing her in place for a moment. Adrienne's eyes flickered from yellow to brown and then a soft gasp escaped her lips. The female's body went slack, first shoulders slumping forward followed by the rest of her body caving in and finally falling to the side.

Trista didn't check to see if the woman was simply knocked out or dead. No, she sprang to her feet and ran. She ran toward the sounds of roars and snarls, bear against wolf. She knew her mate would win, knew that a bear could defeat a single wolf. But could a bear battle a gun and come out the winner?

She clutched the rock in her hand, the stone coated in Adrienne's blood. She'd use it on Reid, if needed. Use it over and over until he too remained prone on the ground. Then she'd pray he didn't get up.

She emerged into the space, stumbling past the last few trees and finally sliding to a stop. The sight had her heart freezing mid-beat as a new type of pain overtook her.

Keen was a bear, a massive, glorious animal that stood tall on his back legs. A bellowing roar escaped him, shaking the earth itself with its volume.

That awed her, but also exposed the fact he was injured. Blood coated his fur, darkening until matted and black against his skin.

Reid had done that to her mate, hurt him.

The beast inside her released its animalistic cackle that eventually pushed past her human lips. The sound halted the battle before her as the males flicked their attention to her. Keen faced her, focused and intent as he took in the condition of her body. Reid glanced over his shoulder, giving her a good look at his bloodied and bruised face, but it also told her other things.

He was on two feet, so he obviously hadn't fully shifted, but his face was still mostly human, as was the hand clutching his gun. She took a moment to take in more of him, noting the shredded clothing and the gray fur covering parts of his tanned skin.

She connected the dots in that split second. While she fought Adrienne, Reid and Keen went at it as animals and then, when Reid realized he was on the losing end, went back to two feet. Two feet and no paws so he could aim that fucking gun at her mate once again.

Reid's eyes roamed over her, one flick up and then down. His expression told her he didn't see her as a threat and she had to admit that battered and bloodied, she didn't look like much. Except he hadn't counted on pure stupidity and animalistic rage. He hadn't anticipated a half-shifter woman not giving a fuck about his power or his strength.

He hadn't considered her.

The moment, the instant his attention was on Keen, that instrument of death aimed at her mate, Trista sprinted. Not away—no—right at Reid. She truly flew over dirt and grass, feet hardly touching the ground before she was mid-stride. Then she leapt, going airborne

243

and aimed at the Alpha. The arm holding the rock came back, the stone tight in her hand, and when she was upon him, almost frozen in the air, she brought that weapon down. She struck his head, rock colliding with his skull just before her body crashed into his. She was over two hundred pounds of furious, hyena-souled woman and this wolf had threatened her male.

He was hers and she'd be damned if someone took that away from her. She'd finally learned to trust and this *bastard* thought he'd ruin that? No. Just... no.

Again she hit him, the wolf flailing beneath her, rolling and shoving at her. His hands weren't claws, they were human and *nothing* compared to the she-wolf.

Was that all he had? No, he'd bloodied her mate. She'd simply surprised him. So she'd surprise him again, she'd hit and scratch and bite and...

A streak of brown teased her periphery and she caught site of another bear, not her mate, soaring over the ground, racing toward a snarling, bleeding wolf speeding from the forest.

Adrienne.

She hadn't killed the woman. The hyena was disappointed.

A cry collided with a snarl and she pushed that fight from her mind. She had Reid beneath her and she wanted him dead, craved his blood and wanted to bathe in—

Human hands hauled her from atop the Alpha, pulled her and shoved her behind a naked, red-stained back. Keen. Keen kept her from the man who'd tortured her year after year and—

The scrape of metal on metal told her Keen had racked the slide on the gun, making sure a bullet lived in the chamber. She didn't know a lot about guns, but that sound was familiar.

"Fucking move and I will fucking end you." Keen's voice held more than a little of his bear.

A wailing yelp raced on the heels of Keen's last syllable and Trista looked toward the source, saw a massive, rapidly shifting bear standing over the limp body of a wolf, its neck tilted at an unnatural angle. In moments, she met Van's stare. He'd wanted Trista dead and now he'd killed to protect her.

Trista focused on Adrienne's lifeless body. The woman was gone and she couldn't find any sadness over the loss of life.

In fact, her hyena rejoiced.

Trista let it.

chapter seventeen

The trek from the lake to the clan house seemed endless. Lethargy pulled at Keen, the loss of blood combined with the adrenaline crash sapping his energy. But he refused to lose focus. Pain or not, protecting Trista and remaining at her side trumped all.

She leaned against him, her weight comforting his bear as they made their way to the den. He sensed her pain, her exhaustion, yet she refused to let him carry her.

The bear was both pleased and enraged by her strength. It wanted to hold her close, ensure she was safe and whole. Instead, she'd pushed away his hands and simply leaned against him as they forced one foot in front of the other.

Males rushed from the house, racing toward them. The scent of their panic and worry reached them a bare moment before they stood before him and his mate.

"Keen?" Ty's gaze swept over him and then Trista. Trista with her battered body and exposed skin. Ignoring his brother's question, he demanded the man hand over his button-down shirt. "What? You want…?"

Keen nudged Trista behind him. He didn't give a damn about his own nudity, just his mate's. "Give me the fucking shirt."

Ty's attention shifted from Keen to Trista and back again, eyes widening. "Oh."

It took seconds for his brother to strip and Keen turned toward Trista, assisting her into the massive button-down, covering her seeping wounds and bare skin from view. As he clothed his mate, he spoke to Ty. The men who'd accompanied Ty had already raced off to assist Van and left him to give his report.

"Reid and Adrienne attacked. There's a twisted history between Trista's father and Reid's mother. The man's rage was justified but his methods were anything but." Keen slipped the last button through the hole and turned to Ty. "Van took care of Adrienne."

"I see," Ty murmured. "And you two are okay?"

Keen snorted. They were both bloodied, bruised, and torn apart, but at least they were alive.

He focused on Trista, on her upturned face and the clear blue of her eyes. Fear no longer lurked now that the imminent threat of death was gone. Reid couldn't fight her despite the amount of hatred he harbored. The male was going to be locked up and presented for judgment when Terrence arrived. If Trista was the man's niece, the Alpha attacked someone in the Southeast ruling family. The Itan would not tolerate such an infraction go unpunished.

No, fear didn't linger, but tiredness and vestiges of pain did. Dirt dotted her pale skin, hiding the depth of her bruises, but he knew they were just beneath the brown surface. He wished Adrienne still breathed so he could exact his own brand of justice.

"We're as good as can be expected, I guess."

Ty cleared his throat. "What do you two need? We'll sort out the mess here, but what can we do for you?"

Keen cupped his mate's cheek, brushing away a clump of dirt and grass. The scent of her blood taunted the bear and the animal urged him to get his mate away from these others so they could assess her injuries. He reminded the beast they had a few of their own to inspect, but it didn't give a damn. The inner-animal was more concerned with Trista.

"Have some first aid supplies brought to the guestroom." His voice was imbued with his bear's growl.

"Do you want Mom to tend to you?"

"No." He shook his head while remaining focused on his mate. He knew his mother would do a good job cleaning them up, but he needed to be alone with Trista, needed to reassure his animal and remind the bear she was alive and on her way to being well. "We will take care of each other."

"But—" Ty tried again.

Keen straightened the shirt covering his mate and then spun to face Ty. "We're good. If you could take care of Reid, I'd like to take care of my mate."

"Of course, of course…" Ty nodded. "I'll have supplies brought to you. And if you need anything else…"

"We'll ask." He wouldn't suffer out of pride. Trista was more important than his ego. If she needed something he'd either hunt for it or ask someone to provide for them.

Ty stepped aside and Keen led his mate away, easing past the rapidly growing crowd. No one stopped them, no one uttered a sound. Murmurs of the gathered people followed them, Ty's a hint louder than the others, and then one of the resident guards jogged ahead of them.

He kept his steps even with Trista's, not hurrying his mate as they approached the den. The back door was held open by the guard and the male followed them in, pausing to speak with Gigi.

Keen still didn't stop. No, he carefully led Trista down the hallway and into the room they'd share.

Quiet reigned, the lack of sound comfortable and almost soothing.

Button by button he undressed her, sliding Ty's shirt from her shoulders before going to work on her clothing. Marred flesh peeked through the large tears and his bear bristled, growling with the desire to tear Adrienne to pieces.

He eased her toward the bed and urged her to settle on the soft mattress. Then, ignoring his own pain, he dropped to his knees and reached for the cloth clinging to her.

"Keen?"

"Hush," he whispered. His claws came out without asking his animal for help. He easily sliced away the remaining fabric, parting it to reveal her once pale skin. "Oh, Tris."

His eyes stung and he told himself it was because of dirt and not the emotional agony coursing through him. Leaning forward, he brushed a kiss near one of her healing wounds and then moved to another, gently begging her forgiveness with each touch. "This shouldn't have happened. I failed you."

"Oh, Keen." Soft, dirt-caked hands stroked him, brushing over his cheeks, and he allowed her to tilt his head back. "There was nothing you could have done. They wanted this and they got it. This isn't you or me, it's *them*. *They* did this, not you."

"I…" *I should have protected you better.*

"Now you hush." She grasped one of his hands, pulling him away from her hip, and she brought it to her mouth. Soft lips brushed over his palm and then she forced him to rest his hand over her heart. "Can you feel my heart?"

Of course he could. He lived for her, and was aware of her on infinite levels. He knew her heart still beat because his beat for her. If her life ever ended, his would crack into a thousand pieces. "Of course."

"Then you know I'm alive, I'm here, and I'm with you. This"—she gestured to her body with her free hand—"is nothing as long as you and I are together. Nothing."

A rustle of cloth had him dragging his attention from his mate and to the bedroom door. He noted a flick of pale fabric disappearing from view just as he recognized a familiar first aid kit resting inside the doorway.

Another reminder that he'd failed his mate, that he hadn't kept her from harm. Seemed that'd been happening a lot lately.

"I need to take care of you." He slid his hand from beneath hers, but she curled her fingers around him, halting his retreat.

"Like you said, we'll take care of each other." Trista pushed to her feet and the tattered remnants of her clothing drifted to the ground.

He was going to hell for staring, going to hell for looking at the patches of pale skin and becoming aroused with the sight. She was so gorgeous. Even battered, broken, and bruised, she appealed to him, to his bear.

"Grab the kit and let's go into the bathroom." With those words, she stepped around him and shuffled toward the bathroom.

In a flash, he snatched up the kit and followed her, holding her arm as she stepped on the smooth tile, ensuring she didn't stumble.

"Easy. Don't fall." He kept his voice low and soothing even though his bear was full of rage. Now that she was nude, more of her injuries were revealed. Cuts and scrapes hidden by fabric were illuminated and he swallowed the snarl that filled his throat.

When Trista gasped, he realized she'd finally seen the damage to her body.

"Oh my God." Her voice quavered and she slumped forward, hardly catching her weight on the counter.

251

"Shh…" Keen wrapped his arms around her, careful of her healing injuries. "I have you. I have you."

"How can you even look at me?"

"Because I love you," he murmured. "I love you and you're alive and we're together, Tris. That's all I need." He shifted his hold slightly, taking more of her weight. "Lemme clean you. The bear is frantic to take care of you."

It was, it scraped and clawed at him, furious that their mate was not only physically injured, but emotionally as well. It really, *really* wanted to hunt Adrienne and kill her again. Then he'd go after Reid.

Trista nodded, but otherwise remained silent. Carefully he eased her toward the toilet, lowering the lid and then helping her sit. The moment she was settled, he went into action, snaring and then wetting washcloths, tugging out supplies and laying out everything he needed.

Then he turned to her, to his mate, and prepared himself for what was to come. Keen was already healed—dirty, but only slightly achy—while Trista had seeping wounds that were gradually knitting together and forming scabs.

He snared a damp cloth and padded toward her. "I dunno where to touch you and not hurt you, Tris."

"You're not going to be able to." Trista glanced at her body and then brought her gaze back to him, to the washcloth in his hand. "That isn't going to do the job." She shook her head. "Turn on the shower."

The bear liked the idea of a wet mate. It acknowledged that she was in pain, but as water washed away the grime…

"It might not be best to have you wet and naked, Trista." The bear stretched inside him, pressing against his skin and urging to keep his human mouth shut. He felt the stirrings of lust, the desire to reaffirm his claim growing with every second. Keen wanted her, his bear craved her, and stepping into the shower would begin a series of events that he wouldn't be able to stop. He'd take her, make her his once again, and hate himself for every joyous moment of it. "I can't keep my hands to myself if we do that. I... the bear..."

He squatted before her, leaning close and pressing his forehead to hers. It was the only point of contact he'd allow himself for the moment. His cock was already stirring, thoughts of touching her further sliding through his mind. He fought the urge to reach for her, to allow the animal control.

"He..."

*

Trista knew the thoughts spinning through Keen's mind because they mirrored her own. She recognized the first hints of his desire and was surprised to find her body reacted in kind.

"He needs to be reminded I'm alive." She reached for him, running her fingers along his cheek. "I'm still breathing, Keen. And those feelings? The need? I feel it, too." Her inner-animal chuffed and whined, wanting to sink her teeth into his flesh, to feel him inside her. Breathing. Living. Loving. "Turn on the shower. Turn it on and then we'll wash today away. The worst is over now. No matter what Quinn says tomorrow, no matter what happens, we have each other and that won't change."

His eyes met hers, brown swirling with the midnight of his bear. Keen's skin rippled, as if his beast were just beneath the thin veneer. His gaze never wavered and she knew he was weighing the truth of her words, hunting for any hint of a lie.

He wouldn't find any subterfuge. Her hyena wanted him, craved him. They'd battled Reid and Adrienne and came out alive.

Trista opened to him, let him see every emotion in her heart. "Go start the water."

He remained still for another moment and then two before finally going into motion. His muscles flexed and tensed, rolling beneath his skin as he moved. Fur rippled across the tanned expanse, hints of brown appearing and then sliding away. If she hadn't known he was a shifter, the event would have alarmed her. As it was, the appearance of his bear only served to urge her to go to him, touch and stroke him. Her beast didn't give a damn about the wounds she'd sustained, it brushed them aside as if they were nothing. And truly, compared to the thought of touching her mate, they were inconsequential.

The knitting of flesh itched and stung as she healed and she knew bright pink lines would soon cover her. Yet the sludge of the fight clung to her.

In moments Keen had the water running and steam filled the air. He returned to her, hands gentle as he helped her stand, yet firm when she wavered.

"Easy…" His voice was low, rough and smooth at the same time. Bear and man.

Her hyena responded to both, purring inside Trista's mind. She couldn't shift, couldn't access the furry part of her animal, but she was closer to it than ever before.

Her mate brought out the beast in her.

"I'm fine." She managed to hide the hint of pain that coursed through her body.

"Uh-huh." Or not.

Keen eased her into the shower, holding her steady when she would have fallen, and blocking the initial spray of water with his own body. She looked him over, noting the already healed wounds, the pink lines lightened before her eyes until they were simply scars.

Beautiful. Deadly. Hers.

More of her strength returned with each passing second, her body drawing on his power, her soul reaching for his. Trista leaned toward him, rested her front against his, and merely breathed in his scent. His pure flavors mixed with the crisp water surrounded her in comfort and love.

"Tris…" His voice was nearly drowned by the raining water.

"Hmm…?" She nuzzled him and breathed deep.

"You can't…" He sounded as if he were being strangled and she dragged her attention to his face.

Want warred with need and fought against emotional torment. His cock stirred, hardening against her hip, and she knew what plagued him.

"I told you I want you."

He grimaced. "You're covered in blood, Tris. My God, she almost killed you and I couldn't get to you."

Guilt wasn't something she'd tolerate.

Her hands traced the lines of his body, running up his arms, across his shoulders, and down his chest. So much strength, so much power… And it was hers, all hers.

She spied the mark she'd placed on his shoulder, the lines of her teeth barely visible beneath the dirt. That was unacceptable. The water washed some of it away, but not fast enough.

She focused on that spot and brushed her fingers over the small divots that represented her teeth. A shudder went through Keen with the contact and his cock hardened further, warm and stiff against her.

"Baby, don't." He twitched as if to move away, but she repeated the action.

Instead of backing up, he eased forward as if searching for another touch. His movements were in complete contrast to his words and she knew the bear had taken control. Her mate's human half was much more considerate while the bear acted on pure emotion and cravings.

"You're mine, Keen Abrams." She scraped her nails over the spot.

"You're hurt."

Trista nipped his chest, digging her teeth into the flesh, but not drawing blood. She knew it'd bring the animal out even further. "Not too hurt."

"Trista," he growled.

She sucked on his skin, nibbling once again. "What?"

"You need to stop."

No, she needed to continue, needed to show him that despite everything that'd happened, she was strong enough to be his mate.

"I need you."

"Damn it, Tris."

"Damn it, Keen." She reached for his neck and gripped the back, digging her nails into his skin. "When we mated, we washed away the past. Now I need you to remind me that I belong to you, that I'm yours. After everything, after the pain and Reid's words, I need to know it doesn't matter. Whatever he did..." She wasn't going to cry, not for Reid's mother or her father's actions. "Whatever he did, it wasn't me. You need to remind me of that. Remind me that I belong to you."

Keen's gaze softened, more of his human side easing forward. "You do. You always will."

He showed her then, showed her by easing her hands from his body and then encouraging her to carefully step beneath the tinkling water. The heat stung for a moment and then spread through her body, easing the lingering aches.

He stroked her skin, pressing kisses along one healing gash after another. At some point, the gentle kisses became more urgent, determined as his tongue slid over her. Her body reacted to the change, to the gradual shift from soothing to passionate.

Keen knelt at her feet, water raining on him, plastering his deep brown hair to his head. But those chocolate eyes gazed at her, hints of black encroaching on the brown hue. There were no wounds on her hips or lower stomach, no scrapes on her thighs. And yet that's where his mouth was intent. He scraped a fang over her hip bone, sending a blossom of arousal through her blood, and then laved the small ache away.

"Yes," she hissed, wanting more from him.

His gaze remained intent on her, eyes entirely focused on her face, and she knew he was weighing her expression for himself. He cared for her, loved her, and he refused to do anything that would cause her harm. She loved and hated him, a little, for that.

"Show me it doesn't matter." She reached down and ran her fingers through his soaked locks. "Show me you love me despite it all."

Keen snarled, glaring at her yet still gently laving her with his tongue. He rained kisses from one side of her stomach to the other, tasting her skin, forcing her to burn for him. Her nipples pebbled and hardened, quietly begging to be touched, while her center heated further. Her pussy grew heavy and hot, clit twitching, and she wanted to force him to where she desired him most.

His nostrils flared, chest expanding and brushing her legs with his deep inhale. He expelled the breath in a rapid gust and growled a single word against her skin. "Mine."

He eased her back, crowding her until her back rested against the cool, slick tile. The low temperature offset the sting from the pressure and she relaxed against the solid wall. The moment she was settled, he went back into action. He nudged closer, prodding her legs until they were spread wider, until he could ease between them.

"Mine." He growled and leaned forward, his gaze intent on the juncture of her thighs.

"All yours." His and his and his again. Forever.

He brought his mouth to her heat, nose nuzzling her short curls while he blew a heated breath over her moist flesh. Then... He lapped at her slit, tongue teasing the very top and she shuddered, unable to suppress the involuntary movement. Pleasure unfurled, blossoming, and spreading from her pussy to sink into her body.

He slid his hands along her legs, skimming her inner thighs and finally resting them beneath her ass. Then he shifted his shoulders, forcing her to spread her legs even farther.

"Lean back," he growled against her lower lips. "Got you," he rumbled. He pushed again and she knew she was two seconds from tumbling to the shower floor, but he caught her, his massive hands gently cupping her ass and giving her a seat. She was unsure of her balance, simply waiting to see if he'd buckle beneath her weight, but she didn't have much time to ponder. His tongue was back, sliding between her labia and flicking her clit.

"God, yes."

Keen hummed against her flesh, licking and tasting, doing evil, wicked, wonderful things to her pussy. He savored every inch of her core, flicking here, gently laving there, and sucking on the tiny bundle of nerves.

With each pass, she gave him more of her weight, relaxed into his hold and let him do what he would to her body. She didn't care. She had pleasure coursing through her veins and her mate giving her more with each passing second. Life, despite the remaining aches, was good.

"Keen," she gasped, sucking in a harsh breath when he scraped her clit with his fang. "Yes," she hissed.

Keen growled and repeated the action, gifting her with more and more bliss.

He shifted his hold, forcing her to spread for him completely, and she rested one leg on his shoulder, searching for leverage. She found it, pushing her heel against his back as she sought to ride his tongue. Hands buried in his hair, she took what she desired.

Trista rolled her hips, aching for his tongue to be *there* and then it needed to be *there* and one more second *there* and... She moaned and trembled, enjoying when he tongued her clit and loving when he circled the very center of her pussy. Then he'd repeat the action, flick, circle, lap...

The pleasure of his touch gathered, coalescing and growing within her. It formed a small bubble surrounding her clit, increasing with each bliss-inducing touch until it spread. The joy slid along her veins, stroking her nerves, forcing her muscles to tremble and twitch with the sensations.

"Keen, please..."

He growled against her, drawing a deep moan from within her chest and adding to the ecstasy that threatened to overwhelm her.

"Need you..." She did, more than anything she needed him stretching and filling her, claiming her again. Once wasn't enough, it'd never be enough.

Keen sucked on her clit, the move rough and hard, and she jerked with the overwhelming pleasure that bombarded her. He released her with an echoing pop and his gaze bore into hers. "Come for me. Come on my lips and then I'll give you whatever you desire." His tongue flicked out, the pink disappearing between her sex lips and stroking her sensitive clit. "Give it to me, Tris."

When he returned to his ministrations, his mouth moving over her, his growls and moans adding to the sensations, she found it wasn't hard to follow his instructions.

One lap became two became twenty and each one forced a whimper and moan from her lips. She arched and rocked against him, taking what she could and gathering each snippet of pleasure he gifted her. But it wasn't enough. She wanted more and more and she didn't think she'd ever be satisfied.

He settled into a seductive rhythm, drawing her pleasure forward with every recurring stroke and circle. It was exactly what she needed, exactly what would push her nearer to release once again. The familiar tingles started in her toes, crawling through her flesh, leaving rolling waves of pleasure in their wake. Her pussy clenched and tightened, releasing more of her juices in preparation of his possession.

He alternated hard sucks with gentle licks, pushing her toward the edge, and she was more than ready to leap off the precipice. It was close, her orgasm rushing nearer and nearer with each second that passed.

"Close…" She pushed the words out with her next panting breath.

That caused him to increase his attentions, give her more, shoving instead of gently encouraging her release. He doubled his actions and she could do nothing but be carried away with the wave of sensations.

She trembled and shook, tensed and twitched. Her toes curled while she involuntarily arched her back, pressing her heat to his lips. Her body was no longer her own. No, it belonged to him, wholly and completely.

The bubble of pleasure swelled to bursting, stretching and threatening to pop at… any… moment…

But then Keen was there. In one fluid rush, he released her and hauled her to him, seating himself inside her pussy in one rapid shift of muscles and flesh. He filled her, stretched her cunt and she screamed with the possession. Not in pain, but in pure unadulterated pleasure as her release overcame her.

Trista lost herself to the joy, reveling in wave after wave of bliss that accompanied his thickness deep inside her. She screamed with her orgasm, shouting his name for all the world to hear and howling with the ecstasy that overtook her body.

The pleasure went on and on and she had only one thing to say to her mate, the male she'd spend the rest of her life with. She opened her eyes, stared into the blackness of his irises, and said a single word that refused to be silenced. "More."

*

Keen nearly came. Right then, right there, with Trista's eyes flashing copper and her animal peering out at him, he nearly filled her with his cum. She spasmed around him, baring her teeth with the demand and he refused to spend himself like some kid.

She wanted more? He'd give it to her until she begged for mercy. There was nothing he wouldn't do for his luscious mate.

He shifted his grip, one palm cupping her ass while he slid his other over her back. His fingers encountered her mostly healed wounds and he was careful as he found a smooth swath of skin. With his new grip, he allowed himself to take pleasure in her body, snatching bits of euphoria while giving her just as much in return.

He slowly withdrew from her clinging heat and then shoved home again, testing her responses. He smiled when she did nothing but gasp and dig her nails into his shoulders. He repeated the action, a slow withdrawal and fierce advance, liking the way her breasts bounced with the movement.

He wanted one in his mouth, his tongue circling a hard nipple that teased his chest. Damn it, what was with him and taking her standing up? And water, what was with the water?

Then it didn't matter because she was hissing and baring her teeth, small nails digging into his skin and her pussy fluttered around his cock. Each tense and relaxation teased his shaft, milking him and seeming to beg for his cum. He'd release soon enough. As soon as she came again. He wanted that, his beast craved it. They'd tasted her first wave of pleasure and now he was desperate to feel her come apart in his arms.

He withdrew and thrust forward again, working his hips, pushing his cock in and out of her soaking sheath. Each ripple and stroke reached into his soul, pleasuring his body and his very heart. His possession of her body didn't give them just pleasure, it was physical proof of her trust in him. There was nothing deeper, more profound, than a woman accepting a male into herself.

And he was the last who would have that pleasure with Trista. She was his and his alone.

"Mine," he snarled, the beast needing to voice the truth aloud.

Copper eyes flared brighter. "Yours."

No words were necessary then, their bodies speaking for themselves. She fluttered around him, pussy milking his cock with every thrust and retreat. His balls were high and tight and his release was within reach. He wanted to come, wanted to let go and possess her fully. Hell, the bear was in *full* agreement.

But he waited.

He wanted her with him.

So he changed his angle, tilted her hips the tiniest bit and was rewarded with a deep moan followed by a roaring shout. Yes, he'd found the perfect spot. With each entrance he pressed against her clit and stroked that bundle of nerves within her sheath. Now he could relish in the pleasure, now he could allow his body the freedom it desired.

His bear pushed forward, anxious to be a part of their joining, and Keen didn't fight the animal. They were one and the same, two beings sharing a body and soul.

"Need you…" she gasped. "Need more…" Trista's hold shifted, hands no longer clinging to his shoulders, but gripping the back of his neck. She tugged and yanked on him, pulling him closer.

And then he realized what she desired.

"Tris," he grunted and pushed deep, another shudder of pleasure overtaking him. God damn he was close. His balls pulsed, desperate for release, while his cock twitched and jerked inside her. She was hot, wet, and tight, and perfect for him.

"Need it, Keen. I'm yours. Forever yours." Trista pulled again, yanking hard this time.

He stared at the spot, at the creamy shoulder already marred by his claiming bite. She wanted another, another piercing of her flesh with his thick, sharp teeth.

"Please…" she whined and then gasped with his fierce thrust. "*Please.*"

The second begging sound accompanied by her deep moan broke his control. His bear rushed forward, transforming human teeth to animalistic fangs. He struck, sinking into skin and muscle while rapidly slamming their hips together. Bodies met while blood filled his mouth. His bear's mental roar warred with Trista's echoing scream.

Her pussy tightened around him like a slick fist, squeezing him, and then spasms overtook her. She came on his cock, his woman finding pleasure in his body and bite.

Keen let go, released his iron control and pure ecstasy encompassed him. He flew with Trista, cock pulsing as cum filled her. The bliss of his orgasm wrapped around him in a joyous blanket and he didn't want this moment to ever end.

With every pull on the bite, her pussy clenched and his dick twitched. It continued, the never ending circle until Trista became nothing more than a trembling mass in his arms.

And still he wanted more. The bear craved his mate's sounds and reactions. At least until she became slack with a final whimper. Carefully, he slid his teeth from her flesh and lapped at the wounds, anxious and immediately regretting his actions. When he pulled back to stare into her eyes, he found them half-closed and her face pale.

He cursed himself for being a selfish bastard. She'd been through so much, hurt by Adrienne, and he fucked her against the wall.

"Tris?"

"Hmm…?" Her head lolled back and rested against the wall.

"Tris, love. Baby?"

She sniffled and leaned forward, resting her head against his shoulder. "Wha?"

"You okay?" Worry had him softening, and he carefully eased her legs to the ground, gradually lowering her until her feet rested on the cool tile. When she went lax and didn't catch her weight, he tightened his hold. "Tris?" He reached behind him and stretched, shoving at the shower knob and turning off the water. "Trista?"

Trista didn't answer and instead harrumphed and nuzzled his chest.

Anxiety mounting by the moment, he slid the shower door aside and slipped out. He didn't bother grabbing a towel or even drying them.

Keen swung her up into his arms and carried her through the bathroom and into the bedroom. He didn't stop until he was able to place her on the bed, soaked body slumping onto the mattress. Then he examined her, hands sliding over her damp skin, pressing and feeling every inch.

She whined and pushed his hands away, fighting him with every touch.

"Tris, what's wrong? Where do you hurt? Do you need a healer?"

He was such an asshole. The biggest asshole known to man. She'd trusted him to take care of her and he'd assured her she could lean on him, that he'd protect and care for her. Well, who would protect her from *him*?

"Trista? What do you need?" He ignored the panic filling his tone.

She finally opened her eyes, the copper slowly bleeding to blue, and grinned at him. "Wrong? No, it's very, very right. Can we do it again?"

He froze. "What?"

"Again. That's what I need." She nodded, a slow, lazy rise and fall.

"Are you kidding me?"

She shook her head and rolled toward him, extending her hand. "Never. I'd never tease about *that*. Now, c'mere."

Keen narrowed his eyes and without thinking reached out. His palm connected with her rounded ass before he had a chance to think through the motion. But when a pink imprint of his hand rose and contrasted against her pale skin, he decided he wasn't all that sorry. Especially when the blue bled back to copper.

No, he wasn't sorry at all.

Trista squeaked and rolled to her back.

He grinned and leaned over her.

From there, things got really interesting… and naughty.

One kiss turned into two and eventually, they needed another shower.

chapter **eighteen**

Trista woke snug in Keen's arms, his body spooning hers and his heat enveloping her in a warm, soothing blanket. Her body ached, parts of her throbbed, but she was alive. Alive and safe and...

Thinking of being alive reminded her of who'd died and her heart squeezed at the loss of life. It was stupid to feel bad about Adrienne's death, but she did. Even if the woman hadn't fallen at Trista's hand, it was still Trista's presence that set the she-wolf on that path. Trista and Reid.

She glanced toward the window, hunting for any indication of time and noticing the sun cast long shadows across the earth. It was late then, definitely after noon, and she wondered how long they'd slept. They'd made love well into the night, coming together again and again, confirming that the other still breathed.

She eased from Keen's arms, gently rolling to face him, stare at his strong features and the new scars that marred his skin. She'd traced each one with her tongue, thanking and praising him with her attentions. In sleep, he looked sweet and gentle, but she knew that could change in an instant if she was threatened.

Her stomach grumbled, announcing its hunger, while her bladder decided it was time to get out of bed and take care of things. She hated to leave him, but she'd snag some food and scurry back to their makeshift den to eat in private. She couldn't stand the idea of being surrounded by people.

She slipped from the bed and dug through the drawers. She remembered Mia telling her about extra clothing earlier in the week and... She smiled in triumph when she found sweat pants and T-shirts. Not the greatest looking clothes, but comfortable.

Now dressed, she snuck into the hallway, softly closing the door behind her. She padded down the hallway, feet sinking into the plush carpet, and toward the soft tinkling of utensils scraping against plates. The murmur of voices reached her just before she turned the last corner that dumped her at the entry of the kitchen.

The family sat around the kitchen table, Gigi working in the kitchen and laying out platters of food as she took things out of the oven or slapped together sandwiches. She glanced at a nearby clock, noting it was just after one p.m.

With Trista's appearance, everyone fell quiet and focused on her. "Um..."

She wasn't sure what to say. *Gee, thanks for killing the psycho woman last night, can I please have a few ham and cheese sandwiches to go?*

Anna saved her from having to figure it out. "How are you feeling, dear? Are you hungry? Here, let me fix you a plate."

The woman hustled toward the bar and snared a dish, quickly placing morsel after morsel on the surface.

"Keen's still sleeping, I thought I'd..."

His mother looked back at Trista with a smile. "Of course, I'll put together something for him, too."

The quiet became oppressive, suffocating and bearing down on her with a weight she wasn't sure she could stand. Did they hate her for the trouble she brought to their door?

A quick glance around the table didn't reveal anything. Ty and Van's features were blank masks, some emotions escaping, but not enough for her to discern their feelings. That near indifference brought words to her mouth.

"I'm sorry for the trouble I caused. I didn't mean..." To tear their family apart.

Keen's father grunted and shook his head then leveled a glare across the table. His anger was focused on Ty and Van, the laser-edged expression skipping over the women with ease before returning to her.

"Nothing to be sorry about." The older man pushed to his feet and came closer. From what Keen said, George Abrams was a gruff, frequently grunting man, but mostly harmless. Unless his family was threatened. Threatened like it'd been last night. Did he think of her as family?

He hauled her into a hug and held her tight. It was sweet and warm and the closest thing to a father's touch she'd ever received. That snarly part of her calmed with George's touch and Trista raised her arms to return the embrace.

George released her and patted her back, nearly sending her tumbling to the ground if not for his hold on her arm. "We take care of family and you're Keen's mate which makes *you* family. All there is to it."

She wasn't gonna cry. She wasn't.

The older man checked his watch and then looked to her again. "Terrence said he'd try and get here by five, but if he isn't, we just gotta stall a little bit. He'll be here and sort all this out."

"I don't know if I want to see him."

George smiled and shook his head. "And I don't wanna get old, but it's gonna happen no matter what I say."

269

Anna pushed her way between George and Trista. She thrust heaping plates into Trista's hands and ignored her husband. "There you go, sweetheart. I put Keen's favorites on there. He may be a meat eater, but the man loves his potato salad. I'll teach you how to make it before we go home. That kitchen of yours is just gorgeous."

The woman beamed, flashing a big, carefree smile as if she knew at the end of the day, Trista would be right where she desired. Here. In Grayslake in the home she owned with Keen.

"Thank you." She snared the plates and took a step back. "We'll eat and be ready by the time Quinn and Malcolm show up."

"Sooner if Terrence gets here." George raised an eyebrow, as if daring her to object.

Trista was smarter than that and merely dipped her head in a nod. He didn't want to get old, she didn't want to meet the man who'd likely turned his back on her mother and, by extension, her.

Without another word, she retraced her steps, carefully navigating the turns. She'd have to knock on the bedroom door since she'd tugged it closed when she left. Darn it, she'd wanted to feed Keen lunch in bed.

"Aunt Trista?" The voice was soft and a hint high-pitched, childlike in its tone. Which made sense since, when she turned to face the speaker, she found herself hip-to-nose with Parker Abrams.

Anxiety immediately hit her in the gut, slamming home and forcing her heart to race. Her first encounter with the little cub hadn't gone well. She looked around the hallway and noted she was alone with the boy who, only days ago, wanted her as his next chew toy.

"Hey, Parker." She tried to keep her tone light as she took a step closer to the guestroom.

"I wanted to say I was sorry." The little boy kicked at the carpet, digging his little toes into the thick weave. "It was wrong to try and hurt you. I can't let my pre-juice fingerpaint my windows."

270

"Um..."

An exasperated Mia waddled around the corner. "Parker, it's prejudice, paint, and views. You can't let your prejudice paint your views and you shouldn't have made such a skewed judgment about Trista without getting to know her."

The little boy rolled his eyes and sighed. "What Mim said. I'm real sorry. I promise not to bite you anymore and I won't even try and hurt other hyenas that show up."

"Um, okay." She let her gaze drift from Parker to Mia and then back to the little boy. "Thank you?"

Mia sighed. "Parker, help Aunt Trista open the door to her room and then come back to the kitchen. Everyone's done eating."

The child groaned. "That means I hafta wash dishes."

"Only half if you quit whining, help Aunt Trista, and hurry back," Mia added.

That got Parker moving. Suddenly a small hand fisted the extra material on Trista's pants and urged her to turn around. "C'mon, Aunt Trista. We gotta scoot our boot."

Scoot our boot?

She'd have to ask Mia about that one later. Like when Trista's world wasn't still balancing on an edge that could crumble at any moment.

Parker dragged her to the end of the hallway and immediately reached for the knob. Small hands wrapped around the shining metal only to have it snatched from his tiny grasp.

The panel swung wide to reveal a half-dressed Keen, but Parker wasn't impressed.

"Hey!" the cub whined. "Mim won't lemme only do half the dishes if I don't do my job."

Keen raised his eyebrows. And Trista quickly explained, leaving out Parker's convoluted apology. She didn't want to laugh at the poor boy and she knew she'd bust into giggles when she retold the story.

Her mate reached out and ruffled Parker's hair. "Tell your Mim you did your job and we'll be out soon."

When Keen gave her a look filled with heat and promise, she realized "soon" was a relative term.

With a smile, Parker disappeared, leaving her alone with her mate. It took moments to get settled in the room, for Keen to sit in a plush chair, pull her onto his lap, and then spend the next half-hour feeding one another. It was teasing without being sexual, it was sweet and not quite chaste, but soothing and relaxing. Especially after what they'd faced. Their bodies reconnected throughout the night and now their souls were coming together again.

Whispers were shared, words interspersed with nuzzles and the gentle brush of lips on skin. Reality would intrude soon, break the thin barrier the door created, but until then, they had each other.

Keen popped the last strawberry into her mouth and she savored the sweet flavors that burst across her tongue.

"Delicious," she hummed.

That had him kissing her, his tongue thrusting past her lips and exploring her mouth. She accepted the passionate kiss, realizing the time for sweetness was apparently at an end.

They tasted one another, discovering flavors while also stoking the other's arousal. It was heaven and she knew even more could be had. Later.

She moaned against his lips and slowly eased the fiery kiss. "We need to shower and they're expecting us soon."

Keen growled, but she realized he did back off a little. "Damn them all."

"No." She pressed a hard kiss to his lips and snared his plate before rising. "We have to deal with this. Reid's still in the basement and Quinn and Malcolm are on their way and…"

"And I'm going to wash your back. Then I'll put that sweet mouth to good use. I didn't get my good morning kiss and I think you need to rectify that." He pushed to his feet and snagged the plates back from her.

"What was all that?" She waved toward the chair.

"Lunch kisses. They don't count toward morning kisses. Morning kisses are"—he bent down and rubbed his nose against hers, pressing their foreheads together—"naked."

Naked. She could get behind the idea of naked.

* * *

The shower took longer than anticipated. Well, longer than *she* anticipated. Keen seemed to be in no hurry to join his family and had loved her thoroughly. Twice.

Running a towel over her hair, she scrubbed the strands in an effort to soak up some of the moisture. She hadn't found a hair dryer under the sink and she hoped Mia wouldn't mind lending Trista hers. It seemed like the woman liked her as did Keen's parents if not his brothers.

The rumble of approaching vehicles and the crunch of their tires over the gravel driveway had her going to the bedroom window. A half-dozen SUVs pulled to a stop before the house, making a neat row of vehicles. Massive men, males larger than the Abrams brothers, alighted from a few of the vehicles and moved to encircle the center SUV. One other vehicle was given the same treatment while the last was simply left alone as two men stepped out.

"Keen?"

He strode out of the bathroom, towel slung low on his hips as he too towel dried his hair. "Hmm?"

"There's…" She pointed out the window.

He padded closer and peeked through the curtains. She watched his expression, saw the spread of his lips into a wide smile, and she let some of her gathering anxiety float free of her body. "They're here."

"They?"

He pointed out the window. "That end one is Mia's father and my brother Isaac."

The brother who'd been permanently scarred by Trista's family. "Keen…"

Keen dropped the towel in his hands and embraced her. "Hush. I already talked to him. You know this. Isaac is a Healer so he's used to acting like Switzerland when it comes to people. He can push his feelings aside and do his job. That also means he doesn't hold grudges and he knows what happened had nothing to do with *you*. Out of everyone, you shouldn't fear him."

Trista turned her head to focus on the other vehicles. "And the rest?"

"Probably Terrence and his entourage. Not sure who else he brought with him, though," he murmured. "Let's find out."

"I'm scared." There, the words were out.

"Give me a little trust, Tris. He's a good man and a better bear."

Trista rested her chin on his chest. "You're sure?"

"I wouldn't let you out of this room if I wasn't."

With a sigh, she stepped back and reached for her borrowed clothes. "Okay, let's see what they have to say and..." She swallowed and prayed Keen would abide by her wishes. "And even if he is my family, you won't force me to spend time with him? I don't think I can after..."

"Tris." He stopped her with a gentle touch and cupped her cheeks. "I love you."

She felt that love to her bones and beyond, it filled her from head to toe and she hoped his feelings would never end.

"I love you and if you never want to see him again, we won't. For now, we'll use him for our safety and to sort things out. After that, even if he is your uncle, we can walk away." When he kissed her, she leaned into the touch, drawing strength from his body.

All too soon, their meeting came to an end and they separated to dress. It took moments to become presentable and they went to the bedroom door. Traveling along the hallway, they were met by Ty halfway to the common area of the house.

"Terrence is here." Ty's voice was low, but audible as he spoke to Keen. "Mia's dad and Isaac, too." That's when Ty's concerned gaze flicked to her and then back to his brother.

"And you know our brother," Keen countered. "I'm not worried about his reaction."

The Itan sighed. "And I know our brother." He relaxed for a moment. "But those aren't the only extras who appeared with him."

"Who else?"

Trista wasn't sure she wanted to know. New people meant new trouble. They already had enough with Terrence and his inner-circle.

"His mate and sons," Ty continued and Trista's stomach clenched. "And," the Itan heaved in a deep breath, "and Jessa."

275

Panic welled inside her. It was stupid and unnatural and there was no reason to be wary of Jessa's presence, but she was. Keen had only thought himself in love with the werebear long ago, but the woman had proven she wasn't the one for Keen. So why was Trista worried Keen would suddenly decide that he wanted Jessa instead?

Because he'd craved her once.

Rough hands grasped her and backed her up until her back collided with the wall. Keen loomed over her, a fierce expression on his face that looked like a cross between anger and frustration.

"You're mine." He fisted her hair.

"Yes." She belonged to him, wholly and without question.

"Which means I'm yours." He tightened his grip just enough to cause a slight sting. "*Yours.*"

She gazed at him and watched the fury drain to be replaced by love. The love they'd professed and shared across pillows and against bare skin.

"Okay."

"She's nothing now, Trista."

"Okay," she rasped, knowing he spoke the truth. She may not have recognized it earlier, but she did now.

The rough grip transformed to a soft caress, one that slid over her shoulders, down her arms, and ended with their fingers twined together. "Ty? Thank you for letting us know."

The Itan grunted, sounding very, very much like his father. With that, Ty turned and headed back the way he'd come.

"I want to introduce you to Terrence. He's a good male and no matter what position he has in your life, I'm asking you to give him a chance." His voice held a plea, one she couldn't deny.

What if Keen hadn't given her a chance? What if he'd scented a hyena and run her off without a second thought?

Trista nodded. "Okay." She took a deep breath and released it slowly. "Let's meet the Southeast Itan."

The path to the kitchen was familiar, as was the route to the living room. The murmur of voices reached them first, the deep baritone of the males offset by the high alto of the women. The tone was subdued, but seemed to be imbued with a hint of excitement, as well.

The excitement made her nervous. The Southeast Itan was a powerful man and if she wasn't who they all thought she was, how would he retaliate?

"Shh… I'm right here. You'll be fine." Keen squeezed her hand.

They paused as they neared the threshold and she fought to ignore the massive males who lined the hallway. Guards. Of course the Southeast Itan wouldn't travel without guards. And each one appeared more deadly than the last.

Her mate must have sensed her growing unease and he was quick to reassure her. "Tris?" She tore her gaze from the suit-clad men. "We're in the clan house, with my brothers inside that room. I know they would protect you with their lives. Knowing that, knowing you'd be safe, I could take on every male in this home and win. Nothing would get past me." He stroked her neck, fingers gliding over the new scars that decorated her skin. "I'm sorry the bear was torn in two different directions by Adrienne and Reid and couldn't keep you from harm, but that wouldn't happen here. Here, they'd all die."

That had the guards growling, the sound rolling and echoing off the tiled floor, but Keen ignored the sounds. "Are you ready?"

Trista nodded. She wasn't, but she didn't think she'd ever be ready. Not really. "Yes."

Before they could take the last few steps, a younger man stuck his head through the arched entry to the living room. "Dad wants to know why you guys are growl—" He swallowed his words and simply stared at her with wide eyes. His gaze shifted from her to Keen, widening even further, before settling on her once again. "Oh. *Oh.* Dad?" With that, he disappeared from view. "Dad!"

They followed the man, more of a boy, into the space to join the rest of their visitors. In reality, Keen dragged Trista into the room, but she refused to admit her cowardice.

At their entry, everyone froze, all conversation stopped, and dozens of eyes were intent on them, one set seeming more focused than the others. Focused on her.

The man was older, easily matching Keen's father in age. She had no doubt the stranger was pushing through his sixties and closer to seventy. His hair was white, but there were hints of a familiar burgundy hue scattered amongst the pale strands. His eyes crinkled at the edges and the slope of his nose was one she'd traced when she was a child. Except, when she was little, it'd been on a decidedly female face. The lips were the same, the cut of his chin. His features were harder, sharper, but still very, very familiar.

Terrence, it was obviously Terrence, the Southeast Itan and her mother's brother. She wasn't sure she could ever call him "uncle."

"My God…" The man's voice was hoarse and filled with shock.

Trista felt the same surprise, had that exact emotion clogging her veins and stealing her breath. But while he voiced his astonishment through two words, she had only one. One that she'd wondered from the moment the theory had been presented to her.

"*Why?*"

"You look just like her."

"*Why?*" She threw the word into the air once again.

He grimaced and opened his mouth to reply, but she couldn't hold back the anger any longer. Instead of waiting for a response, she tore herself from Keen and stomped toward him, her anger and grief filling her more and more with every step. Every struggling moment of her life coalesced into this moment, this time that melded the past and the present until she was before him.

Tears coursed down her cheeks as she released her gathered fury and emotional agony. She yelled and screamed, but had no idea what words were released. But words didn't matter, pain did. The pain she'd endured, the pain she'd lived and breathed through year after year. The pain of losing her mother and almost losing her own life.

"Why did you abandon us? Why did you—" Emotion clogged her throat, stealing her breath.

"I didn't know." His eyes were too kind and regretful. "If she would have come to me—"

"She needed you. *We* needed you." She didn't try to disguise her anguish.

"I'm sorry. If I'd known I would have—"

"Fuck you!" She spat the words, flinging them without hesitation. "Fuck you and your fucking 'sorry.' She'd be alive if you'd helped her. She'd be—"

She unleashed it all on the most powerful man in the southeast. And he took it. Took every bellowing shout.

Snarls battled her yells, growls answering her sobs.

It wasn't until the scent of blood, not her mate's but an unfamiliar male's, hit her nose that she finally stopped. She gathered herself, pushed free of Terrence's easy hold, and sought out her mate. No,

279

he wasn't bleeding, he wasn't hurt, but the Southeast Itan's guards were.

Keen stood before them, his massive bulk having shoved everyone away from Trista and Terrence as she'd fought him. He had them cornered while the rest of the group was spread before them. One of the guards tried to venture close again and Keen batted the male away. At least her mate had kept his claws out of play.

"Keen…" When George stepped forward, Keen raised to his back legs, stretching to his full height as he released a bellow louder than any she'd ever heard.

That had Keen's father easing back into the crowd. The others shifted, squirming beneath Keen's temper, and she was so proud of her mate. He'd been so crushed when she was hurt and now his bear was doubly determined to keep her from any threat.

Trista brushed Terrence's presence from her thoughts and focused on her mate. She could beat on the Southeast Itan later. Right now, she had a mate to calm.

Placing a hand on his haunch, she dug her fingers into his fur and tugged, snaring the bear's attention. It turned to her with a snarl on his lips that he quickly cut off the moment he recognized her. In that instant he went from deadly werebear to a sweet kitten. Well, half-ton kitten, but he was still gentle as he lowered to four paws and turned so he could butt her stomach with his head.

"I'm fine."

He huffed at her and nudged her once again and she rubbed one of his ears, earning a soft chuff. Movement from the crowd, one of the suited guards easing closer, had him swinging his attention to the approaching male. With another roar, he batted at the man.

That had Terrence responding. "I didn't realize you were all trained to be stupid," he drawled. "If he'd wanted me dead, I would be. Some of you are mated. Don't you know better than to threaten a were's mate?"

Keen grunted and she sensed the laugh lurking in the sound. The scent of blood reached her once again, the aroma fresh and still flowing. She glanced around the room, hunting for the person injured by Keen. The male was resting against one of the far walls, hands cupping his nose.

"Keen? You shouldn't have hurt anyone on my behalf." She lowered her head and rubbed her cheek against his muzzle. "But thank you."

"Oh," someone spoke up and Trista looked for the speaker. She found it in a younger man who looked to be hardly fifteen. "He didn't. He broke his nose while running from your mate. *Boom.* Right into the wall. Crunch was kinda nice to hear."

"That's your cousin, Bane." Terrence murmured from behind her and she refused to acknowledge him. Not just because her emotions were in turmoil and anger rode her like a wild beast, but also because embarrassment was beginning to set in. It plagued her while also reminding her of everything she'd been taught by her mother. She'd assaulted the Southeast Itan. Uncle or not, she'd gone after a very powerful male and she didn't want to think about punishment for such an infraction. "Bane is…"

The thump of car doors shutting alerted them to someone's presence. The confrontation had obviously masked their approach, but everyone was now aware of the approaching visitors.

"We can discuss your cousins… everything… later," Terrence murmured and then stepped around her and a still shifted Keen.

People burst into movement then. They righted furniture and straightened clothes while someone ran off to find something for Keen to wear. In moments, Anna reappeared with sweats and a T-shirt for her son. As her mate dressed, she focused on Terrence speaking with George near the entryway. George nodded and moved toward the front door while Terrence turned to the room at large.

"We'll do this outside. Jessa, with me."

That was the first time she noticed the woman cowering in a corner, her features hidden by a curtain of hair. Isaac crouched nearby and extended his hand, assisting her from the ground. Her hands shook, knees wobbling, but she approached Terrence despite her unease.

The Southeast Itan took her from Isaac's arms and led her away. As if their disappearance was permission, they all filed after the couple.

Keen tugged his shirt into place and then held out his hand to her. "Ready?"

"No." She had to be honest with that one.

"Too bad. Let's go."

She followed him for two steps and then stopped, tugging on his hand. He turned back to her and she released the words growing in her chest. "Thank you for keeping me safe."

Keen raised their joined hands to his lips and brushed a kiss across her knuckles. "Anything for you, Tris. Anything."

* * *

Keen would do anything for her including destroying the two men who slithered from Quinn's vehicle.

Adrenaline still rushed through Keen's veins, pulsing and throbbing in time with his heart and the bear was more than willing to simply end Quinn's and Malcolm's lives if given the chance.

They stepped outside in enough time to see the cocky, slick smile fall from the men's faces. Fear coated Quinn's features while a sneer overtook Malcolm's. Both men were disgusting, poor excuses for bears. Keen admitted and accepted guilt for the mistakes he made as a teen, but these men had carried their hatred and disgust in their hearts year after year.

"Quinn, Malcolm." The Southeast Itan released Jessa and crossed his arms over his chest. "What can I do for you?"

"Itan Jensen." Quinn tilted his head to the side and dropped his gaze. A little past submissive and on to disgusting in Keen's opinion. "What are you doing here?"

Ooh, good question, wrong tone.

Terrence's response was swift and cutting. "Visiting my niece, Trista." Malcolm gasped, his eyes widening, smirk falling away. Terrence kept speaking, ignoring the male. "The better question is what are *you two* doing *here* and why are you intent on causing a disruption in this clan."

"Terrence," Malcolm spoke and even Keen recognized that use of the Southeast Itan's first name was not smart.

Trista curled into him, her body reminding him that she played a part in his drama. It'd been his enemy who set them on the path that ended the previous night. Or had it? They still had Reid locked in the basement and he hoped Terrence would handle that matter before he left as well.

"Oh, you don't get to speak." The Southeast Itan pointed at two suited guards and gestured at the two men. "Hold them."

Both males struggled, but the much larger men held them with ease. With that, Terrence traveled down the steps, pausing long enough to assist Jessa down.

"You two, as well." The Southeast Itan captured Keen's gaze for a moment and the bottom of his stomach dropped.

He didn't want to relive this. Not again. Trista squeezed his hand and he sighed. He didn't want to, but with Trista, for Trista, he would.

The path to the males parted and their small group moved forward until the four of them stood before Quinn and Malcolm.

From there, the power that existed inside Terrence Jensen overrode everything. With the coldest voice he'd ever heard from *anyone*, the

Itan spoke. "Quinn Foster, you're charged with negligence, falsifying clan records, impersonating a member of the inner-circle, and abuse of a member of the ruling family. Do not think about pleading not guilty. Your only option is to plead for mercy."

"But, I didn't— Falsifying? Impersonating? Abuse?"

The seething fury that whipped through the air nearly brought Keen to his knees.

"Jessa is here to affirm she never spoke a word about a plot against you. In fact, she has publicly and readily forgiven Keen for what transpired all those years ago. Jessa wants to come home and I have granted her permission to do so. As to the others, do you deny that you've relied on first Trista's mother's help with your job? And then Trista herself? Do you deny orchestrating the attack on Trista? *Do you deny any of it?*"

Quinn made the stupid mistake of opening his mouth and then Terrence was there, face against the cowering male's, his temper swirling around the two men like a midnight tornado intent on destroying everything in its path. "Think before you speak. I will cut you down where you stand without hesitation."

Quinn whimpered and clamped his lips together.

It was wrong of Keen to wish for the man to speak, to make the mistake of uttering a single sound so the Southeast Itan would end Quinn's miserable existence.

Then Malcolm erred as well. He shifted, a slight twitch of muscle that caused his clothes to rustle. It drew Terrence's attention and brown fur suddenly coated Terrence's neck.

"And you... I find it interesting that the child of a dead woman stands beside me. The child of a woman who supposedly died thirty years ago. You found her, didn't you, Malcolm? You traced my sister through the territories and there was nothing left to bury, you said. She was taken by hunters, you said. All you had for me was her jewelry and a tattered, bloody dress."

284

Trista went slack beside him, her knees buckling, and he caught her by the waist before she could fall. "Stay strong, Tris."

Terrence's attention strayed to them for a moment, but he quickly refocused on Malcolm. "I mourned her, Malcolm. I knew she didn't want to mate you and she ran. She was young and I was stupid enough to think I could force her to do something she obviously detested." The man's face twisted and he fought the guards holding him steady, but he couldn't escape. "I let you hunt her, but she wasn't dead, was she? She fought you and I know you hurt her enough to make her bleed. And because of you, because you damn near killed my *own blood*, she was too scared to come to me."

Trista whimpered, her hand going to her throat, and Keen's heart ached for his mate. Tear after tear coursed down her cheeks, leaving shining trails on her skin. "Her neck, her face." The words trembled, but they were loud enough to draw the male's attention. "She had a scar for as long as I could remember." Trista touched with three fingers, starting at her temple, she drew a line down along her jaw, digits spreading as she lowered her hand. "It…" She hesitated and then finished. "It would have bled a lot. Even now, I don't know how she survived."

Malcolm's panicked voice rose. "That doesn't prove anything. That doesn't mean I cut the bitch. It hit her jugular, she was dead. She was—"

Terrence's roar was the loudest he'd ever heard, even louder than Keen's own. "*Silence!*" Not even the birds dared disobey the Southeast Itan. The moment the echoing roar quieted, Terrence spoke again. "Release him to me."

Keen saw one of the guards raise an eyebrow, but he did as his leader directed and pushed Malcolm into the Southeast Itan's arms.

"Come, Malcolm. You and I have your sentence to discuss." Terrence sounded calm, but the claw-tipped fingers digging into the flesh of Malcolm's neck belied the soft tone. Amidst Malcolm's whimpers, the Southeast Itan paused to give another of his

285

entourage one last order. "Come find me in an hour. It should be done by then and I'll deal with Reid Bennett when I return."

Silence followed the two men. No questions needed to be voiced. Everyone knew that two men walked into the forest and only one would walk out.

* * *

When Reid was brought to the front yard and forced to kneel on the gravel, Trista was disappointed to see he wasn't battered or bloody. He was worn, tired, and appeared defeated, but still in one piece.

Damn it.

After hearing the battle in the forest, the roars of the two fighting bears—Malcolm and Terrence—as well as watching several trees disappear from the landscape, Trista's inner-animal was craving blood. It disgusted yet excited her, the beast wanting to see the male die while her human half fought to hold back the heaving of her stomach.

But regardless of her desires, one emotion cut through them all. Happiness. She was *glad* Malcolm was being punished, she was *glad* Quinn would be forced to pay the price for his involvement, and she was *glad* Reid would face Terrence's wrath.

She'd never been this bloodthirsty before. Now she wanted to kick them all for turning her into a raging, violent bitch.

Terrence strode from the forest, almost exactly sixty minutes after he'd entered, and he looked the same. His polo shirt didn't have a single wrinkle and the crease in his khaki pants was sharp and crisp. He buckled his watch as he emerged, shaking his arm to settle it in place. Not even his face was flushed with the strain of battle.

He looked like any well-dressed sixty-year-old man taking a stroll.

Trista glanced at his family—her family?—to see their reactions and they appeared more bored than anything else. As if they knew the outcome and were ready to move along with the proceedings.

As soon as the Southeast Itan drew close, the youngest of his sons cut through the waiting silence with a whine. "Daaad, I'm hungry."

Instead of snapping at his child, he sighed. "Drew, you're always hungry. Lemme deal with Reid and then we can talk Gigi into feeding us."

"You can just order her to. You're the Southea—"

"Quiet," Terrence barked.

The kid didn't even act cowed. He merely slumped the way kids do when they're annoyed, shoulders falling and head lolling back.

It was surreal, watching the man's family and guards treat him like any other bear, father, when he'd just dispatched Malcolm. They were crazy.

Keen leaned down to her, his warm breath stirring her hair. "They look at you the same way."

She glanced at him, brow furrowed. "What?"

"They see me, they see how quickly I lose control. Then they look at you, at you touching me and not caring that five minutes ago I was ready to tear anyone to shreds. They wonder if you've lost your mind."

Trista narrowed her eyes. The animal part of her was ready to tell everyone that her mate was the sweetest thing since hot chocolate by carving the words into their skin. "It's not like you're going to hurt me."

"And he's not going to hurt anyone who doesn't deserve it. They know that."

Trista drew the connection, seeing that violence and death didn't necessarily mean everyone's death. Just those who broke the law. Otherwise, Terrence Jensen was just... Terrence Jensen, mate, father... uncle.

She wasn't ready to think of him that way. Not yet.

"Get him on his feet." Terrence's voice whipped through the air.

Two burly guards hauled Reid to standing. The Alpha shrugged off their holds and then straightened fully. She sensed the man's power, felt it swirl over the ground. Fear trailed down her spine, sending a tremor through her body. It was menacing and dark and she could see why Reid Bennett ruled the wolves.

The Southeast Itan changed then; he shrugged off the mantle of father and friend and shrugged into the role of leader. He strode up to the Alpha, met him toe-to-toe and nose-to-nose as if he didn't fear the large male. Then again, why should he? Even if Terrence was older, he was still stronger, faster, and the rage inside him definitely gave him an edge. The emotion was palpable, encompassing the area, digging into everything and she felt her animal cower in its presence.

"You killed my sister." The tone seemed calm, but the words were hard.

"My *Beta* killed your sister."

"At your orders."

Reid shook his head. "It was his decision. He acted of his own accord. A purge was ordered, it was his method of handling the process."

"And you didn't stop him," Terrence countered. "You, as a leader, are responsible for every wolf in your pack. How many died because of your indifference, *Alpha*?" The title was a slur, a mockery of its true purpose.

"I stopped him, but not soon enough." Did she hear a hint of remorse in the Alpha's tone? No, no way. She'd seen him as nothing but a monstrous brute for so many years. She didn't think he had a regretful bone in his body.

"How many?"

Reid didn't answer right away and the Itan roared. "*How. Many?*"

"Too many." The Alpha bit off the words.

"And you didn't think to notify the families?" Terrence's words were soft, but Reid flinched.

"No. They were all—"

"They weren't."

Trista knew what he was trying to say. Trying to express that those Morgan killed were hyenas. It was a purge, it was allowed, and there was no law that said they *couldn't* kill those they found. But it'd been so many years since a purge had been handled that way.

"Now." Terrence managed to somehow get closer. The two males faced off, gazes locked, but it was Reid who looked away first. "Tell me why you hunted my half-sister, a half-werebear, and her daughter, one-quarter werebear, for over twenty years?"

Trista had the same question, the same burning need to understand. She accepted that she was Brigham Scott's daughter. She accepted that she was half hyena. But one-quarter werebear? And her mother was half? She'd only scented "mom" when she hugged her mother close and it'd always been tinged with a hint of her own hyena scent. She'd never connected the dots and realized the hint of something extra was her mom's inner-bear.

Her world shifted, jarring and shaking her as this new information clicked into place.

Reid said, "The bond between wolves and bears is new. And she scented more like a hyena than a bear. I realize now it was because of her constant contact with Trista and the hyena pack. She doesn't even have your last name."

"She carried her mother's," Terrence snapped back.

"I didn't know she was your—"

Emotions she'd buried, ones that she'd shoved aside and pushed to the back of her mind, surged. She was moving before she realized she'd tensed. Agony tore through her, scraping her heart and churning her gut. Pain, oh God, the pain assaulted her, spurring her to go faster, to push her body.

She shoved Terrence aside as if he were merely a flower dancing in the wind. He stumbled and while the Itan was distracted, she pounced on the wolf Alpha.

He wasn't expecting it, wasn't anticipating someone like her, someone small and fragile, to attack him head on—this wasn't a sneaky confrontation with a rock in hand—but she did. She went after him with human nails and blunted teeth and she sobbed. She cried. Hate and grief poured from her heart, transferring into the prone male with every strike and punch.

She didn't know what she said, didn't know what she screamed and yelled as she did her best to destroy him. Words flew, soaking the air with her sounds, but the syllables didn't matter; only Reid Bennett did.

Trista wasn't sure how long they let her pummel him, how long they allowed her to vent her grief and frustrations on him, but rough hands pulled at her. They tugged and yanked until she was lifted from the Alpha. Still she fought, battling the limbs holding her captive.

"It shouldn't matter!" She yanked against the fingers encircling her bicep. "She was a *person*! She was a living, breathing *mother*!" She strained, aching to be free. "Decent human beings don't go around *killing people!*" Warm arms wrapped around her, stealing her pain, washing it away with the single embrace. Keen. Her Keen, her mate. Her bone-deep anguish settled with his touch and she slumped into his arms, uncaring about the tears coursing down her cheeks. "We're just people." She slumped into Keen's arms, letting him support her, and her voice fell to a hoarse whisper. "Hyena or bear, we're just people. Why can't you see that?"

Her mate tugged her back, urged her to turn in his arms, and she buried her face against his chest. He stroked her back, soothing her with his touch, but she wasn't sure she'd settle. Her nerves were alive, buzzing and twitching. Raw and exposed, she didn't think she'd ever calm again.

The rough scrape of movement, the crunch of gravel, told her Reid climbed to his feet once again, but she couldn't face him. Not yet, not ever again.

"For what it's worth, I'm sorry."

She was empty, empty of caring and feeling and drained from it all. She pulled her face from Keen's sanctuary and looked to Reid, glared at his depressed form, at the paleness of his features. "It's worth nothing. Your words are worth nothing. A man, a *person*, is measured by his actions, the way he affects the world. You could have made it a better place, you command an entire pack. Now," she shook her head. "Your very existence means absolutely nothing."

Trista clung to Keen, using him as her support. Her heart was broken, but she knew he'd help glue her back together. "Take me inside. I can't do this anymore."

In a split second, she was in her mate's arms and she clutched his shoulders. The crowd parted for them, leaving an open path to the front door. She didn't care about what went on, she just wanted to be held by Keen.

"Trista?" Terrence called to her and Keen stopped, slowly turning until they faced the Southeast Itan. "Debra was my sister, and she was your mother. I can't end his life for allowing her death, not even for his attack on you and Keen, but I can inflict a non-fatal punishment as I deem fit."

Trista looked at Reid, stared at the man who'd allowed so much to crumble, and realized she was just... done.

She turned her attention to Keen, searching his gaze for a hint of his feelings, but he was quick to give her words. "Whatever you want, Tris. Whatever will help settle things for you."

She nodded and, not tearing her eyes from her mate, spoke to Terrence. "I want to know where my mother was put to rest and then I want him out of Georgia. He's an Alpha, I can't do anything about that, but I can't look at him. I don't care where he goes or what he does, but I can't turn the corner and find him on the street." Tears, God she'd never cried so much in her *life*, sprang to her eyes. "I just can't."

No one moved, it felt as if no one even breathed, until the Southeast Itan spoke once again. "As you wish. Take him."

She assumed he spoke to the guards, but it didn't matter because they were moving again, Keen carrying her to the house, up the stairs, and across the porch. Their movement seemed to be permission for the others to move as well.

The scrape of stones and booted feet on the gravel overwhelmed the front yard and the scent of Keen's family slipped around them. The brothers and their mates, their parents, all followed her and Keen into the house. They made it to the entryway and a handful of steps down the hallway before a few words had them all freezing in place. Shock from both the words and their meaning made them all speechless. Because 1) they came from Mia and 2)... they came from Mia.

"Oh fuck, my water broke."

chapter **nineteen**

Keen held Trista in his lap, one arm curled around her back, hand resting on her hip while the other hand twined with hers. Her head was pressed to his shoulder and he'd never known such comfort. The house was a whirlwind of activity, people racing through the space, but they had their own sanctuary here. Tucked in a corner of the living room, hidden from those who rushed by.

The moment Mia's amniotic fluid hit the ground, Isaac took over. His brother was no longer merely there as emotional support for him and Trista, he was now a general in command. Orders were barked and immediately followed, shifters racing to execute the Healer's directions.

Terrence kept his guards out of the way and occupied them with preparing the prisoners for transport. Keen wasn't sure why Reid was being hauled in with Quinn instead of escorted out of state, but he didn't care.

Trista was quiet, simply breathing him in as they waited for things to settle and then the real waiting would begin. At least, that's what his father said. That was just before the man escaped and he heard the back door thump shut.

The heavy tread of an approaching male had him raising his head and searching out the source of the sound. Terrence neared them, four guards in his wake who took up position by the entry to the living room and the massive window that revealed the front yard.

The Southeast Itan looked tired, exhausted really. Bags hung beneath his eyes, making him look even older than his sixty years. He settled on the coffee table before them and rested his elbows on his knees.

No one said a word for a while, quiet invading the area while the chatter of the others in the house drifted to them from the kitchen.

Keen glanced at Trista and found her eyes closed, but he knew she wasn't asleep. Tension still had her muscles hard beneath his hands.

Terrence sighed. "This… did not go as anticipated."

Trista snorted, betraying herself, and Keen pressed a kiss to the top of her head. When it came to his mate, he couldn't keep his lips to himself.

"You think?" Her voice wobbled, but he didn't notice another round of tears. It tore his heart out to see those droplets of moisture in her eyes. She raised her head and turned toward her uncle. "What did you expect?"

The Southeast Itan wove his fingers together. "I expected to find my Keeper causing problems with the assistance of my Second. At worst, I was going to give them shit and shove them in a cell for a while. I also expected to warn off a wolf who was getting too big for his britches." His eyes softened, affection sliding over the hardened gaze. "I wasn't expecting to find my niece. They sent me a picture of you but," he shook his head. "I buried your mother over thirty years ago."

A shudder traveled through his mate, but she remained strong. Man, he loved her. Loved her strength. She'd lost her mind a few times today, but she'd beat that part of herself into submission as well. He wasn't sure how she managed to keep a hyena and bear at bay inside her small body, but she did.

Just… amazing.

"Did he tell you what I wanted to know?"

Terrence nodded. "Yes. He at least knew that."

Another tremor, but she held it together. "I want to go there. I want to see."

"Whenever you're ready."

No one said anything else and Keen sank into the silence. It wasn't strained or charged with tension. They'd all expended whatever energy they had in the last few hours. Now it was simple exhaustion that overtook them.

At least, for a moment. Because then the Itan spoke again, his words hesitant, but they came forward anyway. "I have something I'd like to discuss with you two."

Keen focused on the male, eyes taking in the lines of his posture and the expression on his face with renewed interest. That type of statement was never followed with good news and he was poised to defend Trista if needed. He'd shield her physically, *and* emotionally, for the rest of his life. Even if that meant keeping this powerful man away from her.

"I came here to settle the issue with you two, but I also needed to see Mia's father. He made a decision recently, as did Isaac, that affects the family and Cutler." Terrence paused as if searching for the right words. "They're returning to Grayslake. Permanently. Which means Cutler is without a Guardian, a temporary leader, until Parker turns twenty-five."

Keen did not like where this was headed and neither did his bear. With Trista's further stiffening, it seemed she'd jumped to the same conclusion.

She spoke before he could. "No, we're not going anywhere."

"Hear me out before you say no."

Keen didn't need to hear a thing. He didn't want to leave Grayslake even if happy memories were few. He was making his own happiness with Trista in their new house. That's all there was to it.

Terrence must have taken their continued silence as permission to speak. "I can't approve their request and leave the town unprotected until I have a replacement. I know Grayslake holds a lot of pain for you two..."

Trista was shaking her head and Keen squeezed her hand. He wanted to give the man an immediate "no" as well, but he *was* the Southeast Itan.

The male kept talking. "And I also know your abilities are underutilized. Ideally"—Terrence focused on Trista—"I would have you as a Keeper in my circle. You have survived by intuition, pure inner strength, and an in-depth knowledge of the laws alone. And Keen..." Now it was his turn to suffer beneath the powerful man's gaze. "You're one of the strongest bears in the country." Keen shook his head and Terrence nodded. "You might not know it, but you are. You endured retraining camp, which was destroyed long ago. You persevered and made something of yourself despite your bear's reluctance to keep itself under control. If you Challenged me right now, if you Challenged the National Itan, you'd probably win. Not because you're younger and stronger, but because you've never been limited by others' perception and ideals. You're a pure bear when you shift and you've lived through that hell. You know what it's like to be a regular member of a clan while also being privy to the inner workings of the power structure. While I would want Trista as my Keeper, I would like her mate as my Second."

Keen's gut clenched, tightened, and his heart froze.

I would like her mate as my Second.

The handful of words echoed in his mind. The gravity, the meaning and trust and faith, filled him. "I'm..."

He didn't know what he was. Over twenty years of being overlooked, ignored, and forgotten, of pretending to be something he wasn't, and now the Southeast Itan wanted him, them, with him.

Keen tried to speak again. "You can't…"

"I can do whatever I want. I want a Keeper who knows the laws and has both prospered and suffered beneath them. I want a Second who is unencumbered by everyone else's ideologies while also able to adhere to them when necessary." Terrence's gaze bore into him. "Retraining you was wrong."

Keen nodded. He thought so at fourteen and even at twenty-four.

"And you could have destroyed the camp, everyone inside it, without much damage to yourself."

He looked away from the Itan, but there was no escaping the truth. Yes, he'd been that powerful, then and now. "Yes."

"But you stayed because those above you, those who created the rules, told you that was your punishment. You hated it, could have ended it, but you endured because it was the right thing to do."

"Yes." He bit off the word. The bear grumbled and growled inside his mind, not liking that this male, this slightly weaker male, made them think of that time.

"And then you worked within your limitations, not caring about what others thought if it meant keeping them safe."

"Yes." Another snap.

Trista slid her hand over his chest and up his neck, stroking his jaw with her thumb. That touch soothed him and calmed the beast, reminding them he wasn't in the past, he wasn't fourteen. No, he was grown and mated and… being asked to help the Southeast Itan rule. Rule and someday take over for him.

It was a heady feeling, exciting, and made his bear puff up with pride.

Cocky asshole animal.

"How would that work?" Trista filled the silence. "I'm half-hyena. Would your bears actually listen to someone like me? And if we went to Cutler, how would he be the Guardian and Second in one?"

"You're still part of my family and you're your mother's daughter. You wouldn't allow them to *not* listen. Neither would your mate." Keen agreed with the Itan's words. If anyone even let a hint of disgust for Trista emerge, he'd be there to put an end to it. Permanently if necessary. "And Cutler is only an hour from my home and most of the work we'd do is long-distance. This…" He waved at the house. "This is the exception to the rule. As was the incident with Mia's family. Normally, I sit in my office and have conference calls with the Itans and inner-circles. As part of *my* inner-circle, that'd be your only job. Ty and Van manage Grayslake *and* their work with the Sheriff's office. Your primary responsibility, your devotion, would be to the Southeast first and your town second. Those would be your only jobs."

Trista looked to him, indecision in her eyes. A hint of hope and excitement lurked there as did a small dose of sadness. She was unsure and Keen refused to make a snap decision within the whirlwind of activity.

"We'll discuss it and get back to you." He spoke to Terrence, but didn't tear his gaze from Trista. The relief was easily seen and the scent of her emotions wrapped around him.

"Okay, it's the best I can hope for." He pushed to his feet and stared down at them. "I sent your cousins and aunt to the hotel for now. Ty invited us to come back tomorrow once his cub is born." Trista lifted her gaze from Keen's and he did the same, focusing on the male. "But I won't come if it'll make you uncomfortable, Trista."

It was the closest thing to a question Keen had ever heard from the man.

"I…" She hesitated and he stroked her arm, reminding her of his presence and support. He didn't care about her decision, just that she was aware he'd be there for her. "I would like that."

The man's smile transformed him from a deadly, threatening bear to a—dare he say—sweet, joyful male. No one would ever believe him, but one of the most dangerous bears in the nation looked like a young cub when he smiled and radiated happiness.

"Good, good. I'll tell Marjorie and wait for Ty's call." He reached forward, hands easing toward Trista, and then he pulled them back. "I'll see you tomorrow, then."

Before he knew it, Trista was out of his arms and wrapping hers around Terrence. His bear grumbled at the loss of her touch, but accepted that she needed to connect with her uncle. The Itan froze for a moment, shock coating his features, before he finally hugged her back.

His gaze locked with Keen's over her head and he pretended the man's eyes weren't shining with moisture.

"Thank you." The Itan drew in a harsh, audible breath. "Thank you for loving her and taking care of her."

Trista eased from the larger male's arms and stepped back until she folded herself onto his lap once again. His mate turned her attention to him and the words wouldn't be suppressed. "Loving her is the easiest thing I've ever done in my life."

It was the truth. Hard, cold—no, warm—truth. His heart warmed when he looked at her and his body burned with her every touch. She was his everything.

And didn't that sound corny.

A low throat clearing drew their attention and had the guards stiffening. Apparently the guards had been listening intently to the conversation between Terrence, Trista, and him and weren't focused on protecting the Itan.

Keen would have to talk to them about that when he became...

He shoved the thought from his mind. The position as Second was tempting, but he needed to discuss things with Trista before he let his thoughts drift that way.

Keen focused on the woman in the doorway. Jessa hadn't changed much through the years. Her body had filled out to that of a lush female, but her bow-shaped mouth, sweet face, and long blond hair remained the same. She was simply a grown-up version of her sixteen-year-old self.

With the exception of the pale scar that peeked from the edge of her top. He knew how far it traveled, that it went from the curve of her breast to her lower stomach. He also knew how wide they were and the distance between each.

He'd been a big bear at fourteen.

"The, um, baby is here. A girl. Mother and baby are fine."

Keen raised his eyebrows, disbelief filling him. "Isn't that a little fast? Her water broke not"—he glanced at his watch—"an hour ago."

Jessa shrugged. "It happens that way sometimes. Women in my cla— the other clan have been in labor for eight hours before they have a C-section and then there are those like the Itana who take less than an hour. Ty is helping her clean up and Isaac is checking them over. She'll be ready for visitors in thirty minutes."

With that, the woman disappeared from sight. She was poised, strong and sure as opposed to the snotty, simpering girl she'd been.

It made him realize that people changed. Hell, he'd changed over the years and he'd transformed a thousand times over since Trista came into his life.

"I'll leave you all then. Let you visit with the baby. Enjoy time with your family." Terrence turned from them and Trista gave him a look, wide eyes and hope shining in the orbs.

"Terrence," he called back the Southeast Itan. "Why don't you have Marjorie and the boys come back tonight? It *is* a time for family and you're..." Trista gave him a tiny nod. "You're family."

He got another one of those smiles, ones Keen never imagined to grace the Southeast Itan's features. "All right, then."

Shouts rose from deeper within the house, celebrations kicking off as news of the baby spread.

The Itan glanced toward the entryway. "And maybe I'll have them swing by and grab a cow or two. Your cousins can *eat* and I think we'll be celebrating for a while."

Yeah, they would. Not just because the future had been brought into the world, but also because the past had been laid to rest.

* * *

The baby—Sophia Cate Abrams—was adorable, though red and pointy-headed, and the party lasted well into the night. Trista managed to survive the joy, to push through the pain still plaguing her heart. Smiles graced everyone's faces and she forced one to her lips as well. It was easy to pretend to be happy. She'd been doing it for so long, it was second nature.

It was nearing six a.m. and they'd finally torn themselves away from the celebration. Clan members were still milling around the house and yard, drinking and munching while waiting for Gigi to create an early morning feast.

She'd managed to snare Keen's hand and led him toward the front of the house. He was just as exhausted as her, but he would have stayed, not wanting to leave before the Southeast Itan. Trista had no such compunction. She didn't care if it was bad taste or not, she was going home. To her home. The one she'd share with Keen for... as

301

long as he wanted to stay. It was something they hadn't been able to discuss in the middle of the clan.

Now they were in their new home amidst boxes and randomly placed furniture. It was obvious Anna and George had stuck around after Keen dragged her away. The boxes were definitely less plentiful and several rooms had already been organized and decorated with what they'd purchased.

The master bedroom was put together, the bed made with their new linens and their clothing tucked away. It was like a fairy housemother had come in and created a perfect home. She'd have to thank the woman later. It was obvious they'd gone to a lot of trouble to make the home perfect for them.

When they came upstairs, they bypassed the bed and moved to the balcony. The outdoor chaise they'd snagged was positioned on the patio to face the back yard and Keen lay down before pulling Trista before him.

They relaxed, breathing in the morning air, and she listened as the birds woke for the day. The sun slowly eased above the trees, painting their new yard in shades of pink and orange. It was beautiful and breathtaking and *theirs*.

She'd never seen anything so gorgeous.

"I love it," she whispered, unwilling to break the beauty of the moment.

"Me, too."

Trista voiced the one question she'd focused on since hearing Terrence's—her uncle's—offer. "Can you let it go?"

Keen nuzzled her, sending a sliver of trembling desire through her. His warm, moist breath tickled her skin and the soft nip of his teeth drew a contented sigh from her lips. "Can you?" He buried his face in her hair. "Can you let it go and create a new home in Cutler? Work for Terrence?"

Could she? Of course. There was no doubt she could do the job. Hell, she'd been doing it—sort of—for years. The better question, she realized, was whether she wanted to.

So, that was what she asked. "Do you want to let it go?"

"I..." He hesitated and she let him take a moment to gather his thoughts. This discussion, while probably the first of many talks about their future, was too important to rush. "What do you want to do?"

She chuckled. "Pushing it off on me?"

She sighed and focused on their surroundings, on the birds fluttering to the ground in search of food and the way the trees rustled with the wind. She looked at the distant roof peaks and the rich green color of the grass. She imagined a joyful, fulfilling life here, one that was dominated by tumbling cubs and interfering relatives.

"I want to stay."

Keen took a deep breath. "There's a lot of pain here for you. The hyena pack, the way the wolves and bears treated you..."

"And for you." Not that he needed the reminder, but she wasn't the only one who'd suffered.

"And me." He nodded.

"But happiness, too." Just because they'd been forced to alternate towns didn't mean she had no good memories of going to the diner and eating at the counter with Nellie. Or playing with the kids at school, or Friday night movies with her mother.

When he remained silent she wondered if he couldn't say the same thing. "What about you? I don't want you surrounded by bad memories, Keen. I'd rather leave than—"

"Hush." He nipped her. "Give a guy a chance to answer." She felt his smile rise and then fall. "I don't have a lot here, but I think I could. I think we could make our own happiness here. We could start a family to be proud of and maybe work on becoming part of Ty's and Van's."

"They're your family already, Keen."

He shook his head. "No, not right now, not really. But someday, maybe. I think we should stay and find out. Going to Cutler," he sighed. "It's an amazing opportunity, but even with Terrence nearby, it wouldn't be home."

No, no it wouldn't and maybe that was another thing holding her back from tossing her hat in the air and racing across the state. "It wouldn't."

"Are we being selfish?"

"I…" Were they? Her heart squeezed. Mia's father and Isaac wanted to return to Grayslake. Probably just as much as they wanted to stay. "I don't know. I would like to think they'd understand. But even if they don't, I'm going to allow myself to be a little bit selfish. I've lived my life based on the desires and rules of others and right now, with you, I'm not doing it."

The scent of his relief was hot and sweet and he released the air in his lungs with a great heave. "Good. Good."

"I want to raise our children here. I want them to play in that treehouse—after you make sure they won't fall through the floor—and I want to see this sunrise every day, just like this. If that makes me selfish, then I am. Right now, I am and I won't apologize for it."

Keen tightened his hold, arms squeezing her gently. "Me neither."

"Now…" Her stomach tightened. "We just have to tell Terrence."

More quiet, more birds singing and filling the morning air. "Maybe you calling him 'uncle' will help our cause."

304

Trista snorted. "Maybe."

But unlikely.

"When do you want to tell him?"

Never.

"Tonight. I think they're coming to dinner and then heading out right after. He'll have a plane waiting for them at the airport."

"We could travel like that all the time," Keen added.

"I know." That was very appealing. "But we couldn't do this every morning." Trista turned in his arms until she was able to look him in the eye. She hoped he saw the truth and devotion in her features. "I couldn't wake up every day and be reminded that there's no harm in trusting—leaning on—a man when he loves you just as much as you love him. The proof is right here, and I don't want to ever be anywhere else."

Smiling wide, Keen's love for her shone in his gaze. "So, we tell Terrence he's roaring up the wrong tree and needs to find someone else. What do you think?"

Trista tackled him then, sealing her lips to his and sinking into the feel of his body against hers, his taste invading her mouth. That was her answer. It didn't just sound good, it didn't even sound like a great idea. No, the decision was wondrous and glorious and… perfect.

* * *

Keen kept an eye on Trista, watching her coo and smile at his new niece. He couldn't wait for them to have a little cub of their own, see her grow large with their baby and then later cuddle the child close as she fed the little one. It would be beautiful and perfect because it was her, and the cub was theirs.

305

Just the idea made his heart ache with emotion and his bear chuff in excitement. Both of them were in agreement. They wanted a family sooner rather than later. As many times as they'd made love, he didn't think it'd take too long. Mia got pregnant within days of mating Ty and it'd only taken Van a couple of months to get the job done.

He figured he could the same and God knew he'd been trying.

At the same time he accepted his craving for a family, he also resolved to train his cub, focus on loving the child. Hell, if they were blessed with more than one, he'd love each as much as he could and as hard as he could. Not one of them would grow up wondering if he or she was loved and cared for. Knowing Trista's past, he had no doubt she'd be the same way.

He let his attention drift over the gathered crowd. Three quarters of last night's partiers had gone home leaving family behind along with Terrence's protection. It was a hell of a lot less crowded, but still noisy as all get out. He couldn't wait to return to their place, finish setting up the house, and snuggle in for the night. They'd napped, falling into bed exhausted and ready to crash, only to have to get up and come back to the clan home.

He was dog—bear—tired and wasn't afraid of admitting it.

Keen relaxed into his seat, remaining focused on his mate, while he took a sip of his beer. He'd accepted the bottle because the family was celebrating, but he didn't have a taste for it. He was too damned tired to want to drink alcohol and get dragged down further.

It was a good thing, too, since his father decided to wander over about that time and settle on the end of the couch. The man grunted, one that asked Keen how he was doing.

"I'm fine." He tilted his bottle toward his dad. "Thanks for working on the house for us. I know I dragged Trista out of there, and I'm sorry for run—"

Dad looked at him like he was crazy, so he shut up.

306

"I was a bad father. We were bad parents."

sank

The objection jumped to his lips before the apology sunk into his brain. It was an automatic reflex. "You weren't bad parents. You did what you thought was right."

That earned him a narrow-eyed glare. "I did at least teach you not to lie. Maybe we weren't as bad as some, but we sure as hell weren't good."

He kept his mouth shut and didn't respond. When he didn't make a sound, his father gave a grunt of approval.

"Terrence offered you the job in Cutler." Now he wasn't sure if he should say something, but his dad kept talking so he figured he shouldn't. "That's your choice. You and Trista have to do what's best for you. But your mother wants to move back to Grayslake because of the grandcubs." And what his mother wanted, she got. Dad may have been the Itan once upon a time, but Mom really ruled the den. "And it'd be nice to have everyone here. Give us a chance to fix what we broke."

Keen leaned closer and lowered his voice. His father had only mentioned the position in Cutler, not the rest of the Southeast Itan's offer. "He wants me as his Second. Trista as Keeper, Dad."

His father sat back and blew a long breath through his mouth. "Hot damn."

Apparently giving birth meant Mia's ears were back in fully working order. Or she finally had enough energy to yell across the room. "Language!"

Dad grimaced. "Love that gal, but…"

Yeah, but. "We have little ears hanging around. Can't have your grandcub's first word have only four letters."

He grunted and then got serious. "We want you two here, I want to get to know my son for the first time, but we don't want to hold you back, either. I'll tell your mother about things. She'll understand. We can visit y'all and—"

Keen shook his head. "No, we haven't said anything yet, but we're going to—"

Of course, that's when Terrence strolled over and butted into their conversation. "You've made a decision, then?" The man raised a single brow. "And based on your sudden frown, I don't think I'll like it."

Keen grimaced, stomach twisting, and his bear growled at him over acting like a pussy. "No, we decided to pass. You're roaring up the wrong tree with us. I know Mia's father and Isaac will be disappointed, but we…" He met Trista's gaze, one that was filled with love, hope, and happiness, and a sense of calm blanketed him. "We want to build a family here."

"I understand that." Terrence nodded. "I don't like it, but understand it. Honestly," he sighed, "I thought that might be your answer." The Itan glanced to his right, looking at his own family. "My eldest is a good man. Not meant to take over the Southeast, but good nonetheless. He's got a mate in Cutler. They'd planned on settling in the compound and working for me, but maybe it's best for them to take over things there while Parker grows up." He sighed and looked at Keen's father with a rueful smile. "I have to let him go sometime, eh, old man?"

His dad gave a disgusted grunt and stood. "I'll show you old, ya bastard." Dad shoved at Terrence and then threw his arm around the leader's shoulders. "There's a good spot out back. Lemme kick your ass before dinner."

"Language!" Mia's voice rang through the room once again and his dad grunted in return.

Trista padded toward Keen, an uneasy smile on her lips, and he held out a hand for her. She rushed across the remaining feet and sunk *sank* onto his lap, curling against him like she'd been made for him.

"What did you two talk about?" Her voice was low, small.

"I told him and everything's fine. He's going to work out the details with Mia's dad." He pressed a kiss to her temple. He couldn't keep his hands, or his lips, to himself when it came to her. "And his son might take over. He's disappointed but understands."

The tension left her with a low sigh, body deflating and molding to his. "So, it's okay."

"It's okay," he confirmed.

"We can start our life now."

Keen looked around the room, taking in the sight of family and friends enjoying each other's company. Yeah, it wouldn't be the easiest life, there was still a lot of healing to do, but it'd be theirs and that's what mattered. "Yeah, Tris, we can."

Just then, Gigi hustled into the living room and raised her voice to be heard above the low din. "Dinner's ready, y'all."

As one, everyone moved, rising from chairs and pushing away from walls as they headed toward the doorway. Only Mia's voice halted them.

"Wait! I got something to say before you all eat. The minute you stuff yourselves, you'll be heading home, taking a nap, or disappearing to parts unknown." The small woman pushed through the crowd and finally spun to face them. "So, before you get all comfortable, we have something to settle." Keen noticed her arms were empty and then he spotted an exasperated Ty nearing Mia. The movement caught the Itana's attention and she frowned at him. "Do you have the invoices?"

"No."

The Itana narrowed her eyes. "Why?"

"Because we're not billing them."

"We are."

"Nope."

Mia planted her hands on her hips. "I'm the Itana and I say—"

"I'm not invoicing my family for cursing."

The Itana straightened her spine. "I started the swear jar months ago."

"And forgot about it."

"Hush. The point is I remembered now and I kept track. It's time to pay the piper." Mia scanned the room and finally settled on Keen.

Shit.

"Keen, you and Trista owe me *375.50 and that's only for the last week. I'm giving you a break. It should be triple that, but you get a discount as a mating present. You can make the check out to—*"

"Mia," Ty growled and approached his mate. In one quick move, he had an arm around the woman and eased her from the room. All the while he whispered about the fact that they needed to discuss things in private and naked.

Chuckles rolled through the room and the space slowly emptied as the crowd followed the Grayslake ruling pair. Before long, it was just him and Trista, still wrapped in each other's arms with smiles on their faces.

"It's not too late to escape. If we stick around, we'll end up owing Mia enough that she could put a lien on the house or claim our first born." Keen was only half kidding.

"No, this is home. With you, right here, right now, it's home. And I don't want to ever leave."

"So, we won't."

Life wouldn't be easy, it never was, but it was theirs. And it was in Grayslake.

The End

If you enjoyed Roaring Up the Wrong Tree, please be totally awesomesauce and leave a review so others may discover it as well. Long review or short, your opinion will help other readers make future purchasing decisions. So, go forth and rate my level-o-awesome!

By the way… here are a couple of links to help you hunt up the first two books of the Grayslake series:

No Ifs, Ands, or Bears About It: http://bookbit.ly/noifszon
All Roar and No Bite: http://bookbit.ly/arnbzon

about celia kyle

Ex-dance teacher, former accountant and erstwhile collectible doll salesperson, New York Times and USA Today bestselling author Celia Kyle now writes paranormal romances for readers who:

1) Like super hunky heroes (they generally get furry)
2) Dig beautiful women (who have a few more curves than the average lady)
3) Love laughing in (and out of) bed.

It goes without saying that there's always a happily-ever-after for her characters, even if there are a few road bumps along the way.

Today she lives in Central Florida and writes full-time with the support of her loving husband and two finicky cats.

If you'd like to be notified of new releases, special sales, and get FREE eBooks, subscribe here: http://celiakyle.com/news

You can find Celia online at:
http://celiakyle.com
http://facebook.com/authorceliakyle
http://twitter.com/celiakyle

copyright

Made in the USA
Las Vegas, NV
31 January 2022

42754592R00187